FOUR MOTHERS AT CHAUTAUQUA

FOUR MOTHERS
AT CHAUTAUQUA

ISABELLA ALDEN

LIVING BOOKS®
Tyndale House Publishers, Inc.
Wheaton, Illinois

ET

Visit Tyndale's exciting Web site at www.tyndale.com

Tyndale House Publishers edition 1997

Living Books is a registered trademark of Tyndale House
Publishers, Inc.

ISBN 0-8423-3191-3

Printed in the United States of America

01   00   99   98   97
6   5   4   3   2   1

Yours in memory of
Chautauqua days
Isabella Macdonald Alden
"Pansy"

CONTENTS

FOREWORD

To all friends of the Pansy Series who followed the fortunes of *Four Girls at Chautauqua* and *The Chautauqua Girls at Home* years and years ago, the writer of this chronicle wishes to explain that Ruth Erskine, Eurie Mitchell, Marion Wilbur, and Flossy Shipley, in due course of time, took to themselves husbands and became "Mrs. Burnham," "Mrs. Harrison," "Mrs. Dennis," and "Mrs. Roberts"; that they passed through varied and marked experiences, trials, temptations, joys, and sorrows—both before and after marriage—as indeed *Ruth Erskine's Crosses, Judge Burnham's Daughters,* and other volumes in the series have already told. That, as the years passed, their sons and daughters grew to manhood and womanhood, became husbands and wives—some of them; became perplexities and problems—certain of them; and on a certain summer day in the year 1912, those same "Four Girls," with their children and their children's children and aunts and cousins, made up a mammoth "family party" and returned to the spot that had become historic ground to the original four.

The record of certain of their experiences there, the changes they found, the people they met, together with quotations from some of the words they heard—words that will go on influencing their lives and other lives forever—is carefully set down in this volume. The account is complete in itself; still, if any should wish to know more of the years that are gone—as regards the "Four Girls"—a glance at the books of the Chautauqua Series will recall their story.

Four Mothers at Chautauqua is especially designed for the thousands who met there during the summer of 1912 and for the thousands who wanted to go but could not. For widely differing reasons, that special summer will ever be memorable to those who spent it at Chautauqua Lake.

To the members of the dear class of '87, whose twenty-fifth anniversary was celebrated that summer—who certainly did what they could to make all Chautauquans remember "The Pansy Class," and who have strong hope of celebrating their fiftieth anniversary—a few of them in the "city by the lake," many of them in the "city, which hath foundations"—this volume is especially dedicated by their friend and classmate,

PANSY

April 1913

WELCOME

by Grace Livingston Hill

As long ago as I can remember, there was always a radiant being who was next to my mother and father in my heart and who seemed to me to be a combination of fairy godmother, heroine, and saint. I thought her the most beautiful, wise, and wonderful person in my world, outside of my home. I treasured her smiles, copied her ways, and listened breathlessly to all she had to say, sitting at her feet worshipfully whenever she was near; ready to run any errand for her, no matter how far.

I measured other people by her principles and opinions, and always felt that her word was final. I am afraid I even corrected my beloved parents sometimes when they failed to state some principle or opinion as she had done.

When she came on a visit, the house seemed glorified because of her presence; while she remained, life was one long holiday; when she went away, it seemed as if a blight had fallen.

She was young, gracious, and very good to be with.

This radiant creature was known to me by the name of Auntie Belle, though my mother and my grandmother called her Isabella! Just like that! Even sharply sometimes when they disagreed with her: *"Isabella!"* I wondered that they dared.

Later, I found that others had still other names for her. To the congregation of which her husband was pastor she was known as Mrs. Alden. And there was another world in which she moved and had her being when she went away from us from time to time; or when at certain hours in the day she shut herself within a room that was sacredly known as a Study, and wrote for a long time, while we all tried to keep still; and in this other world of hers she was known as Pansy. It was a world that loved and honored her, a world that gave her homage and wrote her letters by the hundreds each week.

As I grew older and learned to read, I devoured her stories chapter by chapter, even sometimes page by page as they came hot from the typewriter; occasionally stealing in for an instant when she left the study to snatch the latest page and see what had happened next; or to accost her as her morning's work was done with: "Oh, have you finished another chapter?"

Often the whole family would crowd around when the word went around that the last chapter of something was finished and going to be read aloud. And now we listened, breathless, as she read and made her characters live before us.

The letters that poured in at every mail were overwhelming. Asking for her autograph and her photograph; begging for pieces of her best dress to sew into patchwork; begging for advice on how to become a great author; begging for advice on every possible subject. And she answered them all!

Sometimes I look back upon her long and busy life, and marvel at what she has accomplished. She was a marvelous housekeeper, knowing every dainty detail of her home to perfection. And a marvelous pastor's wife! The real old-fashioned kind, who made calls with her husband, knew every member intimately, cared for the sick, gathered the young people into her home, and loved them all as if they had been her brothers and sisters. She was beloved, almost adored, by all the members. And she was a tender, vigilant, wonderful mother, such a mother as few are privileged to have, giving without stint of her time, her strength, her love, and her companionship. She was a speaker and teacher, too.

All these things she did, and *yet wrote books!* Stories out of real life that struck home and showed us to ourselves as God saw us; and sent us to our knees to talk with him.

And so, in her name I greet you all, and commend this story to you.

Grace Livingston Hill

(This is a condensed version of the foreword Mrs. Hill wrote for her aunt's final book, *An Interrupted Night*.)

1

"WHERE ARE THE GIRLS?"

ERSKINE Burnham guided his auto skillfully to the side entrance, gave his chauffeur directions for the evening, and came presently into the living room with the air of a man who had reached home again and was glad.

"Where is—" he began after greeting his wife, then with a barely perceptible pause changed the form of his sentence: "Where are the girls?"

His wife knew that he had begun to ask: "Where is Mamma?" Over the changed question they both smiled.

"They are in the sunset room," Mrs. Burnham said, "supposed to be engaged with a gorgeous sunset, but in reality they are having an animated conversation. Mother has a new idea about vacation."

"What is that?" her husband asked as they went together toward his dressing room. "It seems early yet for vacation plans, but I presume the season will be upon us unawares, after all. What does Mamma want?"

"Chautauqua," his wife said, laughing. "She aims for family parties; children, grandchildren, and all the aunts and cousins, and believes that to spend the summer there together would be ideal."

"Chautauqua! Why, isn't that a good idea? The 'Four Girls' all back there together after the lapse of years. I wonder what Mamma hasn't planned for that before."

"Oh, they say that they have tried dozens of times to plan it; that they meant to go back the very next year, all together, but something prevented, and has always prevented; it really seems as though they might be able to carry it out this time. Aunt Flossy thinks this is the best possible year for going, because her husband and Dr. Dennis are both to be away all summer; she said the 'Four Girls' could be together, much as they were in their girlhood. She confided to me her feeling that Mother and Aunt Eurie would not so keenly miss the husbands gone to heaven, when hers and Aunt Marion's were not there as constant reminders. Isn't that exactly like Aunt Flossy?"

Erskine Burnham's face wore a tender smile. "It's peculiar, isn't it?" he said, "and like her. I should never have thought of it. But Aunt Flossy will find it a difficult matter to try to live youthful days over again; there are too many children and grandchildren—and memories," he added gravely. Then, after a pause:

"How many could we muster, do you suppose?"

"Children? Oh, I don't know; quite a company, I should think. Grace and her family will be sure to want to go wherever Aunt Marion does; you know Aunt Marion gave up the trip to California because Grace couldn't take the baby; and Maybelle and Erskine will go; Flossy says they have been considering it; Erskine has always wanted to go because his father and mother met there. She says there is a streak of sentimentalism about Erskine; she fancies he had a schoolboy notion that he would go there someday, as his mother did, and meet his fate. I spoiled all that, she says, by bringing Maybelle to them, and if you could have seen her face when she said it, you would realize more than ever how glad she is that it was spoiled. As a matter of fact, it was she who brought them together, you know."

"They are mated, all right," the father said with the air of one who was satisfied. "And for me, I am glad to think that you had a hand in it. How about our respected namesake? Can he be considered in the Chautauqua plans?"

"I am sure I don't know. Aunt Flossy is planning as though she expected them all, but I heard her tell Mother that Burnham hadn't said a word yet about summer plans, and she did not like to speak of them first. I suppose she is afraid he will be set against anything that he fancies she wants him to do. That boy will have to be managed by contraries, if at all."

"And does Aunt Eurie expect Eureka, the independent, to follow in her proposed train?"

"Who can tell? Nobody knows two hours ahead what Eureka Harrison will or will not do. Isn't she the strangest girl you ever knew?"

"I hope so!" Mr. Burnham said, laughing. "I should not care to know another like her. Queer study in heredity it would make to furnish specimens like her and Burnham Roberts; think of Uncle Evan and Aunt Flossy being father and mother to him!"

"I wonder if there isn't a great deal more to Burnham than appears on the surface," his wife said thoughtfully.

"Oh, there is enough to the fellow to make a man, if someone or some *thing* could get hold of him. The only person thus far who seems to have much influence is the one of whom we are all afraid."

"I don't think that Eureka really *influences* him," Mrs. Burnham said, still speaking as one who was thinking aloud rather than talking. "It is the unconventional, the *wild* in her, meeting the same strain in him, that attracts."

Mr. Burnham laughed gaily. "You are growing too metaphysical for me, Mamie dear; is there anything but wildness in Eureka Harrison?"

"She is her father's daughter, Erskine."

"Yes, and her mother's. I fancy that Aunt Eurie had a good deal of the unconventional mixed up with her girlhood. Mamma confessed to me once that before the four went to Chautauqua together, she used to avoid Eurie Mitchell in public as much as possible because she was always a little afraid of what she might say or do next. Still, I do not mean to convey the impression that she was ever like Eureka. Heredity and environment are both strange studies; it won't do to be sweeping in conclusions about either of them. Well, Mrs. Burnham, I have brushed away the outward soil of the city at least; shall we join 'the girls' and help them plan? They will find in me a strong candidate for the Chautauqua scheme; at least it will be a splendid place for the children of the party."

At the same time that this conversation was taking place in the dressing room, two young people were lingering among the cushions piled luxuriously about the "sunset porch," drawn thither ostensibly by the glorious view to be had of the sunset and lingering after its glories had faded and the other watchers had departed, because of their propensity to seek each other's company. These were the two whose characters, or at least reputations, had been more than hinted at by Erskine Burnham and his wife: Eureka Harrison, Eurie Mitchell Harrison's only daughter, and Burnham Roberts, Flossy Shipley Roberts's younger son.

Eureka Harrison was not a girl to be lightly passed over at any time, yet one hesitates to try to describe her; she was one of those persons who make always a distinct impression yet who refuse to be classed and whom the conventional forms of description do not seem to fit. Certainly she would not be called beautiful, although observers were sure to remark upon her singularly beautiful eyes and to add that, but for her nose and mouth, she would be strikingly handsome. Yet there was nothing the matter with either nose or mouth that they did not seem to fit her face.

"That's the trouble with everything about me," the girl said one day, joining gaily in the discussion that was being had at her expense. "I'm a misfit; nothing that belongs to me is quite what any other part calls for; and what is worse than all the rest, it extends to my character so that I don't exactly suit anybody."

There was truth in this statement. "We really *can't* ask Eureka Harrison," said one set of her schoolmates; "she talks so loud and laughs so much and says such unexpected things."

"Don't let us ask Eureka," said another set; "she is too straitlaced in her notions for a frolic of this kind."

She was not tall, although slightly above the medium height, but she could be very stately when she chose; or she could have no more dignity "or sense of propriety than a monkey," as one annoyed acquaintance expressed it. Her beautiful eyes could flash fun or fire; but they could also be as cold and expressionless as steel. Always people wanted to turn and look again at Eureka Harrison.

"She is not in the least like her mother," said those who knew Mrs. Harrison. "And yet," said those who had known her as Eurie Mitchell, "there is something that suggests her."

Flossy Roberts once made a remark that Erskine Burnham said expressed all that was to be said on the subject: "In some ways Eureka Harrison is an exaggeration of her mother, and in others she is a sharp contrast to her."

The young man is more easily described, or at least announced, as strikingly handsome. He was almost faultless in form and feature and carried himself in the manner that is hinted at by the word *distinguished*. Of the four children who made up the Roberts household, Burnham, the second son, was easily the one who had inherited most physically from his parents, yet a more striking contrast from them in character could hardly be imagined. The other son and two lovely daughters had been, all through their developing youth, the joy and comfort of their father and mother. The girls were now happily married and conducting happy homes of their own; and Erskine, the minister, was, with his wife, Maybelle, the idol of a flourishing church. It remained for Burnham, the youngest born, to fill the lives of his father and mother with anxious care. Through his aggressive babyhood and imperious childhood, his parents, wise in their experience with three others, had tried in vain to apply the principles that had helped to tide the others through shoals and hidden rocks into the safe waters of responsible manhood and womanhood. Burnham simply would not be guided, would not follow, and he *would* lead. Always and everywhere he managed to secure his own way. Pleasantly, if he could, sometimes with the winsomeness of an angel, often, it must be confessed, with the wisdom of a serpent. In the secondary schools he had—through endless troubles and some painfully severe attempts to subdue him—for the most part managed his teachers. He was reasonably fond of study and had the gift of rapid acquirement, yet, with these and all the other advantages which were his, he barely succeeded in passing the college examinations, and twice during the four years was suspended for insubordination. It was only his father's powerful influence and strenuous effort that secured his return in time to graduate with his class.

Now that the fact had been accomplished, the question among his acquaintances was: What is Burnham Roberts going to do next? In the Roberts household it was a painful question.

Poor Flossy Roberts! Whatever way she looked at it, or for that matter at her youngest son, her heart throbbed with foreboding. Never since the day that her girlish faith took hold of God with a firm grasp and made him her life's center had she been so sorely beset with fears.

For her other children she had an assured faith that could ride serenely above the ordinary happenings of life, but the ever-present question that sent her most often to her knees in agonizing prayer, and that had as yet received no satisfying answer, was: "What is to become of Burnham?"

Mr. Roberts, noble Christian though he was, far from being often sorely disappointed in his son, and from having to come constantly to his rescue from conditions that meant disgrace and were shadowed with dishonor, had acquired a habit of sternness and an air of authority in dealing with him that antagonized the boy and made him show his worst side to his father. Also it made the open rupture between them that the mother feared seem increasingly imminent as the months passed.

It was therefore with almost a sense of relief that she had listened early in the year to the business plans that, if carried out, would take her husband in company with one of his sons-in-law halfway round the world. The plans developed, and it was settled that their second daughter should accompany her husband. After that, many and earnest were the entreaties that "Mamma" would go too. It would be such an opportunity to visit those mission stations in China and Japan, in which she had for so long been interested. Mr. Roberts, although he seconded his daughter's and son-in-law's efforts, did so halfheartedly; he knew they would fail and was glad; because however much it would add to the joy of the travelers, there was that ever-present question, what might not the boy do, with his mother at the other side of the world?

For "the boy" loved his mother; with a fitful, irresponsible, selfish sort of love, it is true, but such as it was, there were times when it held. He had been known to break away suddenly, unreasoningly, from plans into which he had entered with zest, just as they were ready to mature, thereby upsetting the whole scheme to the disgust of his boon companions, who accused him of deserting without a cause. Had he owned the cause, it would have been a look on his mother's face or a wistful word that she let drop unawares and that chanced to reach him at the right moment. There were other times, and these, to lookers-on seemed by far the most frequent, when he did not hesitate to move directly across his mother's plans and disregard her expressed wishes, although he knew that in doing so he was blasting some of her dearest hopes.

So much for the two who lingered on the sunset porch, after the sunset and their elders had departed to discuss the summer plans from their point of view.

"Have you heard of Aunt Ruth's latest, that includes us all?" This question came from Eureka.

"The summer plans, do you mean? I have heard of nothing else the entire day; the *maters* all seem to have gone wild over the same theme. But how did you discover that the scheme included all of us?"

Eureka flashed a half-scornful glance in the young man's direction and put vim into her reply.

"Oh, I didn't mean to include you. I knew that Aunt Flossy would like very much to have your company this summer since your father is to be away, and by the same token I knew, of course, that you would plan differently. All that seems to be necessary to start you in an opposite direction is to have your mother hint a preference."

He laughed carelessly, but he was watching her face without seeming to do so as he quoted, "'Is Saul also among the prophets?' Did you never hear about people who live in glass houses?"

"Oh, I know what you mean, of course; but I don't go to work deliberately in cold-blooded indifference to stalk across my mother's wishes. Mother and I have endless arguments about things and try to make each other see that 'my way' is the best; but Mother is very different from Aunt Flossy."

The young man laughed again. "That is true," he said significantly. "Still, don't let's quarrel, not tonight; I'm too weary; that last game of tennis exhausted me. I think we would better go in; the air is getting quite sharp and, I see, is affecting your nerves. As a matter of fact, my mother has not mentioned the word *Chautauqua* to me; all the same, you are right about my intentions; they do not include that magic name; to be frank, I don't believe yours do either; from all that I have heard, I cannot imagine a summer resort less suited to our capacities."

"What do you know about the place?"

The young man shrugged his shoulders. "Haven't I been housed with the 'Four Mothers' for almost the entire day, while you roamed at large? I know *everything;* and I never fancied that I should be happy in heaven. Listen! that's Mrs. Erskine Burnham singing, isn't it? Let's go in."

2

 ◆━❈━◆

"LET US GO"

IT WILL be remembered by those who are acquainted with the "Four Girls" that they went, during the closing years of the last century, to the far-famed resort in New York state known as Chautauqua. It was by no means so well known then as it has now become.

In those early days the "Four Girls" who, by what seemed to be the merest chance, planned to spend a two-week vacation together there, carried away with them experiences that not only left deep impressions but that altered the entire course of their lives. Small wonder that, as the years passed, they looked back to those days with an ever-deepening sense of interest and made many plans to revisit the place that had become to them almost sacred ground and that their children had learned to regard with peculiar interest.

But it had not been found easy to accomplish this. Vacation plans that reach into four widely differing homes and touch interests as diverse as four households are likely to represent are not easily made to harmonize; and as the households grew and married and intermarried and set up continually more homes that yet were included in the peculiar circle of friendship, the difficulties increased. Each of the girls was unwilling to break away and go without the others; and as each mother in after years wanted not only the husband and children, but the children's children to share her mecca with her, the hope of accomplishing it dropped into the background. Thus it came to pass that until this eventful year of nineteen hundred and twelve, the happenings of which are now in part to be chronicled, the original party had never revisited Chautauqua.

By the middle of June they, "the girls," knew that they were to go; taking with them what portions of families they could muster. No husbands were to be of the party. Evan Roberts, as has already been told, was in China representing his firm in extensive business operations that would hold him for the entire summer; and Dr. Dennis was carrying out his own long-cherished hopes in joining a party of choice spirits who were engaged in scientific research in Egypt and the Holy Land. For the others, Judge Burnham had been long gone, and it was now nearly three years since Eurie Mitchell Harrison had been left a widow. Her husband, too, had planned earnestly for that visit to the Holy Land—not the extended and expensive journey that the company of scientists had undertaken; just a vacation flight to Palestine for a few wonderful weeks while the party lingered there, and he could have the advantage of their experience. To this end the Harrison family, always without financial resources equal to their growing needs, planned and economized in ways that vividly recalled to the wife and mother the pinched years of her girlhood.

But it came to pass that economizing, with the

Holy Land in view, had not been necessary; suddenly, after only two days of illness, Dr. Harrison was called to the immediate presence of him whose footsteps have made the shores of Galilee sacred. Instead of a flying trip to the "Holy Land," he went there to dwell. Eureka was away at school; and so swift had been his summons that there had been no chance to recall her in time for her father's farewell word and kiss.

She came home in the middle of a term and did not return. Throughout her mother's dismayed efforts to plan how the broken college course could be resumed, she had been resolute.

"I am not going back, of course," she had said to her favorite brother, who was trying to help plan, and who was as much straitened financially as his mother. "I ought not to have gone in the first place, and I told Mother so; it was a continual added strain upon Father to meet my bills, and he had strain enough without them, goodness knows. There are times when I can be almost glad that he has gone where he won't have to study and twist and deny himself at every turn to meet necessary expenses. I am glad you are not a minister, Neal; I hope to live to see you a rich man."

"There are other consolations than riches," her brother said gravely. "I don't believe my father would have exchanged his possessions for money when it came to the end."

Eureka looked at him sharply. This was quite unlike the usual manner of her naturally gay and carefree brother, who generally met her recklessness halfway and enjoyed it. Was he going to forsake her and join the church people? This was the phrase she used when she thought of the separating family line. The others were earnest workers in the church, as ready to sacrifice for it as their father and mother, but she and Neal had held aloof, sturdily resisting all efforts in their behalf, and both of them careless, often to the verge of irreverence, in speaking of sacred things. Eureka had been more outspoken than her brother, knowing no restraint except her father's presence. She had loved him with a fierceness that resented, sometimes bitterly, his being called upon to endure the annoyance and sacrifices and petty economies common to the lives of most ministers; yet with that curious blindness often seen in children, she had never been able to see that she was her father's greatest trial and that he was afraid of her influence upon her brother.

Neal had felt this and, now that his father was gone, mourned over it. There were moments when he wondered if it were too late even then to make his father glad by a deliberate choosing of the way so long pointed out to him. Was it conceivable that a man like his father had gone where he did not care anymore? Neal did not believe it, and it was this train of thought that had induced his grave response to his sister. If she had met him with a touch of sympathy, he might have voiced the half-formed resolve to make what tardy atonement he could for having ignored his father's eagerly expressed wishes. But Eureka's response had been sharp.

"Do you think any serious harm would have resulted to the 'possessions' if Father had been allowed a little money also, or that it is a sin for a good man to have salary enough to support his family? I'm sure I hope that all the expectations he had about the other world have been fully satisfied; he certainly suffered enough here to demand full payment there. I know that there are people in the church he left that I would go a mile out of my way to avoid meeting. Neal, you have been away from home so much since you grew up that you don't realize how hateful church people can be! Some of those psalm-singing missionary women just worried Father's life away! I never want to belong to a church as long as I live!"

Neal did not know how to talk on such themes; did not even know how to separate personal religion from mere church membership. His vague half-formed purpose to "say something" to Eureka passed, and the vague desire to honor his father's memory by choosing his way faded. After all, Eureka was half right; some of those people in the Fourth Church had plagued the life out of his father; Eureka thought he did not understand, but he knew all about it; why should he care to be one with such a set?

Three years later, when his mother wrote him about the Chautauqua trip, he had given up all thought of making good his father's teachings; yet he joined heartily in the vacation plans; indeed, they would go; it would be a lovely place for a family gathering, and no spot could be more healthful for the baby. His wife sighed a little and hinted that she had expected to go to the coast this summer, but he forestalled all serious objections.

"You can go there for June, Kathie, and again in September if you choose; those are ideal months for the shore; but I think I ought to give my mother July and August; it is the first time she has planned to leave home, you know, since she was alone. I'm especially glad to go with her to Chautauqua, because she has always wanted to go back there and been prevented."

"But, Neal, isn't that place entirely given over to religious meetings? What will we do all summer?"

Her husband laughed lightly. "Who could have posted you about Chautauqua? Not the Barnards, certainly. Ned told me today that his mother was not going there anymore because the place had drifted away from its old ideas and was becoming 'a mere fashionable resort.' It's a resort, all right; since I received mother's letter it seems as if though half of New York had told me they were going there for part of the season. Our kind of people, you know; there must be attractions there."

Others besides what Neal Harrison called "their kind of people" were planning for Chautauqua. Miles away from the Roberts home in New York lived the family of Mr. Joseph Bradford—father, mother, two young-lady daughters, and an orphaned niece of Mr. Bradford, who had come from California a year before to make her home with her uncle's family. Mr. Bradford was a valued accountant in the great mercantile house of which Evan Roberts was a member. He knew Mr. Roberts by sight; in fact had spoken to him a number of times, and once been summoned to his private office to explain certain figures, receiving from him a cordial acknowledgment of his skill. If in passing it is chronicled that when Mr. Bradford reported this at home his wife's comment was:

"Words are cheap; why didn't he raise your salary if he thought so much of your skill?" and the husband's reply:

"Perhaps because he thought I got a very good salary now; I do, anyway"; it will tell as much about the heads of the household as pages of description could.

Mrs. Bradford aspired; not so much for herself as for her daughters; she was a woman of limited education and unlimited capacity for copying the speech, the manner, even the very atmosphere of those whose early advantages had been greater than hers; she not only made the most of her opportunities, but she created opportunities. When Mr. Bradford a year before had, unsought, received a large increase of salary, and the family had moved into a more commodious flat that was just around the corner from a choice street, several of whose residents were "in society," Mrs. Bradford set to work with renewed energy to improve their social position. The church they had attended and near to which they had lived was now three blocks removed, but the one on the avenue was five blocks away. To the one on the avenue, however, Mrs. Bradford desired to go. Why in the world should they trudge back to the old church when they were in convenient walking distance from the one of all others that she would prefer? Besides, it was the one to which the Roberts family belonged; it seemed quite appropriate that people who belonged to the same business house should attend the same church when they could as well as not.

Something like a smile glimmered on the face of the usually grave Joseph Bradford at this, and he said he must tell Moses about that. Moses had opened and closed the doors for the patrols of their retail house for at least a dozen years; he didn't believe it had ever occurred to him that he ought to forsake the little colored chapel where he worshiped and go to the church of the Roberts. The girls laughed, but Mr. Bradford was immediately sorry that he had smiled and been facetious; for his wife had looked severe as she said that she did not see any occasion for turning into ridicule her efforts to help the children. She was sure there was no comparison between Mr. Bradford's position in the great business house and that of old Moses. Expert accountants often rose to a great deal higher positions and commanded large salaries. There was really no reason in the world why they should not attend an uptown church if they chose, but she should not press it, of course. She was not thinking of herself when she proposed the change; she called them to witness that she did not often think of herself—which was true—and if none of them saw the advantages that would result from the change why, of course—

"But, Mother," said Isabel, who was eighteen and a beauty, "what advantage would it be to us to crowd in among people whom we do not know and never will know? They will brush by us in the aisles and wonder who we are and what we are doing there, and that will be all there is of it. I'd rather keep on where I know the young people and am one of them."

"It might give us a chance to study the latest styles in dress," said Josephine, the eldest daughter, who had more than a touch of her father's latent sarcasm. "I'm sure I should enjoy that part, although I am doubtful about the rest. I need some new ideas dreadfully; and I can copy anything I ever saw if I can have fifteen minutes to stare at it. We couldn't afford to pay for a seat, so we could take a different one every Sunday and select the hats and wraps that we liked best. I wonder if they would let us choose, especially if we had a good motive. 'Give me a seat behind Mrs. Roberts today,' I would say, 'I want to copy her Paris hat.'"

"It would give you two a chance to breathe the atmosphere of refinement and culture that you evidently need," the mother said with emphasis. "The careless way in which you speak of the church and its opportunities shows what you need. People of refinement do not choose their church relations as they do their clothing. But I shall say no more about it; I told your father so. It is not the first time by any means that I have tried to plan for the sake of my children and been misunderstood even by them."

However, she did say much more about it, and she carried her point as the girls and their father had known that she would.

The Bradford family, in the course of time, transferred their relations to the uptown church, which was large and divided into sections so widely separated that the brushings past in the aisles without knowing whom one brushed was inevitable. They felt stranded and uncomfortable. The church they had attended had free sittings, and it was awkward in the extreme to be always standing around waiting to be seated; yet Mr. Bradford flushed almost to the roots of his gray hair the first time he returned to ask the price of a pew in the new church and heard the amazing answer. How could they ever feel at home in such a church? Yet perhaps even the girls did not realize the greatness of their mother's compensation when she said in answer to a question from one of her old neighbors:

"Oh, yes, I know Mrs. Evan Roberts; we attend the same church, you know."

But when in the breathlessness of a June morning, the Bradford family at the breakfast table were appraised of their mother's latest proposed venture, Isabel said it took what little wilted breaths they had away.

"Let us go," said Mrs. Bradford, "for a month to that Chautauqua that the Carpenter girls were always talking about."

3

ANOTHER MOTHER

"WHY, Mother Bradford!" This was Isabel's exclamation. "Much contriving has certainly made you mad, Mother." This came from Josephine. Then Mr. Bradford added, "How in the world, Sarah, do you think we could accomplish that, especially this year, when we have had such extra expenses already?"

"I know," said Mrs. Bradford, pouring coffee with the composure of a general who foresees his plans successful, "but there are always extra expenses, you remember, and always must be; we might as well plan for them; but we have been saying for years that next year we would surely take a vacation like other people, and I think the time has come. We ought to get out of town this summer on Isabel's account; when she had that cough early in the winter that hung on so long, you remember; I resolved then that she should not spend the long, hot summer in the city."

Then they all looked at Isabel, whose bright eyes and glowing cheeks were the very embodiment of health. The girl laughed in appreciation of the joke and then assumed a languid air and drawled—"How can you be such a hard-hearted father? Don't you see that I'm in a decline?"

Even Mrs. Bradford had to laugh, but she called herself to order briskly, and the others as well.

"Fun is all very well, but really, this is no laughing matter; I mean just what I said about Isabel; her cough worried me a great deal. She looks well now, but before the summer is over, I expect her to wilt."

"You hear, Father," murmured Isabel, "I shall wilt." Mrs. Bradford ignored her.

"And anyway, we all need the change. The trip I am proposing is not expensive; I've been inquiring into it. They have what are called Chautauqua tickets, round trip, you know, for almost half the regular fare; and they last all summer long."

Mr. Bradford's face continued to wear its troubled look. "But, my dear, the traveling expenses are a very small part of a summer's outing."

"Not as we shall arrange it. Chautauqua is a unique place, you will find. They have cottages there, small ones as well as large, and rooms for light housekeeping, somewhat on the plan of flats, I suppose; and in fact they have done everything they could to lighten the expense of living. One of the ladies who goes there every summer said to me:

"'Students and people of literary tastes very often are short of money, and it is that class of people who are attracted to Chautauqua.'"

It was a delight to this aspiring woman thus to class herself among people of literary tastes. But the hard-hearted father still demurred. He had simply no money for literary tastes, or any other kind; he was sorry, but she knew how it was, the extra premium on his life insurance had come in this year with all the rest and made things very close indeed.

"I know all that of course, Joseph, but we have got to live, I suppose, somewhere; what I am pointing out to you is that the paltry sum needed for these Chautauqua tickets, which you yourself said wasn't worth counting, is all the extra expense we need have—except the rent, of course; but that must be a very trifle for just a month, especially in a place where they try to help people of limited means. The cost of milk and vegetables and things is so much less in the country that I have no doubt it would offset the rent entirely. I believe I can manage so that there will be nothing extra at all."

"Except clothes," interrupted Josephine. "We shall all have to get new clothes."

"Well, Josephine," her mother said with a kind of despairing patience, "we all have to wear clothes at home; I don't see that that makes a great difference."

"Not so many," the girl said with an expressive shake of her head. Then, feeling sorry for her mother, she added:

"But it would be heavenly, of course, and I'm sure I hope we can do it. I've wanted to go to Chautauqua ever since I heard the Thorn girls rave over it. By the way, Father, Julia Thorn got her certificate by studying at the Chautauqua summer school. I might do something of that kind, perhaps, and earn a little money."

She felt, rather than saw, the cloud on her mother's face; she had begun by wanting to second her mother's efforts and spoiled the sentence before it was completed. One of the ambitions of this ambitious woman's life was so to manage finances that her daughters should not need to earn money through any of the plebeian channels that could be expected to open to them. Their school days had closed with high school. Isabel would have been glad to continue her studies, had opportunity offered, but she had not cared enough about it to make the opportunity for herself; and Josephine frankly owned that she had had enough of school life. Teaching was therefore out of the question for them, and as it was almost the only ordinary occupation open to women that had their mother's approval, it followed that they seemed compelled to wait at home while their father worked hard to support them.

The talk of the summer plans, or plan, continued. Mrs. Bradford had much to say; she had been busy about it for weeks and was ready to explain away any difficulty that might arise. For the most part they listened quietly, however; Mr. Bradford spoke but twice, each time to bring to light an additional expense that would have to be met.

His wife, who had already made up her mind and was beyond reaching by commonplace facts like those, was glad when he suddenly discovered that it was later than usual and he must run for his car; she could talk over things better with him away; when everything was arranged, it would be time enough to bother him with details.

"Where is Hazel?" he stopped to ask on his way to the door. "I haven't seen her this morning."

"Hazel stayed with Mrs. Hammond last night; the baby was so ill she thought she might be a comfort to her."

Mr. Bradford turned back with his hand on the doorknob to say:

"Not to sit up again, I hope. I don't want you to allow that, Sarah; the child is much too young for night work."

"O dear, no! she was simply to be within call if Mrs. Hammond needed help; don't you worry about

Hazel, Joseph; I shall see that she is not overworked in any way. There's your car! You'll have to run."

It might have been this episode which suggested Josephine's next question. "Mother, what about Hazel if you carry out your Chautauqua scheme?"

Mrs. Bradford's reply was so long in coming, and her face expressed so much annoyance, that Isabel broke into a laugh as she said:

"Mother forgot Hazel."

"I only wish I could!" said the lady with energy, "but I have by no means done so. I am almost certain that Mrs. Hammond would like to have Hazel stay with her this summer if it could be brought about. It would be a nice pleasant home for her—she is so fond of the baby—and it would save the expense of travel and all that; though Mrs. Hammond could not pay her much, I suppose. Of course she has not hinted at any such thing, but I believe I could arrange it if—"

"A nurse girl!" Isabel broke in. "Oh, Mother!"

"Well, what now? There is no disgrace in being a nurse girl is there? although I didn't call her by any such name. Poor Mrs. Hammond is obliged to stay in town all summer, and with that frail baby to care for, I can see that Hazel would be a real comfort, under the circumstances."

"I daresay she would," said Josephine. "I should think any help that the poor thing could get would be a comfort. How would it do to have me stay with her and let Hazel go in my place?"

"Josephine!" And at this exclamation, Josephine laughed. "Why not, Mother? I am older than Hazel and ought to be more valuable help; and the cost would be just the same in either case. There is no disgrace in being a nurse girl, you know." She could not resist the wicked pleasure of pricking an occasional bubble of her mother's, to see it burst.

But Mrs. Bradford was equal to the occasion.

"The very fact that you are older than Hazel makes it important that you should have advantages for which she can afford to wait," she said in her most dignified manner and with what Josephine called her "company tone."

Then Isabel turned discomfort into a new channel by saying with emphasis:

"Father would never in the world agree to have Hazel stay in town, with all of us away."

"I don't suppose he would," Mrs. Bradford admitted. "I did not mean that I was seriously considering it." She sighed as she spoke, because she had very seriously considered it; but it had been almost, if not quite, put aside, because she knew just how far she could influence her husband, and just when he would become as adamant.

Isabel returned to the charge.

"Then, Mother, Hazel will just *have* to have a lot of new clothes. She will, anyway, for that matter; she has nothing decent to wear. I was ashamed of her last Sunday in that skimpy white dress that she has outgrown."

"Dear me!" said Josephine, "you don't pretend to think that anything can be too skimpy for these days, do you?"

Isabel laughed. "Well, they can skimp in the wrong direction, and hers all do. Mother, seriously don't you feel that Hazel must have a lot of new clothes?"

"I feel that she cannot have new clothes, Isabel; I wonder that you mention it after what your father said. I need a new suit myself, and fully expected to have it; but I intend to sacrifice it for the good of my children; and if I can go without new dresses, I see no reason why Hazel shouldn't do the same."

"But, Mother, Hazel is positively shabby. She could not go anywhere as she is now."

"She will not need to go anywhere in particular. I do hope, Isabel, that you will have sense enough not to talk before her about dressing and going. I shall keep her at home with me a great deal of the time. There will be a good deal to do, remember, if we take a cottage or have housekeeping rooms, and Hazel is a young girl with no thought as yet of dress and society; see that you do not put such things into her mind."

"Hazel is just three months older than I am." Isabel's tones were significant. Her mother resisted the temptation to box her pretty daughter's ears and tried to speak calmly.

"Isabel, what is the matter this morning? You seem bent on contradicting everything I say. I know Hazel's age, of course, and I repeat that she is a young girl, much younger than you and still clinging to notions that you put away with your babyhood. You ought not to need to be told that the age of young people is measured by the way they mature rather than by years. Hazel Harris is a child, as her mother was before her, and there is no necessity for forcing her into woman-hood. I shall have to tell you, as I did your father, that there is no occasion for worry; I feel myself entirely capable of taking care of her."

Josephine, who had remained unusually silent for some minutes, suddenly broke up the conversation by rising rapidly from the table as she said:

"Well, I must confess I am getting tired of living on my father's and mother's sacrifices. I may as well give warning that this is the very last season I mean to do it. I'm going to learn dressmaking, or millinery, or *something,* and earn my own living. I'd rather be a shop girl at a notion counter or nursemaid outright than to have you pinching and struggling to try to make a fine lady of me."

This was a sore subject with Mrs. Bradford; she was dismayed over the spirit she had aroused, but she was also very much annoyed, and she answered with lofty dignity.

"Don't talk nonsense, Josephine. I'm sure no one said anything about sacrificing; when I complain, it will be time enough for you."

To her younger daughter she added as the door closed after Josephine, "That girl keeps me in hot water half the time. I'm just expecting her to make some reckless move that will undo all I have tried to do for her. Motherhood certainly has its trials."

"Don't be worried," said Isabel lightly. "Nothing dreadful will happen; I don't believe there is enough to either Josephine or me to make a decided move out of the regulation line; the life we live is much too comfortable to disturb. We are only consoling our consciences by threatening every now and then to go to work in the only ways open to us. All the same, there is one thing that has got to be said. Whether we go away this summer or stay at home, Hazel must have at least one new dress; I don't see how she is going to get along without more, but that, at least, is a necessity; I'm going to talk to Father about it and see if it can't be managed right away. I'm ashamed of her."

This is but one of the many talks that ensued during that June month, which most of the time was unusually warm, inciting the Bradford family to more or less irritability and argument for argument's sake. A few stormy scenes were lived through, chiefly after Mr. Bradford had caught his ear, before the managing head of the house steered her ambitious little craft into settled waters.

That she would accomplish her purpose in the end they had all felt reasonably certain, but it had been harder work than she had expected. For several weeks the girl, Hazel, had loomed up before her as an almost insurmountable difficulty. By ripping and pressing and turning and dyeing, the harassed mother felt that she could accomplish at least respectability for the girls—as she called her daughters—but that child's wardrobe was—well it was what ought to have been expected of Hazel Harris's daughter—disgracefully inadequate when she first came to them and made up of material that even a child ought to have known would not wear well. The crisis was reached on the day that she sent Hazel on an errand which would take the entire morning and, looking into the girl's speck of a room, went over her wardrobe piece by piece. It did not take very long; evidently clothing for both Hazel and her mother had been limited; the troubled schemer came to the sad but inevitable conclusion that Isabel was right; if the girl went away with them, there must be one new dress. If she had but known it, she need not have wasted that morning and almost choked her conscience in trying to decide otherwise. Isabel had been true to her word, and that very evening Mr. Bradford handed to his wife a twenty-dollar bill with the brief statement that it was every cent he could spare just then, and that every cent of it must be spent on Hazel. He was not up in young women's wardrobe, poor man! It must be confessed that he looked for results from that twenty-dollar bill that his wife and daughters knew were impossible to attain.

4

ON THE THRESHOLD

THERE can never be a more perfect summer day, at least for the "Four Girls," than that one on which the four white-haired matrons whom their children lovingly called "the girls" stood together on deck and watched the steamer slip swiftly through the waters of Chautauqua Lake toward the Chautauqua pier.

For the most part they were silent. There had been constant chattering during the day and continual visiting among themselves by the company that quite filled a drawing-room car and roused the interest and curiosity of other travelers.

"Don't you think they are a family party!" was one of the items concerning them that floated through the train. "They must be, they all call one another by their first names and are very intimate indeed, as none but relatives ever are."

Other items were added from time to time.

"Those people are all going to Chautauqua for the summer; won't they have fun? It is delightful to see such a large company going together. I wonder how they came to choose that resort?"

Later, someone solved this problem. "It seems that those elderly ladies were at Chautauqua years ago when they were young and now they are going back with their train; isn't that interesting? I wonder what sort of place Chautauqua is? Why don't we go there some summer?" Marion Dennis overheard this and reported it.

"Evidently we are missionaries," she said. "Our mission is to introduce Chautauqua to the benighted; I didn't suppose there were any people of intelligence who did not know a good deal about it by this time. But you mark my words, another family party will spring up among these travelers someday *en route* for Chautauqua; which will be a good thing for them."

They laughed a good deal about being missionaries and did what they could to interest strangers in their summer plans. They laughed a great deal that day, much more than was usual with them; it seemed to take very little to arouse their mirth. Part of the time laughter covered deep feeling, and much chatter was for the purpose of preventing others of their party from thinking too much and pointing contrasts too keenly.

Mrs. Ruth Burnham's scheme for gathering the forces for a summer at Chautauqua had prospered beyond her highest hopes. Not only children, but grandchildren and aunts and cousins had responded heartily.

"The very trainmen are astonished over us," Eureka Harrison proclaimed, "because of our all-togetherness. I overheard two of them romancing about us. I presume they think we are Mormon recruits on our way to Utah, there are so few of the male persuasion among us. Erskine here will do for the 'elder' who is marshalling us across the continent; you look dignified enough for the part, I am sure, and some of their missionaries are quite young."

As the day drew toward the sunsetting the party became quieter; until, when the four matrons drew instinctively near together and stood watching the glory of the western sky, they were almost silent.

Very few among the younger ones could appreciate the feeling that the well-remembered landscape awakened in the hearts of those four women, whose memories were entwined with so much that sobered them. Erskine Burnham was one of the few; he darted an annoyed, almost angry, glance once or twice at Eureka Harrison as her penetrative voice and light laugh sounded continually from a few feet away.

"I wonder if it is impossible for that girl to be quiet under any circumstances," he said to his wife. "One wearies of her everlasting chatter, especially just now."

"She does not understand," his wife said gently. "She is young and has no experience of life, as yet, to think back to."

"And no depth of feeling in any case," he said, speaking irritably. "I cannot imagine how a girl like her is going to fit in at Chautauqua."

For himself, he was entering into his mother's mood with almost painful sympathy. From a child he had responded in a way that was unusual to every chord that touched her, and he had been trained from early boyhood to an almost worshipful memory of his father. He could almost feel the throbbing of his mother's heart at that moment over the thought that *one* was not there to share this joy with her; yet there was Eureka Harrison, whose father had been so few years away from them, throwing off sparkling little sallies to make the more thoughtless laugh! Evidently she had not a thought of her mother. He felt justified in frowning at her and in thinking that it would have been better if such a discordant element in their party had dropped out.

All of which goes to prove how very little we know about one another. Just at the moment that Eureka Harrison was succeeding in having a monkey, made out of her handkerchief, climb an imaginary pole made of her arm, to the shrieking delight of some of the grandchildren, her heart was saying:

"Poor Mother, how often she described this very scene to Father and how many times she planned to take this journey with him! It is too hard that when at last she has it, she must be alone. If I could only share her loneliness with her! If I knew how to throw my arms about her and kiss her into comfort, as one of Aunt Flossy's girls would be sure to do if it were their mother! Oh, me! I wonder why I had to be made of stone, apparently, with a raging fire of pity and sympathy hidden away inside?"

They were almost at the pier.

"It is very much changed," Mrs. Roberts said gently, with her hand on Mrs. Harrison's arm.

"Yes," was the answer. "And yet it's the same shore; changed and the same—like us."

Mrs. Dennis spoke quickly, cheerfully. "It is a very different evening from the one on which we arrived before. Do you remember how it rained? You and Ruth wouldn't go out to find the meeting; Flossy and I had to go all by ourselves."

"You will never forget that!" Mrs. Harrison said with a touch of her old brusqueness. "I'm sure we repented in sackcloth and ashes."

"And we stayed in *Mayville*," Mrs. Burnham said meditatively. "What simpletons!" Then they laughed a little over their past follies and their present foolishness in recalling it all.

"Hear those old girls," said Eureka Harrison, "going over their memories of years ago when they were young. I wonder how it feels to be old. I never want to know; I hate the thought." She gave a little expressive shudder, which Erskine Burnham, to whom she was speaking, did not notice.

"They are none of them remarkable for great age," he was saying in what Eureka called his legal tone; he was never quite able to keep from resenting the thought of his mother being an old woman.

"Oh, no, but then their youth is long past, and there is a difference, of course. Mother is growing into an old woman in some respects; I can see it much plainer than she does herself; she draws back now from efforts that she would have made a few years ago without hesitation. I don't like it for her, any better than you do in your mother; I know you see the same thing in her but don't like to admit it. I don't wonder at that; I wouldn't, if I could help it. I hate old age; for myself, I am afraid of it."

The last words were murmured, as though she were thinking aloud rather than talking; and again came that shudder which seemed to suggest a visible shrinking from something inevitable.

This time Erskine Burnham noticed it and regarded her thoughtfully; he had no personal experience by which to understand that state of feeling; he was years older than Eureka, but he had no such shrinking from old age.

"I suppose one ought to order one's life in such a way that when the activities that belong to youth and vigor begin to weary, the brightening future lying just ahead will absorb one's interests." He spoke gravely, watching the girl's face the while. Did she possibly have some serious thoughts? But her laugh was as light, and her tone as gay as usual.

"No, thank you, the present is enough for me; I want to look neither backward nor forward. I think the good old Methuselah times ought to have stayed with me; then our youth would have been so long-drawn out that we should have had a chance to weary of it before it went.

"Fancy having eight or nine hundred years in which to enjoy—Chautauqua, for instance. Do look at those lovely houses on the hill yonder; there must be charming views from those upper porches. I didn't imagine that they had such pretentious houses here. Isn't this Chautauqua that we are approaching? It doesn't look much like the woods that mother was always talking about. I'm afraid they have become dreadfully civilized."

The boat touched the pier just as the sun sank behind the hills, leaving a trail of glory in the western sky and that peculiar soft dreamy light over lake and shore that one seems to see nowhere else, and that no old Chautauquan ever forgets.

Those of Mrs. Roberts's party whose lives were chiefly spent in large cities where they never saw a real sunset were so absorbed in the view as to be hardly able to give attention to the business of gate tickets and baggage. As for the four to whom the scene was not altogether new, they attended to neither baggage nor sunset, but stood and gazed about them in wide-eyed wonder.

"It isn't the same place at all!" was Mrs. Roberts's final exclamation. "Marion, don't you remember the mud we waded through on that first night? We must have gone up that very hill, only, where is the road?

Look at those paved streets! the idea! What is the name on that large building over there?"

"That's the arcade," volunteered a brisk young man who was looking out for possible boarders. "The jewelry store is there, and the art store; and all sorts of fancywork classes meet there."

"Fancywork classes!" repeated the dazed little woman. "Who imagined such frivolities at Chautauqua!"

Mrs. Dennis laughed. "You will have to accustom yourself to more startling changes than those," she said. "Aren't we all going to a hotel for the night? Imagine a hotel of any sort at Chautauqua! I confess I had some fears lest it should not be large enough for our party, but those houses in the distance reassure me. Do you remember the dining halls and the man who told us whichever one we went to we should wish that we had taken the other?"

"I wonder where they were located?" said Mrs. Burnham. "One was on a hill, I remember; the hill must be here still, but I don't seem to recognize even hills."

"It doesn't seem possible that they will be able to accommodate so large a party as ours with all these people here already," Mrs. Roberts said, "but of course they can; I was very explicit as to the number of rooms we should need; I reserved one for Burnham, thinking that he might change his mind at the last minute as he so often does."

"Where is Burnham?" asked Mrs. Dennis. "Isn't he going to come up here sometime during the season?"

"I don't really know what his plans are for the summer; he was very vague. I don't think he is sure of where he shall be; he rarely follows out his own program anyway; but he was very emphatic in eschewing Chautauqua; he has the strangest idea of the place!" The sentence closed with a little sigh.

They had been stopped for a moment by an obstruction in the road; and when they started again, the two ladies walked on together, leaving their escorts to follow. Mrs. Roberts glanced back to see who was within hearing before she spoke again in lowered tone.

"At first I hoped and prayed for his coming here until I found that Eureka was coming; Eurie told me that she hadn't the least hope of her, but it seems that at the last minute she changed her mind. When I saw her on the train, I thought that perhaps that was the reason why my prayers about Burnham coming with me had not been answered. I cannot tell you, Marion, how anxious I am to keep those two apart for this summer, at least; I cannot help thinking that it will be an important summer for them both. It is not that I fear their caring for each other as lovers, you know; I don't think either of them have such a thought; the most that they do when they are together is to quarrel, and Burnham is the most merciless critic that poor Eureka has; but they influence each other for evil continually. Isn't it strange? Do you think that Chautauqua can do much for Eureka? Her mother is so pleased that she came; but—I don't know—every letter from Evan has a word of caution about my being too much disappointed in Chautauqua; he says he hears everywhere that it is very much changed and that I must not hope for the atmosphere that we found. The outward changes are numerous enough, and yet perhaps—"

"Perhaps," said Mrs. Dennis cheerfully after waiting a moment for the completion of the sentence—"we shall find that walks and lawns and buildings can change without materially changing the atmosphere. As for what Chautauqua can do for Eureka, do you think any of our acquaintances expected or even hoped that our coming here years ago would have any good results? Suppose we hope for the best, Flossy dear, and pray for great things, not only for Eureka, but Burnham. The Lord is not limited to Chautauqua, even though we did so singly find him here that we can never forget it."

The troubled little mother pressed her friend's hand as she murmured:

"Thank you. Oh, Marion, pray mightily for my boy."

5

THE UNEXPECTED

AN HOUR later the matrons of the party were together on the upper hotel veranda.

"Isn't it lovely here?" Mrs. Harrison said. "Such a contrast to our old tent with its cot beds and tin-basin toilets! Oh, Marion, I thought once that if ever my gaze rested again on dear old Chautauqua with the prospect of spending a few blessed weeks here I should be perfectly happy. What a mistake it is to fancy that we can ever be that!"

"Until—" said Marion Dennis gently, with a swift, pitiful glance at the widow's robes and the tear-dimmed eyes.

"Yes, I remember that; I am always glad over the word *satisfied;* 'I shall be satisfied when I awake with his likeness;' but oh, there are some things that I want—*here*. Now that I have accomplished getting Eureka here, I am wondering all the time if it was wise. Perhaps it would have been better if she had gone with her aunt to Sea Girt, after all. I should have tried to encourage that, but for one thing; I know that Burnham Roberts was invited to Pal Beach for August, and that is only about eight miles from Sea Girt; if there is any one thing that I hope to accomplish this summer, it is the keeping of those two at least a hundred miles apart. Haven't you noticed that Eureka is a great deal more restless and—well, unlike other girls when she is with Burnham? I think the two are so much alike in their dislike for the conventional that they stimulate each other; that is the only way I can account for it."

Mrs. Dennis restrained the temptation to laugh; two confidences within so short a period, about the same persons, each from the standpoint of an anxious mother, had its humorous side. The utmost she could do was to be noncommittal.

"I am glad that you are to have Eureka to yourself this summer. Let us hope that Chautauqua has something wonderful in store for her as it had for us."

But the poor widow, who found it hard in these days to see a bright side anywhere, shook her head and spoke mournfully.

"I confess I haven't much hope of that; a girl who steadily resisted for years the influence of such a father as she had is not easily moved. She needs something to steady her, but I don't know what it would be."

"Where is she now, Eurie?"

"On the lower veranda with some of the youngsters; they are always in her train. Don't you hear her voice?"

As she spoke, Eureka's silvery laugh floated up to them; it expressed, Mrs. Dennis thought, lightheartedness and freedom from care as well as words could have done.

"I hope you count your blessings, Eurie dear," she said earnestly. "I do think that to have as happy a disposition as Eureka has and a heart that attracts childhood are gifts to be thankful for."

Eurie sighed. "Eureka is nearly always pleasant," she said, "and the children like that, of course—but I think sometimes that she is bright and pleasant because she has nothing to cross her; for she has a very strong will and bends everything and nearly everybody to it; really, Marion, she has her own way always; and so that she gets it, nothing else seems to matter very much to her."

Oh, dear blind mother! The probabilities are that you will never understand what a bitter cross your daughter Eureka bore when she gave up her college course, not because she could not have pushed her way through the difficulties and earned the money with which to do it—but because she felt that home and mother needed her. Having made this heavy sacrifice quietly and so cheerfully that it was not recognized by others as a sacrifice, why did the girl wear out her mother's nerves and heart by daily petty follies and willfulnesses that seemed always to foreshadow something worse? Only the One who fully understands the perversity of undisciplined human hearts can answer that question.

"Well," said Eureka's mother with a long drawn sigh, after waiting a moment for the reply that Mrs. Dennis was not ready to make, "there is no use in borrowing trouble, it comes fast enough; at least I have her for the summer away from the influence that I dread the most; I must try to be thankful for that. Isn't it horrid to have to feel so about dear Flossy's boy?"

"Hello!" said a ringing voice just below them, not speaking to them but to someone on the lower veranda. "All safely landed, eh? That unreliable boat must have got in before its time; I meant to be at the pier to receive you with all due honors. Do any of you happen to know where I'll find the *mater?*"

Exclamations of surprise from the lower veranda and shouts of glee from some of the children punctuated these sentences, while on the upper porch the two mothers who had been conversing exchanged startled and, on the part of one, dismayed glances. Trees obscured their vision, but there was only one voice like that. And then Eureka Harrison's voice put possible doubts to flight.

"Burnham Roberts! Do you ever do, even by accident, the thing that you have declared you will? I ought to have expected you after being so vigorously assured that you couldn't be hired to come to Chautauqua."

"I couldn't," said the youth cheerfully. "Nothing and no one could have hired me; I came of my own free will and design."

"But what in the world brought you?"

"Just what brought you, fair lady, cars first and then the boat; only I have the advantage of being an old resident. I reached here fully twenty-four hours ago. If I hadn't been beguiled by a pretty new maiden to take a longer walk than I had planned, I should have been at the dock, spyglass in hand, sighting your approach. Rooms all right? Is my mother satisfied with them?"

But Eureka ignored his questions and asked her own.

"A *'new maiden?'* Have you found new girls already to fascinate?"

"Scores of them; there are possibilities at Chautauqua, I assure you. Not that any of them presumed to fill your place, of course; it was simply a case of 'the other dear charmer' being away, you see."

"Now, Burnham, seriously, I hope you haven't been talking nonsense to some silly young girl here who doesn't know you and might believe something that you said."

"Dear Grandma, I assure you I have been discretion personified; you would have been proud of me. We talked chiefly about the clubs with which the place is infested."

"Clubs?" repeated Eureka curiously.

"Yes, organizations, you know; there is one for every year of life I think, beginning with the babies in their cradles. Could you, fair lady, direct me the way to find my maternal relative? I am longing to delight her eyes with the unexpected sight of me."

The face of Eureka's mother had settled from dismay into a kind of gloomy resignation.

"There is no use," she said. "I may as well give up the struggle; it seems to be a kind of fate; there he is again, and they have begun just where they left off; it will go on all summer just the same."

"That is the kind of chaff they always talk," she added as the merry nonsense floated up to them. "Not a grain of sense between them."

Mrs. Dennis cast about her mind for some soothing word.

"Perhaps that is when other people are within hearing; they may wax sensible when they are alone. Do you know, I don't understand how a volatile youth like Burnham Roberts can exercise much influence over a girl of so much character as Eureka? I should think it would all be the other way."

She might have added "And the other mother thinks it is," but of course she did not.

Mrs. Harrison made a gesture of dissent.

"What is she influencing him to do, or be?" she

asked pointedly; and as there was no reasonable reply to make to this, Mrs. Dennis was silent.

From that time on, for days together, two young people whom their elders had struggled to keep apart did what they could to justify the anxieties of their respective mothers. They were together constantly. Often, it is true, with a group of delighted children in their train, who served as excuse for all sorts of revelry; but there were long walks and long rows taken without the accompaniment of children, and there were hours long-drawn out when no one knew where they were save that they were somewhere together. They attended very few of the lectures, and even the public recitals of which Eureka was supposed to be fond and the concerts that were expected to attract them both failed almost entirely.

"Yellercutors as a rule are great bores," Burnham Roberts said loftily in response to his mother's petition that he would accompany her to the hall to hear a choice reading. "Especially those of the feminine gender, which you seem to affect here most of the time. Extravagance in pitch and tone and especially in gesture are to be looked for every time. Eureka has heard this one and says she doesn't care to hear her again; and Eureka is a fairly good judge of that sort of thing. They say that man Clark is fairly good; when he comes on, we are going.

"What's that, Mommy? You're alone? Where are all the others? What is the use in there being 'Four Girls' of you together if you can't keep one another company? I'm awfully sorry it happens so, but you see there's a Christian-Science female going to hold forth this afternoon over at Celeron, and I have promised to take Eureka to hear her. Fancy a lecture of any sort at

Celeron! Would it be irreverent to quote: 'Can any good come out of Nazareth?'"

But poor Mrs. Roberts was not thinking of the question. "Christian Science!" she repeated, her tones expressing such unqualified dismay that her son exploded into laughter.

"Why, my dear Mamma, what is the matter? I didn't say we were going to join the cult; even Eureka, who seems to be ready for anything absurd, hasn't got so far as that yet; we are going for the fun of it, of course."

"But, Burnham, what a strange idea to hunt up a talk on Christian Science and leave such a program as we have here today!"

"Oh, the program be hanged! Begging your pardon, Mamma; but all the same, you are being programmed to death on these grounds; there's so much of it, don't you see? Something going on every minute from the time one's eyes are opened in the morning away into the night; I don't know but they keep it going all night; I never saw anything like it! It sort of turns a fellow against it.

"What's that? You wouldn't think I had enough of it to turn me in any direction? Why, Mommy dear, you are growing sharp, sticking pins into a chap in that fashion; I'm astonished at you!

"But in spite of your ill treatment, I'm awfully sorry to leave you alone; wish I'd known of it earlier and I'd have made other arrangements."

Whereupon he kissed her eyes, kissed her nose, kissed her chin, and went gaily off to Celeron.

This state of things lasted for a couple of weeks, and then one morning Eureka came into one of the little reception rooms where her mother was sitting with the daily paper in her hand.

"Chautauqua Daily Assembly Herald," she read aloud

and laughed. "Think of this institution running a *daily*, and such an ambitious sheet as this, too, with a high-sounding name! It's convenient, though. Have you seen it this morning, Mother? I bought one so I could study things up; I've reformed, don't you think? I told Burnham last night that I had wasted all the precious hours on him that I should, trying to keep him out of mischief; and that after this he must play alone, for I was going to work. Do you know that one can study anything under the sun on these grounds? Look at these booklets, besides the announcements in the papers. I have schedules on all the summer-school courses, and there are hundreds of them; they begin with the babies and move straight through to oc-togenerians. There's a woman in her eighties out west somewhere who was inspired here to get an education and entered college last fall; honest, I'm not spinning yarns, it's a real 'tale of history,' as our little Maudie used to say. I've been inspired by it to go to work. I shall take up some study tomorrow. Why don't you look delighted? You've always wanted me to go on with my education; now that I have resolved to do so I ought to be commended."

"Are you in earnest, Eureka?"

"Of course. Don't you know that I am always in earnest about everything? Burnham says that is my worst fault; that I'm too intense."

Mrs. Harrison sighed. "I've never been able to determine whether you were very much in earnest about most things, or not quite in earnest about anything," she said.

"That's a doubtful compliment, but I'll pretend that it was meant for one, thank you. I'm in earnest this time, at least. I'm going to take a course in 'Literary and Dramatic Expression,' if you please; I'm reading from the booklet; doesn't it sound cultivated? It means learning to read, you know. I shall have Professor Clark for a teacher; he is the best reader we ever heard at college, and there were dozens of them that year. I said then I'd like to take lessons of him if I ever had a chance; and the girls hooted at the idea of my having a chance. I wonder what they will say now?"

"You can read aloud now better than most," her mother said. "Your father used to think so, and he was the best reader I ever heard."

"He was prejudiced in my favor," Eureka said softly, a tender smile hovering over her face, completely changing its expression. After a moment she spoke again in her most businesslike tone.

"I intend to make a business of this matter of reading aloud. I have a brilliant idea stolen from that Christian-Science woman we went to hear, much to your dismay. I never realized until I heard her that money could be made by such easy methods. I tell you, Mother, those Christian-Science people are sharp in business, whatever may be said of their logic. They have all sorts of ways of money getting and disciple making at the same time. A very fine reader goes out to read by the hour to a very susceptible and very rich old lady. She selects her most seductive passages and reads aloud in her most charming manner. The old lady absorbs the doctrines, and the reader absorbs the cash; see? I can read their Christian Science puzzles in a way to befuddle the very elect if I try; and I shall not have to try very hard; they seem to me to be written for the express purpose of muddling what few brains most people have."

Burnham Roberts had sauntered into the room in time to hear that last sentence.

"I'm amazed," he said. "After what we heard the

other day, I didn't imagine that you would go back on the Christian Scientists in that fashion."

"I'm not going back on them; I'm immensely interested in their ways of working. What I said was that their books seemed to be written for the purpose of muddling brains; viewed from that standpoint they are a success."

Burnham shrugged his shoulders. "She is sharp this morning," he said, looking whimsically from her to her mother. "I'll tell you what is the matter with her, she has decided to become a yellercutor."

6

"In Spite of Things"

IT WAS Mrs. Ruth Burnham who found her, down on the shore away from the bell tower, curled a limp heap in the grass, her head bowed over almost to the ground, and her tremulous voice sobbing out: "Oh, Mother, *Mother, Mother!* If I could only go to you!"

"My poor child!" said Mrs. Burnham, bending over her. "What has happened? Are you hurt? Are you ill? What can I do to help you?"

The girl came to a sitting position with a quick gasp, then started to her feet, brushing away tears and controlling her sobs with a strong effort.

"I beg your pardon," she said hastily. "I thought I was quite alone and too far away for anybody to see or hear me. I ought not to—"

"Dear child, you have done no harm in any way. Sit down, please, you look too miserable to stand. We are quite alone. I strayed out of the beaten path away down here, much farther than I meant; it looked so pleasant. I think I used to come here years ago. I could not help seeing that you were in some kind of trouble, and I thought I might do something to help you."

"No one can help me," said the girl in a kind of passion of despair. She had dropped to the grass again because she was trembling too much to stand. But she controlled herself and spoke more quietly.

"That is I mean—that I am not—that I ought not to need help; only—"

"Only you are away from home and mother, poor child, and miss them. I know all about it. Where is your mother, dear?"

"In heaven," said the girl, and her eyes filled.

"Oh!" said Mrs. Burnham, and the girl told her, long afterwards, that she knew then for the first time how much tenderness and sympathy could be put into a single monosyllable.

"Forgive me, dear, I did not think. Will you tell me about it? Sometimes it helps to talk things over. Where is your home, dear?" She dropped on the grass beside her and laid a soothing hand on the girl's brown one.

"I have no home," said the tremulous voice. "They are all gone; Father and Mother and home. There is only me."

"My poor little girl! But you have friends, relatives?"

"Yes, I live with my uncle, Father's brother."

"Here, at Chautauqua?"

"Oh, no; they live in New York; we are only here for a month." Instantly Ruth Burnham thought of Flossy Roberts and her lovely New York home and her lovely nature that kept her reaching out always after those less fortunate than herself. Was not here a chance to help this unhappy child? But she must talk commonplaces to her until she was herself again.

"It is a delightful place to come to for a month, isn't it? Especially to those who live in cities. I hope you are enjoying it and taking in great draughts of air and strength for the winter?"

There was a question in the tone, but she did not expect an answer; she meant to talk on quietly for a few minutes to give the girl a chance and to learn incidentally and by degrees in what ways she most needed help. The vehemence of the reply surprised her.

"No, I am not enjoying it; I *hate* it."

Then she sprang to her feet, apparently dismayed over her outburst and spoke rapidly.

"I ought not to say such things, I don't know why I do; forgive me, please. I must go home."

But even as she spoke she reeled and would have fallen, had not Mrs. Burnham's arm saved her.

"Sit down," she commanded gently. "Don't be frightened, you are only faint; you sprang up too suddenly. Lean against the tree and inhale this; you will be better in a few minutes."

"You are very good," the girl murmured as she held the costly trifle to her nostrils and breathed in gratefully its pungent odor.

The clock in the bell tower struck the hour and produced another start.

"I ought to go home this minute," the girl said. "I didn't think it was so late."

"You are not able to go yet; the color has not come back to your face."

"But I must go; I was to have supper ready by half past five without fail, because they have an appointment for the evening, before the lecture."

She made a second attempt to rise, only to reel back with a despairing murmur:

"Oh, I don't know what is the matter with me."

"I do, my dear; you have been overtaxed in some

way, and Nature is taking her revenge. Did you eat your dinner today, as usual?"

A faint color showed for a moment on the girl's face as she said:

"Not a mouthful; I couldn't."

"I suspected that. Will you let me prescribe for you? I want—" But she was stopped by an exclamation of dire distress. The girl had torn the rather shabby white dress she wore, a long, zigzag, mud-stained rent, difficult to mend; but the dress hardly looked worth mending, and the distress on the owner's face was so out of proportion to injury that Mrs. Burnham was puzzled. Could it be that the girl's circumstances made it necessary to attach so much importance to so small a loss?

"It must have caught on that root," she said. "But never mind, we can pin it up so that you can get home in it nicely."

"But I am afraid I cannot mend it," the girl said pitifully. "It has grown so thin that it will not hold the stitches, and my aunt will—oh, I don't know what to do!"

This was genuine distress and hinted at a state of things that distressed the listener; clearly here was an opportunity for a helping hand if one could but find just how to use it with the least pain. Then, as the girl attempted to stand and grew dizzy again and dropped, half sobbing, to the grass, she remembered the sentence she had been about to speak.

"My dear, you are not fit to get supper for anyone tonight, and I am going to take charge of you; consider me your aunt for the time being; then it will be your duty to obey me."

The shadow of a smile flitted across the girl's face, but Mrs. Burnham could not know that it marked to her the amazing difference between her aunt and this stranger.

"I am expecting my son at any moment now; they are out driving, and he was to come this way and pick me up. The carriage is two-seated, so I am going to carry you home with me for a little rest and refreshment; we can attend to the dress, too. The children's nurse is skillful with her needle, and she can have the rent mended by the time you are ready to go home."

"Oh," said the girl, "I *wish* I could; you can't know how much I should like it, but I must not; really, I must go home at once; my aunt would be so—so—and supper must be ready promptly tonight; they are not to be at home until just in time for it. Oh, what is the matter with me? If I am going to be ill, what *shall* I do!"

This last sharp outcry was caused by a return of the dizziness and deathly faintness as soon as she tried to stand. At that moment there appeared around a bend in the road two horses and a two-seated carriage, with Erskine Burnham as driver. A preemptive motion of his mother's hand brought him promptly to her side; meantime, she spoke to the girl.

"You are not going to be ill, my child; but you are going to be sensible and let me give you a little care. I will send a message to your aunt at once, so she will not be frightened. Help her to the carriage, Erskine, she is faint; and drive at once to the hotel, please."

Eureka and her unfailing companion, Burnham Roberts, were together on the porch when Erskine Burnham's carriage rolled down the driveway. Eureka leaned over the railing to call gaily to its occupants but changed her mind and said instead:

"Who in the world has Aunt Ruth picked up now? That woman is getting to be the greatest! She is taking lessons of your mother. What a shabbily dressed girl! Dear me, it's an invalid! Erskine is almost carrying her."

"Great Scott!" said Burnham, "what eyes the girl has!" Eureka gave him a glance of half-amused contempt. "Do you always see eyes?" she asked.

"Not always, nor often such eyes as those. I wonder who the creature is?"

She almost wondered it herself, lying among the pillows of a luxurious couch in a charming room being waited upon by the deftest of handmaids, whom they called "Nurse Norah." Mrs. Burnham's first care had been to learn the address of the rooms where the aunt was doing "light housekeeping" and dispatch two of the children with a note.

"Tell her aunt that we'll take the best possible care of her and send her home before dark, so she need have no anxiety," the girl heard her call after the messengers as they scurried away, and she gave a little half hysterical laugh. If they could know how absurd it was to think of her aunt feeling anxiety about her!

"If she could only lose me forever and *forever*, it would be the happiest day of her life," she said aloud. She believed herself to be quite alone, but Mrs. Roberts, who had slipped softly in at Mrs. Burnham's suggestion, heard the words, felt their pent-up bitterness, and stopped midway in the room, perplexed. How much, or how little did that mean? Was it the cry of a heart half broken or the sentimental wail of a foolish, selfish girl? There were almost equal chances for either. After a moment's thought she went forward and knelt beside the couch.

"Are you feeling better, dear?" she asked. "Don't try to sit up; I am Mrs. Roberts, the one who met you in the hall, you know."

"I am better, thank you," the girl said, "and you are all very, very kind, but I truly think that I ought to go home just as soon as I can."

"Just as soon as you can, you shall," said Mrs. Burnham from the doorway; she was followed by a maid bearing a tray; she pushed a small table near to the couch and arranged dishes on it as she talked.

"Now, for a girl who declined to eat her dinner I order this bowl of bouillon, steaming hot; it will put new life into you; after that, some of these tiny biscuits and a sip or two of chocolate; all girls like chocolate, don't they?"

Presently she seated herself, continuing to chat pleasantly and to note with satisfaction the eagerness with which the girl swallowed the hot bouillon, like one half famished. Before the meal was concluded, she was called from the room.

"I am leaving you in good hands," she said, looking back from the door. "My friend, Mrs. Roberts, has mothered several girls and knows all about them."

"I can't think why she is so good to me," the girl murmured, looking after her with loving eyes. "It feels like a little bit of Mother, and sometimes I miss *her* so awfully! It frightens me to think that the desolation seems to grow worse."

This sentence gave Mrs. Roberts the opening for which she had been wishing, and for the next half hour she exerted all her skill to learn the needs of the girl thus suddenly thrust upon their attention.

But there proved to be a quiet reticence about her, a sort of gentle dignity that attracted, even while it put aside all strictly personal questions. Yet she was frank, apparently, and seemed to tell her whole story.

"I am just Hazel Harris," she said, "an orphan, with no one in the world of my own name or blood; my father's half brother, the only one he had, lives in New York, and I have come there from California to live with him, and that is all."

"Then your aunt is this uncle's wife? And you are at Chautauqua for the summer?"

"Only for a month."

"That seems a short time, yet a great deal can be accomplished in a month. I wonder what you are going to let Chautauqua do for you in that month?" The girl stopped her slow sipping of chocolate and looked thoughtfully at the small lady opposite her.

"What I am going to let it do for me?" she repeated wonderingly.

"Yes. Don't you know that opportunities do for us what we let them? Sometimes we just let them slip." In her heart was a sigh for the boy who was letting them slip.

"I never thought of it that way," the girl said. "I'm just enduring Chautauqua."

"My dear! that needs explaining."

"It is easily explained," said the girl, sitting erect and speaking rapidly. "The place is beautiful and wonderful in ever so many ways, but I am not in it, nor of it; I don't belong; I just stand on the outside, so close to the edge that I am almost pitched off, and watch it going by. Do you think even heaven would be a good place to you if you stood forever and ever on the outside edge and just looked on?"

"I shouldn't," said Mrs. Roberts earnestly. "I should know that I was in my Father's house and had a claim on all its joys."

It was not the sort of answer the girl had expected. It quieted her excitement and flushed her face with a new thought. She gave a little embarrassed laugh and was silent for a moment; then, as the thought took hold of her, she said:

"It *is* different, isn't it? That will be Father's house, and I shall know that I belong inside; thank you."

"Then you are his child?"

"Yes, oh yes! I should die if I hadn't that; and having it, nothing should make me unhappy for very long, should it? But it is very hard to remember all the time. I find that I want my good things here, too."

"You have a right to them, my dear; be sure you take what belongs to you, and part of your inheritance is at Chautauqua; be happy here."

The girl looked startled.

"In spite of—of things?" she asked breathlessly. "Do you think I could?"

"In spite of everything, my child. Your Father means you to get good here, and happiness."

"Then I will try for it," said the girl gravely, with a marked air of conviction and decision. "I had not thought of it in that way at all; I thought I had a right to be miserable, and I hugged my little miseries and made much of them. I won't anymore. Thank you; oh, thank you *so much!* Now I'm sure I ought to go home; I feel real well and strong; all the faintness is gone. Do you think I might have my dress?"

As she spoke, she looked down at the flowing robes of the silk wrapper that enveloped her and blushed and smiled.

"I feel like an Eastern princess," she said, "or like an enchanted maiden in fairyland. I was afraid I should waken suddenly and find all the lovely lights gone out of the world; but I shall not; you have made them stay. Oh, I *thank* you. You do not know what you have done for me."

Just then came Nurse Norah with the shabby little

white dress, wonderfully mended and delicately pressed; the soil of the woods washed away.

"I didn't think it could ever be made to look nice," the girl said, surveying it with delighted eyes.

In the doorway was Burnham Roberts, asking for his mother and looking at the girl.

7

POSSIBILITIES

HE FOLLOWED his mother into the hall with a question: "Don't you want us to see your little protégée home, Mamma? Eureka and I are going to walk and will be glad to take care of her."

But Mrs. Burnham had heard the question and turned to explain. Erskine had kept his horses for the evening; he and his wife were going to drive to Mayville and row home by moonlight. Their route lay directly past the cottage where the child lived, and they could drop her there; it was really too far for her to walk in her present state.

"She is singularly interesting," Mrs. Roberts said when they had watched their guest depart.

"Isn't she?" echoed Mrs. Burnham. "I don't know when I have met a young person who took me so utterly by storm."

"We must know more of her," said Mrs. Roberts. "I think she has great possibilities."

Burnham Roberts, who was still awaiting the movements of Eureka, exploded into laughter over this.

"You two ladies are the limit!" he explained as they

looked at him inquiringly. "You are always finding singularly interesting persons with possibilities. That is Mamma's forte especially, and I think, Aunt Ruth, that you and she are well mated. Now to me this new specimen of yours is just a big-eyed girl going about to see what she can find."

"Very well," his mother said, smiling, "I think she will find it, and I hope she will."

"Well, really!" was Mrs. Bradford's greeting to her niece. "Seems to me you have been creating quite a sensation; fainting away on the grass in a public place and having letters written about you by 'Ruth Burnham,' whoever she is. I hope you told her that you got into such a temper that you couldn't eat your dinner and that was what made you faint."

"You came back in a lovely carriage," said Josephine, "for all the world like a second Cinderella; only the prince was a married man with his wife beside him, wasn't he? What a pity!"

"I do wish, Josephine, that you wouldn't try to fill the child's mind with absurd ideas about romantic adventures. What would a man do but bring a girl home in his carriage who had fainted away before his mother's face and compelled her to look after her? The fact that she brought her illness on herself, even if it were known, wouldn't hinder people from taking care of her of course. I see nothing but a very commonplace incident in it. Are you all right now, Hazel?"

"She is looking wonderfully well for an invalid." This was Isabel's comment. "Her eyes shine like diamonds. Are you sure you didn't play sick, my dear, so as to get to see the world? Did you dine in state in the large dining room?"

"No," said Hazel, "I took my dinner on a couch in

Mrs. Burnham's room and couldn't hold up my head to take it."

"Humph!" said Josephine. "I think they might have taken you in to dinner with them since they set out to be so nice. All rich people are snobs, anyway."

"Don't spoil her vision, Josephine, with your sordid suggestions. Let her dream it out for one night; she has been in fairyland; one can see that by a look at her face," remarked Isabel.

"She ought to be in bed," said her aunt. "That will be better for her than visions and compliments. A good night's rest will make you all right."

"I have been in *heaven*," said the girl aloud in the privacy of her own room, "and, oh, I must be different after this; it is my opportunity, and it will do for me what I let it; my Father means me to get good here. That is wonderful; I must never forget it."

Her face was very sweet as she moved about the place, making ready for bed; she had been uplifted by a new thought.

One looking on would have felt sure that nothing in her surroundings had given her thoughts an uplift. The entire attic was her room; it was large enough to serve, as it had done for years, as the dumping ground of the house. Broken chairs, rickety tables, worn-out trunks, discarded packing boxes, any and everything which by reason of breakage or mutilation of some sort had fallen into disuse had by degrees found their way to the attic and lay in distorted heaps in the various corners. Certainly the room had furniture enough, such as it was, and yet the word *bare* would have been the very one used instinctively in describing it. In the few feet of space that Hazel had chosen for her room, a pitiful attempt had been made at order and daintiness. One of the rickety tables had been set up with a packing box under one end to do duty in place of a missing leg. It had been covered with a sheet of pink paper, and over it spread a fragment of discarded muslin curtain, carefully darned and pressed. On this dressing table the girl had arranged her incongruous toilet belongings. A small, exquisitely framed hand mirror that had belonged to her mother's happy girlhood; a plain, common hairbrush and comb, a cake of cheap toilet soap lying in a dainty silver soap box that had been hers from childhood. A pin tray of delicately carved foreign wood holding the few very plain bits of jewelry that had escaped the wreck of their home. For the rest, the furnishings were meager enough. A common cot made up with the usual common furnishings of cheap attic rooms in summer resorts; a barrelhead, with a cloth spread over it, for a toilet stand; a small, enameled washbowl and a tin pail for a pitcher, made up the list of absolute necessities.

Mrs. Bradford, when she first looked at the rooms offered for light housekeeping, had not thought of the attic as a possible sleeping place and probably would not have considered it had she not been, as she expressed it, at her wits' end. It had been discovered that her ideas as to prices obtaining in country summer resorts did not correspond with facts. She had written many letters and studied many descriptive rental lists and had more than once been almost on the verge of despair, yet had never relinquished, even for an hour, her determination to spend a month at Chautauqua with her family. But there had to be compromises. Mr. Bradford in one of his firm moments had settled it that they must take the vacation without him. It was too long a trip in any case for him to take for two weeks, and he could not afford it.

At first his wife was heartbroken, but after many

arguments with herself, she persuaded herself that it would really be better for him to run down to the shore for each weekend, and for a day now and then through the week, than even to go to Chautauqua.

"It would be taking his vacation piecemeal, you know," she explained to the skeptical Josephine, "so spreading it out through the season; and he would have the sea air which he likes so much, and nothing to tempt him to anything but rest."

"Yes," Josephine admitted, "if Father would only go to the shore every weekend through the summer, it might be better than ten days at Chautauqua. But, Mother, he won't do any such thing; he'll stick in town and work."

"He simply *must* do it," Mrs. Bradford said, setting her lips firmly.

But Josephine had continued skeptical and had spoken her mind to her sister that evening.

"Mother thinks she can make Father take a little care of himself this summer, but I know better. He will stay here and slave himself to death for us; just as he has done all our lives. I hate it! The reason I want to go to Chautauqua is to see if something won't grow out of it that will help me to earn my living."

"How could Chautauqua help you in any such way?" doubting Isabel had asked.

"I don't know," was the half-irritable reply. "If one-third of what I have heard about it is true, it ought to bristle with ideas for people who are willing to work. Anyhow, that's what I'm going to try to find out. If I don't succeed, I'll turn nurse girl, or shop girl, or something, as soon as I get home; see if I don't."

Isabel had laughed. "I shall see," she said significantly.

She had heard much such talk before; she did not

expect anything to come of it. She too "hated" the state of things then existing, but she saw no way out save the one that she knew held her mother's hopes, the determination that one of them should make a marriage rich enough to affect the fortunes of the entire family. Being people with a certain amount of refinement, they never mentioned this darling scheme of their mother's, except in jest; and being girls with a background of honor, they hated all such ideas as beneath them; nevertheless, Isabel had a miserable belief in her heart that their mother would somehow dominate them both. So, after other compromises in the matter of dress and traveling outfits, in the closing days of July they had reached Chautauqua and spent a perplexing day trying to make the accommodations to be had match a very limited purse; limited as it was, Josephine was miserable over it because of her shrewd suspicion that her father meant to sacrifice quietly all his "weekend" days at the shore in order to supply it. From three rooms and a kitchen as being the least that they could possibly manage with, they had dropped to two rooms, then to one, with a tiny kitchenette. As a matter of fact, it was Hazel who had given the casting vote for that one room. It was after her aunt had said despairingly,

"I am sure I don't know what we are to do; I don't see but we might as well give it up and go back home. We could manage in this one room, three of us, with a cot for Josephine, and you sleeping with me, Isabel, but four in a room is out of the question."

"I don't know," Isabel said, slowly pacing off the room as she spoke. "There's a chance for two cots, one at this side and the other at the foot of the bed."

"Yes," said Josephine, "and three of us could line up in the hall while the fourth one got ready for bed; she could shout through the keyhole, 'Next,' as soon as she was ready to hop in."

"Do for pity's sake be quiet, Josephine," said the harassed mother. "If these people downstairs should hear you, what would they think of us!"

Then Hazel had spoken.

"Aunt Sarah, isn't there a place for a cot for me in that attic where the owner said we could put our trunks?" She never forgot the instant look of relief that flashed in her aunt's face.

"Sure enough!" she said cordially. "How bright you are, Hazel, to think of that. It must be a large attic, for she said there was plenty of room for all the luggage. A cozy corner of it might be fixed up for a sleeping room, I should think; and if we did it ourselves, it ought to be without much additional expense. I think an attic is a real cozy place to sleep, especially in the summertime. In fact, I shouldn't in the least mind it myself, if I were younger."

Josephine had demurred. "But up there alone, away from us all? I think it would be forlorn."

"Nonsense, Josephine. Hazel isn't a child, nor a coward. How far away from us would she be, pray? You speak as though the house were a castle."

"We might have two cots up there," Isabel said meditatively, "for Hazel and me; we could keep each other company, and that would leave a princely space for you and Josephine, Mother."

"Nonsense!" Mrs. Bradford said again, more sharply than before. "You'll do no such thing; I don't care to ask them to build their house over to accommodate us; one cot in the attic is all the extra I can think of asking, and if you feel so dreadfully about it, I can go up there myself and sleep."

Then Hazel had made haste to explain that she was

not at all timid, that she would not be lonesome because she would be sound asleep, and that she really liked the idea of a corner quite to herself; and her aunt seemed more pleased with her than she ever remembered to have seen her.

But it must be admitted that the first night of that attic dismayed them all. Josephine and Isabel exclaimed over it as impossible, while their mother was gloomily silent. Hazel was the first to recover and to persist in the possibilities of the room. Moreover, she carried her point, because her aunt was more than willing that she should, and moved to the attic that evening. It certainly had possibilities; hornets and bats had set up housekeeping in the rafters and been apparently unmolested for ages. Rats and mice, of which Hazel had a foolish horror, scurried to and fro almost under her feet in their panic at her invasion. But she conquered her fears, or kept them in subjection, and was not actually unhappy in her retreat, at least not all the time. She had known all the while that the dominant feeling which made her accept this corner was not named self-sacrifice, but selfishness. It was her one chance for "being rid of them all" part of the time. She put it thus baldly, to herself, ashamed of herself the while, for Josephine and Isabel were always kind and occasionally considerate, but she could not help feeling that she did not belong to their world, and escape from them at times seemed almost a necessity.

It is true that when on an unusually warm night, such as rarely visits Chautauqua in August, she felt compelled to keep head and ears closely covered to shut out the sound of little nibbling teeth all about her or the rattle of a roll of papers on the shelf above her head. She told herself that she was paying too dearly for privacy and that she would not stay in that attic another night; yet with daylight her courage revived, and she invested in two five-cent mousetraps, one for the shelf, and another to place just below her pillow and tried again. For that matter, what else was there for her to do?

There were other trials besides that attic at night when bats and mice were abroad; daylight brought its full share of them. Economy in every sense of the word was the order of Mrs. Bradford's light house-keeping scheme; and poor Hazel who had been trained in a different school, or rather in no school at all so far as housework was concerned, was forever "wasting milk and eggs" in alarming fashion and using an appalling amount of butter. Her experience in this line was so unpleasant that the girl gave up the use of these standard articles for herself as much as possible; and presently added fresh fruits to her list of denials. There came to be reason for Isabel's statement that Hazel's eyes grew larger every day. She annoyed her mother by announcing that her cousin was not look-ing even as well as she did in New York, and that "Father" would be distressed over her.

8

THE CLIMAX

"SHE is bound to distress somebody," Mrs. Bradford said irritably. "I never in my life knew a girl with a more ungovernable temper; just because I said the other day that fresh fruits were ridiculously high priced for the country, she flushed up to her hair and hasn't touched a peach since."

Then Josephine: "Well, Mother, you said it just after Hazel had helped herself to a dish of them, and you know you added that it would be well for us to remember that and not serve them as though they were applesauce. I think I should have done just what Hazel did; or else I should have taken three times as much for spite; I think that would have been my style of temper."

"Then you would have proved yourself a rude, hateful–acting girl, just as she did," Mrs. Bradford said firmly. "But I would risk your doing any such thing; I brought you up, thank goodness."

Which phrase, by the way, suggests one of Hazel's heaviest trials.

"I should think even your mother could have

taught you better than that!" was one of Mrs. Bradford's especially trying exclamations—there were others like unto it, all of them containing to Hazel's excited nerves a covert sneer for the mother whose memory she adored. There were hours when she found all these experiences so hard to bear that, in the privacy of her attic room, she told herself with bitter weeping that she could not endure it any longer.

Such a climax had been reached on the day that she flung herself into the grass by the lakeshore and sobbed out her bitter cry for "Mother." Not that it had been a great trial that called it forth, but rather the piling up of many petty ones. Before Mrs. Bradford's table economies reached what Josephine called the "starvation point," a method of relief was discovered. It was learned that among the numerous boardinghouses scattered over the grounds, certain of them furnished fairly good meals for twenty-five cents. They were named lunches, to be sure, but on occasion they would serve excellently well for dinners. Pencil and paper together with a vigorous exercise of Josephine's computation powers proved that seventy-five cents would afford three of them better dinners than that sum would produce in the kitchenette.

"But there are four of us," objected Isabel, "and that would mean a dollar each time."

"That's true," Josephine agreed. "And a dollar seems a great deal more than seventy-five cents, some way. We might take turns, though, and the fourth one eat the scraps at home that don't count. That's the way some of the poor families in New York do; honestly it is. Mother, you needn't look so disgusted; Nettie Goodwin told me that some girls in her grade actually took turns in dresses. They found that one of the children was coming to school for a month, and then dropping out on a plea of illness while the other one wore that same dress to school. That could be managed better with dresses than dinners, though, couldn't it?" and Josephine giggled.

"I don't think it is necessary to compare yourself with the slums," Mrs. Bradford said with dignity. But Josephine's nonsense had given her an idea. She was extremely anxious to secure the occasional dinners; not for their sakes, but for the opportunity it would afford her daughters to make some desirable acquaintances. Since she knew in her secret heart that she had come to Chautauqua for the sake of its possible social advantages for her girls, she must of course embrace every opportunity. It was an actual fact that her expenses were planned on such narrow margins that while she could see her way clear to the occasional seventy-five cents' outlay for outside lunches, to make it a dollar troubled her. Couldn't the taking turns be managed in some way? Hazel unwittingly opened the way. She remarked one day on the almost universal custom obtaining on the grounds among the smaller boardinghouses of serving the heavy meal at midday. She should not think that city people would like it; for herself, she never cared to eat meats and hearty foods at noon and did not believe she should ever learn to do so. Mrs. Bradford opened her lips to argue on the greater healthfulness of the midday dinner where it could be managed, then suddenly closed them again. Was not here an opening for her plan? The very next day the plan matured. Mrs. Bradford announced boldly at the breakfast table that she was going to the Arlington for luncheon; Mrs. Adams, the lady across the way whom she met yesterday, said they served excellent noon meals there, quite good enough for dinners; she had seventy-five cents to spare and could take two of them with her; since Hazel entirely disapproved of heavy lunches, "suppose we leave her to eat whatever she pleases and you two come with me? There is plenty in the house to make a good dinner for one, and Hazel can eat it tonight while we take our light suppers. How will that do?"

Isabel exclaimed in astonishment, and Josephine laughed over it as a joke.

"Mother is actually doing the slum stunt!" was what she said; but her mother frowned. As for Hazel, after a moment of surprised silence, she said it would be all right so far as she was concerned; it was quite true that she did not care for meats and vegetables at noon.

The girls, finding their mother in earnest, made some vigorous protests, but in the end Mrs. Bradford carried her point. The second time the experiment was tried was the day of the climax. It came about in this wise. Mrs. Adams, the lady across the way who had introduced them to the Arlington, stopped at the side porch on an errand which she presently made known.

"Do you lunch at the Arlington today? We thought we should, too; it is too warm to do any cooking. I wonder if I may venture to ask a favor? I notice that your maid doesn't go with you to luncheon, and I was wondering if I couldn't borrow her to sit with Baby while I am gone? Of course I would pay her a little something for her time; though he is always sound asleep at that hour, and she could read or sew all the while. There is really nothing for anyone to do, but I couldn't leave him in the house alone, you know. Would it be possible do you think for me to make an arrangement with her, or is she busy for you during the noon hour?"

Mrs. Bradford was very much embarrassed, was

confused, was at an utter loss what to say in reply. The simple truth—if it had been simple truth—that she kept no maid and that her niece did not go with them to dinner because she did not enjoy warm meals at noon, did not even occur to her to say, because she knew that the real reason for Hazel's not going was to avoid that additional twenty-five cents and to save the child's one respectable dress from a too-frequent appearance at all hours of the day. How could one make such explanations to a stranger? She hesitated, grew red in the face, and stammered some unintelligible words before she finally got out the statement that it would not be convenient for Hazel to leave home at that hour. Mrs. Adams went away perplexed, half offended, and with a feeling that the Bradfords were queer, and she would better have as little to do with them as possible. And then Hazel, who had been within hearing all the while, and who was more angry than she ever remembered being in her life before, pushed open the door of the kitchenette, her eyes ablaze and her voice unsteady.

"Aunt Sarah, why did you not tell that woman that I was your niece?"

"Well, really!" said the astonished and much annoyed aunt. "I suppose I did not consider it necessary to explain our family connections to the neighborhood. I didn't think anything about it. You needn't go into a rage over it, though; there is no disgrace in being taken for a maid; very respectable girls are often maids. If you hadn't been eavesdropping, you wouldn't have heard anything to disturb you."

"I was not eavesdropping, and you know that I don't stoop to such things; I was about the work that you told me to do; and I'm not angry over being called a maid; I wish with all my heart that I was somebody's servant working for wages. What humili-ates me is to live with a woman who resorts to all sorts of subterfuges to save the food I eat, and who tries to palm me off on her acquaintances as a hired servant to keep up false appearances; I was brought up to be honest."

Then there were two very angry people in that hall.

"You were brought up to be impudent," blazed Mrs. Bradford. "I never heard such impudence in my life, nor was ever so insulted; the idea of your actually accusing me of lying! I wish your uncle, who thinks you are such a jewel, could have heard you talk to me! Let me tell you, miss, that if you were my servant you wouldn't be standing there very long. I should pack you off bag and baggage before you had a chance for any more impudence. But unfortunately for me, you are my husband's niece, and I must endure you. I shall see as little of you as possible, though. Have the decency to go out of my sight and stay out until you cool down and are ashamed of yourself; you are like your mother in temper as well as in everything else."

Hazel turned and went. The mention of her mother's name, even in such connection, brought such a sense of pain and shame as to almost overwhelm her. If her mother had been there and overheard it all, how utterly disappointed with and ashamed of her child she would be! The child could almost hear the low, sweet voice speaking the tenderly reproachful words:

"How could my daughter say such things to her uncle's wife, a woman old enough to be your mother?" And again, as Hazel tried to justify herself to herself,

"It makes no difference about the provocation, Daughter. My Hazel is a follower of the meek and lowly Jesus, and he is the only standard by which to measure life."

"And I have broken faith with him," said the girl aloud with a burst of tears. Then she fled to her attic.

The outcome of it was that within the hour she sought her aunt with words of apology.

"Aunt Sarah, I want to beg your pardon for what I said; it was very wrong."

"And false," said Mrs. Bradford pointedly. "I want you to especially remember that you accused me of falsehood. Still, I accept your apology; we will say no more about it; when people allow themselves to get as angry as you were, they are quite apt to forget the truth."

After that they went their separate ways, each believing that she had spoken truth. Hazel was sure that her aunt was trying to pose before this new world of strangers as a lady of ample means who did "light housekeeping" for amusement and kept a maid to attend her; and Mrs. Bradford did not for one moment believe that she had allowed her neighbor's inference to stand because she wanted to deceive, but merely that she was taken by surprise and had not known what to say. The fact is that Mrs. Bradford really believed herself to be a strictly truthful person; and she was consumed with indignation over the charge of falseness. So the peace arranged that morning was rather a surface one. When, later, Hazel was told that she had better eat her luncheon right away so as to close the kitchenette from the flies, she replied with cold dignity that she did not want any luncheon; then she had immediately drawn down the kitchen shade and made the room as dark and cool as possible and fled to her attic. And her aunt had banged the door of her own room a little as a sort of escape valve to her feelings and told the walls that if that ill-tempered girl wanted to sulk all day without any dinner she was welcome to do so. After that, she made ready and went out to join her daughters by appointment at the colonnade and go to that dinner luncheon. A little later, Hazel, in her one white dress very skimpy and slightly soiled, stole out and made her way by the least frequented avenue to the shore and the grass, where she had abandoned herself to bitter wailing.

A more lonely and desolate girl than this one of eighteen years might have been hard to find. There are many, it is true, infinitely worse off so far as the mere necessities of life are concerned, but for desolation and at times an almost suffocating realization of it, Hazel Harris easily stood first. The contrast between her present surroundings and her past could hardly have been greater. The only child of parents who all but idolized her, they had lived for the purpose of having every wish of hers gratified, if possible, even before it was spoken. Always with uncertain income, as the families of landscape artists are apt to be, they were yet at no time touched by poverty in any of its sordid aspects. They were economical—or thought they were—today, because it was necessary; but they were lavish in the extreme tomorrow, when a picture had just been sold; and thought as little about the tomorrows of the distant future as the robins or the snowbirds. The wonder is that they had not spoiled their daughter; perhaps they had loved her too much for soil of any sort to touch her. Perhaps it was because with all their unworldliness, and what might by some be called improvidence, they had yet a simple abiding trust in God as their heavenly Father and Jesus Christ as their Savior and Guide and had trained their daughter to unquestioning obedience to his will that she came to her seventeenth year as sweet a flower as ever bloomed, always in the shielded atmosphere of parental love and companionship, loving books and study as well as her mother had done; loving flowers and ferns and all beautiful effects of sunlight and air and dew as well as her artist father did. She studied books and nature in their company and was their constant companion in all their rovings—and they traveled a great deal—caring almost too little for any other companionship.

And then, suddenly, trouble and sorrow swooped down upon them out of a clear sky. The father was severely hurt in an automobile accident, and after six months of endurance that taxed all his powers, he died. Then it was found that doctors' and surgeons' and nurse's bills had more than swallowed their tiny surplus. There were five more, never to be forgotten months, during which Hazel and her mother struggled bravely with poverty; selling pictures almost from house to house; pictures that were dearer to them than any other earthly things; and they had the unspeakable pain of knowing that their acquaintances bought out of pity for them. The frail little mother shivered and shrank from the ordeal; she grew daily paler and thinner, while Hazel, from being a cherished flower that was expected only to give out fragrance, blossomed into responsibility and burden bearing. There were a few dear weeks in which her mother asked her advice, followed her suggestions, and called her, not only her blessing and her treasure, but her staff to lean upon; and then, all unexpectedly to the girl, her mother slipped away and left her alone! Alone and poor. Their little hoard of money was gone; there were no more pictures to sell; most of the curios had been already sold; during that last hard year they had refrained as much as possible from buying clothing, and their supply had never been large. So at seventeen poor Hazel found herself not only alone and penniless, but almost destitute.

The only relative with whom her father had carried on a fitful correspondence through the years was his half brother, Joseph Bradford, whom in boyhood he had looked up to as an older brother and had always loved. In his prosperous years he had sometimes sent his brother substantial proof of his continued regard. Hazel had heard all sorts of pleasant stories having to do with the boyhood of those two; but of her uncle's family she knew little, save that her mother and her Aunt Sarah did not love each other; even this she learned by inference, rather than direct statement. But there was no denying that she began life in her uncle's home prejudiced against his wife; for how could any woman be worthy of affection who did not love her mother, the dearest, sweetest woman who ever lived!

"I hope I shall never have to stay at Aunt Sarah's for even a week," she had said one day to her father, her eyes flashing over some word in her aunt's letter that the quick-witted girl saw was a covert criticism of her mother. "I know I should almost hate her."

Her father had laughed indulgently; he did not love Aunt Sarah himself.

"Don't you worry, Pussy," he had said with his arm about her. "Daddy is going to get famous one of these days; he is going to paint a picture that will set the world on fire; and when money and fame come pouring in, your Aunt Sarah will discover that we are the choicest people in all the world."

But the picture that was to bring wealth and fame was never painted; for soon after that her father went away.

9

THE PROBLEM

EUREKA Harrison was taking a walk "all by her lonesome," as one of the children of their party put it; she belonged to a group who would have liked nothing better than to relieve the lonesomeness; but Eureka would have none of them that afternoon. She wanted to be by herself; she had problems to think out, one especially, of such a character that no one must be allowed to intermeddle.

It occurred to her as a curious coincidence that Burnham Roberts should have an engagement that afternoon which did not include her; she had wondered how she should dispose of him, and behold, he had disposed of himself and gone driving with his mother without so much as suggesting that she accompany them.

She walked rapidly down the long tree-lined avenue leading from the college to the center of life. Turning by the colonnade, she walked through one of the main avenues toward the amphitheater, where half the world was gathered for an afternoon concert; she did not mean to be beguiled by the concert. As she passed the School of Expression, she smiled over certain conceits of Burnham's that had to do with her work there. He did not half like her spending so much time over lessons and practice; more than once he had assured her that she read quite well enough to suit him, and he did not like to have her manner spoiled. What more did she want if he, and all her best friends, liked her reading as it was? But she wanted a great deal more and knew that she did. She was enjoying the lessons wonderfully and had no little pleasure in the thought that she would surprise him and others one of these days by showing them how far from "spoiled" she was. She was also enjoying to the full the innumerable sidelights thrown out concerning great pieces of literature, in prose and poetry, and the insight she was getting with regard to books in general.

"It is like taking a course in literature," she told Burnham, and he had replied with a shrug of his handsome shoulders that if there was any one thing of which he was more tired than another, it was a course in literature.

"You are tired of everything that is worthwhile," she had flashed back at him; to which he with unfailing good nature and impudence had replied:

"Except you, of course you mean."

She smiled absently as she recalled all this, and then her face shadowed again over the problem. What was she going to do with her lessons in reading? True, they were most enjoyable in themselves, even if she did nothing with them; but they were expensive. She was using for them the money that her aunt, who had wanted her at Long Branch this summer, had sent for her personal use; but she could think of a dozen ways to use it that would have been better for herself as well as her mother unless—but that meant the problem.

Her plan had been to establish herself as a reader for private citizens of wealth and leisure. Half-blind elderly men who wanted the daily papers read to them understandingly and eternally; middle-aged and would-be literary ladies who did not know what to read nor where to find out. Such would, by degrees, find *her* out, and she would see to it that once found, they would hold on to her. She knew how to hood-wink the dear souls into thinking that they really knew a good deal about the book she was skimming for them. "It is an art to know how to skip," the professor had said one day in class; she was learning how to skip. There were other departments in her plan. One, the thought of which delighted her, was the training of little children to love good literature. Pick-ing it out for them bit by bit; introducing them to Longfellow and Bryant and Lowell, and even Brow-ning and Shakespeare before they were supposed to be old enough to know that such names ever existed. What delightful work it would be to turn an immortal poem into a prose story that would capture the imaginations and hearts of little seven- and eight-year-olds, and afterwards introduce them to the poem and its author. She was charmed with the idea as it developed in her mind and was sure she knew already of mothers by the score who, once they understood her scheme, would be glad to pay her for giving their children such an opportunity. She would set about working up her class the very day she reached home. She would borrow the phrase "The Children's Story Hour" from this rich Chautauqua program; also, she would contrive in some way to get in at some of those story hours herself, in order to learn either how to do it, or how not to do it—one lesson would be almost as helpful as the other. Oh, she was sure she could succeed and money could be made out of it that would be sufficient to relieve some of the anxieties that daily pressed her mother. All this she would do if—and there was the problem again that she was not yet willing to definitely think about, although she had come out for that express purpose.

She was nearing the Hall of Philosophy now, and she allowed her thoughts to go back to the last meeting she had attended there. It had been a twilight Sunday vesper service, when air and sunlight and shimmering leaves and singing birds had done what they could to enhance the charm of the whole. The place itself was unique, a many-columned hall roofed over but open on all sides to sunlight and all the witching influences of nature; blue sky arching above it, blue lake glimmering in the near distance, and at vespertime the westering sun making a glory in the sky while yet its lingering beams were dancing among the leaves of the tall, old trees. How beautiful it was! Eureka, who was at all times more susceptible to the influences of the beautiful than most of those who knew her well imagined, had felt almost immediately on that Sunday afternoon the strange and tender spell that the Hall in the Grove has power to weave around those whose hearts are attuned to such ministry.

She had laughed a little at the "Four Girls" when they went into raptures the Sunday before about the vesper service. She and Burnham, instead of attending it, had chosen to take a long tramp along the lakeshore.

"Why should we have been there?" she had asked in response to the exclamations of regret. "We had a lovely walk, and that service isn't different from other prayer meetings, I presume, even though they choose such a high-sounding name for it as vesper service."

"It is not like any prayer meeting in the world," her mother said almost indignantly.

"Why not? Don't they sing and pray and talk? What is that but a prayer meeting?"

"She doesn't understand!" Mrs. Harrison said this with a despairing look at Mrs. Dennis, who suggested that one must attend a Chautauqua vesper service in order to appreciate it.

"There is something about it that words will not describe, my dear." This was said to Eureka.

"Besides," said Mrs. Roberts rousingly, "the Bishop is there, you know."

Eureka's response to this was an outburst of laughter and an exclamation.

"The way you said that, Aunt Flossy, was irresistible! I wish Burnham could have heard it. Honestly, the way that Mother, and Aunt Marion, and—well, all of you, and hosts of others for that matter say 'The Bishop' is just as a devout Roman Catholic would say 'The Pope.' Hearing you, one wouldn't suppose that there was another bishop in this whole round world, ever had been, or ever would be."

"No," said Mrs. Burnham calmly. "That is not the thought; there are bishops aplenty, but ours is *the* Bishop. Go and hear him at vespers, Eureka, and you will understand."

So, on the following Sunday, Eureka went to vespers, Burnham Roberts in her train.

"I am going to this meeting for your mother's sake, not mine," she had said as they sauntered down Clark Avenue, being passed continually by hurrying throngs anxious to secure seats in the hall.

"Indeed!" he had said. "May I be allowed to ask how your presence at a vesper service is supposed to benefit my mother? Except of course as your presence anywhere is a benefit to all concerned."

"Save your pretty speeches for occasions where they will tell better; it is not *my* presence that your mother cares one penny for; it is yours. I chanced to discover that she was particularly anxious to have you hear the Bishop at this meeting; so I decided to ask you to escort me to it as the easiest way of pleasing her."

As she said this, Burnham was looking at her with a curious smile on his face, the full import of which she did not understand; then he said:

"Do you know I think you are awfully good to my mother? a great deal better than you are to your own."

This had vexed Eureka, she could not have told why, save that it always made her angry to have it hinted that she was not good to her mother. So little attention did she pay to the subtle workings of her inner self that had she been told that her anger arose from the fact that her conscience owned to the truth of the charge, she would have been surprised and unbelieving.

To Burnham she had responded sharply. "Much you know about it! I do, and especially have undone, a thousand things for my mother's sake that you never hear of. As for yours, I suppose you think I don't know that your mother would ten times rather see you at vespers—or that matter anywhere else—*without me* than with me; but you see I did not know how to get you there without my obnoxious presence, so I came."

He had laughed good-naturedly, as he always did at her thrusts, and then he had said quite seriously something that puzzled her.

"We don't either of us understand our mothers very well, I am afraid."

There had been no time to question as to his meaning, for they were within sound of the voices in the Hall, and they came, a moment later, under the spell of the service. Organ and cornet were playing, and hundreds of voices were singing the evening song:

> *Day is dying in the west,*
> *Heaven is touching earth with rest;*
> *Wait and worship while the night*
> *Sets her evening lamps alight*
> *Through all the sky.*

Following the song, a voice firm and far reaching, with a certain quality in it that demanded reverent attention, gave forth the startling command with which the responsive reading opened: "Above all things and in all things, O my soul, thou shalt rest in the Lord alway, for he himself is the everlasting rest of the saints."

Eureka had not expected to care for the service; she had honestly sacrificed the long walk that she especially enjoyed at that hour to a good-natured desire to please both her mother and Burnham's by their presence there. But there was something compelling in the words to which she was listening—in the voice that was uttering them. "Thou *shalt*"—actually it was a command!—"rest in the Lord alway." Was her consciousness speaking to her soul ordering this to her? Suppose she could obey and "rest in the Lord?" The word *rest* did not in any sense describe her; she was restless, dissatisfied, unhappy a great deal of the time;

oh, in truth most of the time; nothing satisfied her; nothing ever had, fully and lastingly.

"Thou shalt rest in the Lord *alway.*" Had the Bishop put a special emphasis on that word *alway* or was it because it proclaimed a tremendous fact? "For he himself is the everlasting rest of his saints." Was that it? Was it the explanation of all unrest that people were continually seeking it in the wrong place? *Was* there such a thing as rest in God? What a solemnly glorious thought! *God.* Certainly he could rest a person if he would. "Come unto me, and I will give you rest." Did a voice speak that word just then? Only the voice of her childhood memory speaking to her soul. She was standing at her father's knee beside his study chair repeating the verse she had just learned: "Come unto me, all ye that labour and are heavy laden, and I will give you rest." It was true then; for that call was the voice of God; he was offering rest. "For he himself is the everlasting rest of his saints." But it was all for the saints. Yes, but this child of Christian parents had been carefully trained. She could seem to hear her father's voice in answer to her childish question. "A saint, Daughter, is one who has set apart his life as belonging to Jesus; chosen him, you know, for his Savior and Guide." But all people who had chosen him and followed his teachings did not rest. Her mother? O dear, no! That word would never be used in describing Mother. Aunt Ruth? Well, certainly Ruth Erskine Burnham had borne some peculiarly terrible trials very well indeed; and her face in these days wore a calm that suggested rest. And Aunt Flossy? The critic ran rapidly over Flossy Shipley Roberts's life story as she knew it from her own mother and from observation and decided that Aunt Flossy certainly was different from most other people. More quietly happy perhaps, in spite of annoyances and discomforts; more sure of all things working out toward the final right. "Still, she worries a good deal about Burnham," commented this merciless critic. There was Aunt Marion, too. Eureka knew the history of Marion Wilbur's skeptical girlhood and of the rocks and shoals of her early married life. She had heard of her troubles as a stepmother, and she knew also that her stepdaughter, Grace, adored her now; not only permitting but seeking her aid and influence in the rearing of her own children. It had to be admitted that Aunt Marion had made the sort of success in life that her girlhood had not promised.

On the whole, the "Four Girls," being passed upon in rapid mental review, witnessed well for the honor of their Lord; yet they did not satisfy the critic, who did not realize that she was seeking the perfect satisfaction that can be found only in the Master.

At that point, Eureka's attention had been again arrested by the voice of the Bishop. He was leaning forward with clasped hands and speaking to his audience earnest, tender words, as friend with friends. He was voicing in strong phrases his ever-deepening love for Jesus Christ his Savior, his Master, his Lord. Witnessing to his unfailing guidance through a long, full life. "I believe in him," he said, "in his divinity, in his deity, in his humanity, I believe in him through and through with my heart and mind and soul; I committed myself to him; through a long, full life he has kept the trust; I am persuaded that he will keep that which I have committed unto him."

Listening to the strong, calm voice, full of that assurance which is born of knowledge, studying his face, recognizing the look on it as reflected power, the critic came suddenly to the conclusion that here was one who rested in the Lord and realized in daily living that he was "the everlasting rest of his saints." And if there was one, could there not be others? Why were there not many others? *Were* there many? Was there a place in the world where she could find a company of them, a great throng, each bearing on his face and in his life the truth that he was at rest in the Lord?

"Ye are my witnesses saith the Lord." Oh, the pity of it! *Witnesses,* lame and halt and blind!

10

The Problem Solved

EUREKA scarcely heard the prayer, although if she had listened it might have answered some of her questions. Her mind—not her heart—was busy with the words of the hymn that had just been sung. They were familiar enough to her, but she had never thought of them before.

> *Abide with me from morn till eve,*
> *For without thee I cannot live.*

When one really stopped to think of them, those were wonderful words. Did any person living feel that he could not live without a sense of God's nearness! It amazed her. She moved restlessly in her seat. Almost for the moment she felt as though she could not live because he *was*. She felt afraid of him! Burnham Roberts glanced down and drew her wrap more closely about her; the wind was drawing in fresh from the lake, and he evidently thought she had moved because she was cold. What would he have thought if she had told him that she was afraid? Afraid of God!

She had never before realized his presence; now it seemed to her that he was there. She stole a look at the Bishop as he prayed. Did she imagine it, or was "the fashion of his countenance altered"? Was that the "rest" of which he had been talking that she saw shining on his face? It recalled the words: "For he himself is the everlasting rest of his saints."

When he spoke those words of final petition did he look straight at her, or did she fancy that? "The Lord lift up his countenance upon thee, and give thee peace."

She made only one comment as they moved with the crowds down the avenue. "I understand now why they call him 'The Bishop' in that distinctive way; there is but one."

But though Burnham asked a dozen questions, trying to get at her meaning, she would not explain. Perhaps she could not have done so in words.

The memory of that vesper service and the thoughts it had awakened came back to her with force that afternoon as she sat in the deserted, silent hall. She made an effort to live over again the peculiar sensations that the hour had given her; partly because she did not understand and felt that she would like to study them, and partly because she wanted to put off the consideration of the problem. But they refused to return at her call. She began to ask herself that other question. Why was she continually turning away from a thing that must be thought about? It was really very weak and silly in her! She arose presently and walked on; giving a half-amused glance at the Athenian lamps as she left them, wondering if their use in this day could awaken other sensation than that of fun. Across the park was Alumni Hall. She stopped a moment to survey it and to read the many announcements on the bulletin board near which she stood. Alumni Hall was the home of the C.L.S.C., about which one was beginning to hear so much; the hum of it was all over the grounds; and it was much in evidence on the bulletin board; they seemed to be having class gatherings of all sorts. One class in particular loomed into prominence in all manner of ways.

The bulletin at which she was looking read: "'87's, take notice! Business meeting of importance today at four." "Remember the Reception for the Class of '87 in the Hall tomorrow at three." "Committee of '87 banquet requested to meet in their room today at three-thirty sharp!" She remembered to have noticed a call in the morning paper to "All '87's to 'watch out' for the class breakfast." Also, that arrangements were in progress for a special class reunion at which "every '87 was expected."

"Really!" she said as she read the bulletin, "that must be an aggressive class. I wonder why they are so much in evidence? I wonder if I couldn't manage somehow to get invited to look on at their doings? I mean to look into that Reading Circle before long, anyway. If they really succeed in getting up a class spirit—and this looks like it—a homesick girl who missed what was her due might find a little comfort in it. What if *I* should join it? Burnham and I might read the books together, especially if—" At that moment a carriage came into view on the main road just ahead of her. Two ladies were in the back seat, and the driver, holding the reins lightly, was half turned toward the ladies, as though more interested in conversation than in driving. He lifted his hat to Eureka as they passed, and she saw that it was Burnham. He had his mother in the back seat, and beside her the lovely "invalid" whose eyes had arrested his attention the moment he saw them. He was looking into them now and saying words that made their owner laugh out joyously. The carriage had drawn near enough for Eureka to hear the laugh. It came to her as they swept by that there was room for her on the front seat beside Burnham, and that Aunt Flossy might have asked her, knowing how fond she was of driving; only, she understood perfectly that Aunt Flossy would rather— here she pulled herself up sharply and walked on very fast, plunging presently in among the tall trees of the deeper woods. Seating herself on the gnarled trunk of one that had been lately felled, she determined at last to give her undivided attention to that which had called her away out here alone.

It was her brother, Neal, who had, that very morning, caused her to feel the necessity for such consideration. Neal and his wife had come to Chautauqua for August as he had promised and had found it so much more to their mind than they had expected that there had really been no room for the discontent his wife had imagined she should feel.

She had even heartily commended the Management as she made ready for the entertainment given by the Coburn players for "being sensible enough to cater to several classes of people, those who knew what was worth hearing as well as those who imagined that they did." This was high praise from Mrs. Neal. Both she and her husband had managed to keep themselves so happily busy as to find little time for the mother for whose sake they thought they had come. Neal's action therefore in seeking his sister out that morning with laborious care and proposing a walk together had been all the more marked. Although Eureka had responded with alacrity, leaving the dolly she was dressing for his young daughter and going with him away down the hill to a rustic seat near the lakeshore, she did not help him at all to get started in the "little talk" which he proposed but threw pebbles into the water in utmost unconcern and waited with a lurking smile in her eyes for what might develop. She knew Neal so well that she was sure he had been set a task that was not to his liking and that he did not know how to perform.

At last, after several blundering efforts to approach the subject naturally, he blurted it out in the baldest form.

"I say, Reek,"—this, by the way, was the only nickname that had ever been bestowed upon Eureka. No one had ever apparently thought of such a thing as calling her "Eurie," the pet name of her mother's girlhood, and one that was still used by her special friends. Early in their girl and boy life together, Neal had begun to call his sister *Reek,* "for short." He still used the name on rare occasions, and Eureka, who would tolerate it from no one else, rather liked it from him.

"I say, Reek, what are you going to do with that chap you are toting around with you all the time?"

Eureka raised her eyebrows at him in wondering surprise and sent another pebble shimmering over the water before she spoke.

"Is that a conundrum, Neal? If it is, I give it up."

"Oh, now, Reek, don't be naughty and bother a fellow. I brought you out here on purpose to talk with you about it. Of course you know who I mean, all right. There's only one who is eternally at your elbow. Burnham Roberts is a good-enough fellow; I've always liked him better than some do, but he isn't your kind, of course; isn't halfway your equal to begin with and doesn't mean anything, anyhow; never does, you know. He's simply an awful flirt; and I don't know a meaner name. A girl flirt is bad enough, but when a fellow descends to that sort of thing, it's atrocious. It's the worst thing about Burnham; I believe that fellow would get up a flirtation with a pump handle if there was no girl around. The question is, why do you let him flirt with you?"

Eureka shivered inwardly. She hated that word *flirt*; it did not belong to Neal's natural vocabulary; she knew it was one of his wife's words. She replied quietly enough.

"Do you think he is flirting with me, Neal?"

"Why, sure. What else is there to think? I don't mean he is making love to you; I told Mother, or—that is, I know well enough that you wouldn't allow any silliness; but you see it looks like it to people who don't know you; and he is all the time keeping away good friends that you might have; of course they suppose that everything is fixed up between you. Then, when he gets tired of you and throws you overboard—well, not exactly that, of course, but when he drops you and gets to going with somebody else, where will you be?"

Despite her indignation, Eureka could hardly suppress a smile; she had recognized her mother's hand, even before Neal made his slip, but her mother would never have put it so baldly.

"She ought to have done the talking herself," mused Eureka, beginning to be half sorry for the mother, who was being so lamely represented. Aloud, all she said was:

"According to you, I should think even in such a terrible event I would be just where I am now."

"No, you won't; not by a long shot. A girl can't go around with a boy from morning till night for weeks and months, rowing and playing tennis and concertgoing and churchgoing and all the rest of it, and then suddenly give it up without setting tongues to wagging; that's human nature. If you were a rich girl, they would say you jilted him, but as it is, they will say he jilted you; that's as sure as preaching. Although anything serious between you is absurd, of course, and I told Mother that you wouldn't marry him even if he wanted you to; that won't hinder people's tongues; and it is never good for a girl to get herself talked about in that way."

To say that Eureka was indignant is putting it mildly. She felt herself outraged, humiliated. It was insufferable in Neal to sit there calmly saying such things to her, foreseeing her the subject of coarse and gossiping tongues! It was horrid in her mother to set a man who did not know how to talk on such matters to preaching at her! She felt like blazing out at him as the one and the only one who dared to use offensive language about her; but she did not. She held herself to outward calm and gave attention to another pebble. The very quietness of her manner deceived her brother; he began again with renewed confidence.

"Mother feels it, Reek, very much. You ought to think of her; we are the only ones left to look after her now. She cannot bear to have the honored name, Father's name, besmirched by common gossip; Mother hates such things, you know. For that matter, I cannot say that Katherine and I relish having our family name made the subject of gossip as is being done already. Oh, I know you are simply amusing yourself, but you are doing it at our expense, don't you see? I wonder that a girl with as keen a brain as yours doesn't think of that. It isn't as if you cared; if your heart was in it the least little speck, I'd shoot the fellow before night for presuming to trifle with you; but as it is, I must say that I think for you two to go on in this way without regard to the feelings of either mother is rather too bad."

Then Eureka rose up; she had endured all she could; here was Burnham's mother being thrown at her again, and it was insufferable; but she did not mean to let Neal know how he had hurt.

"Well," she said as she threw her last and largest pebble with surefire aim and watched the widening circle, "what do you propose to have me do? Shall I entice the youth out in a boat and contrive to tip it over and have him quietly drowned? Or shall I look up some other victim and elope with him in order to spare the other mother? Either way would make talk, of course. I don't see from your standpoint how that part of it is to be avoided; but either would materially change the character of the talk; which would you advise?"

Neal had risen also. He looked sorrowfully at the sister whom he fancied he understood and sighed heavily as he said:

"I see I have failed, as I feared I should. I may as well confess that Mother wanted me to talk things over with you and try to make you see that you were doing yourself, as well as the rest of us, a great wrong. I told her it wouldn't do any good; that you didn't listen to me nowadays and seemed to care for no one's society but Burnham's and that—"

But here Eureka had turned away and answered gleefully the call of children's voices from the hill and challenged them to catch her in a race along the shore. They came joyfully up and bore her away in triumph. And here she was, a few hours afterwards, resolved upon reaching a decision before she went home.

Should she, or should she not, marry Burnham Roberts? This was the momentous problem that had been haunting her for days and had reached a climax through Neal. He had done her good service in one respect; he had cleared her vision. She saw now as she had not before the position she occupied in the eyes of others. Neal believed that she was merely amusing herself; he was mistaken; the idea of amusement had not entered into her thought. Her first impulse was born of a good-natured desire to help Aunt Flossy by keeping Burnham out of mischief. Burnham must laugh and talk and sing and drive with some girl; that was a foregone conclusion; he had begun when he still wore kilts. Aunt Flossy foresaw dangers, indeed had warded off several while he was yet a high-school boy; but the propensity increased with his years and made no end of trouble. Eureka, looking on amused, yet pitiful for the mother, had suddenly decided to come to the rescue. Since Burnham must have a special girlfriend, why not one with whom there could be no trouble? Forthwith she set herself to like or appear to like the things that he liked; to read the books that he read; sing the songs he called for; and, in short, entertain him. She succeeded so well that he presently cared steadily for no other society, although there were frequent lapses for a day or two under the spell of a new and pretty face. Meantime, a surprise came to Eureka in that she was finding pleasure in that which she had begun as a sort of sacrifice. Soon after this discovery she began to realize that Burnham, too, was far more in earnest in his friendship than he had probably meant to be. He was really taking many things for granted; appropriating her at all times as a matter of course; looking grieved when she failed him at any point, feeling positively wronged if she planned anything without him. He had a way, too, of referring to their future quite as if it were a settled matter that they were to spend it in each other's company. At first she had received all such advances with mock seriousness, but several times he had startled her by seeming almost hurt. Neal had precipitated matters also by taking it for granted that Burnham cared nothing for her; if Neal, then others. People believed, did they, that Burnham Roberts was merely flirting with her, and that she might be "cast off"! She held her head high, even over such a thought. And then—Neal to hint that she was doing what might sully the honored family name! Why not show them all? She was not in love with Burnham Roberts, not in the silly sense that many seemed to mean, but she liked him very well indeed; quite as well, probably, as she could ever like anybody. He could never be to her what her father had been to Mother; of course he could not! The strange girl actually smiled over the idea of one cultivating for a man like Burnham Roberts the same sort of regard that her splendid father had awakened! Still, there was a great deal in Burnham to grow fond of. It is true that the word she hated applied to him; but married men did not flirt; at least decent married men did not, and she was not afraid for Burnham. There was one very sore point: "Aunt Flossy," as she had been taught from childhood to call her mother's friend, had never looked with approval upon her; every added day made this plain to the girl who had begun by trying to help her save her son.

"Still," she said, as she rose up from the stump of the gnarled old tree, "when once we are married and she begins to see that my influence over him is for good and is strong, she will feel differently, perhaps. Anyway," and she drew herself to her full height and stepped proudly at the thought, "it is no descent in the social scale for even a Roberts to marry a daughter of Dr. Harrison. As for money, thank goodness Aunt Flossy is superior to all such ideas."

And as she walked rapidly homeward, she told herself that the problem was solved. Neal, and all the rest of the world, should be shown just what they both meant.

11

CLOTHES AND PERPLEXITIES

MEANTIME, the youth who was the subject of the problem that had sent Eureka Harrison distraught to the woods for half a day was managing his own affairs quite to his satisfaction. He began with the drive, the sight of which being enjoyed had hastened Eureka's decision.

He had been so fortunate as to overhear his mother say that she was going that afternoon, without fail, to look up their little new friend. Ten minutes afterwards, he came to beg her to drive with him and try a pair of as fine ponies as he had seen in some time. His mother, being at all times eager to secure his company, still looked doubtful.

"I cannot go far," she said hesitatingly, "because I have pledged myself to a bit of effort for this afternoon. I'll tell you, Burnham, I'll take a short drive, of half an hour say, then you can set me down at the little cottage on Terrace Avenue where that child who was here the other day is staying; I want very much to have a talk with her."

"Won't she be at the amphitheater?" questioned Mrs. Burnham.

"I fancy not. From something she said, I got the impression that she did not attend the afternoon sessions very often."

"All right, Mother," Burnham said and went away whistling to order the ponies. When he could get speech with his mother alone, he presented his plan.

"Why wouldn't it be a good idea to take your little protégée for a drive, Mommy? She looked to me as though she didn't have too many of them. You could have your talk while driving better than in one of those tucked-up little places on Terrace Avenue."

That would be very pleasant, his mother said, but would he want to take the time and miss the lecture?

Oh, he wasn't going to the lecture; he wanted to give those ponies a fair trial; he had some thought of buying them. Which statement brought a troubled look into his mother's eyes; the things that Burnham Roberts thought of buying were named legion; and most of them did not have his father's approval.

"You will not care for ponies when you get where you can use your machine again," she reminded him; to which he agreed, and for the dozenth time expressed his mind about the folly of prohibiting automobiles on Chautauqua grounds. It was ridiculous! What if there were innumerable children there? Couldn't they train them to keep off the roads? Children were everywhere. He would so like to take her for a real spin into the country; with horses one couldn't go but halfway to anywhere before it was time to turn around and get back. To all of which his mother agreed and hoped he would forget that he thought of buying the ponies.

He had already forgotten it and was wondering if the little girl had ever taken an auto ride, such a one as he could give her, and how large her eyes would be if he had a chance to show her how it felt! Meantime, his mother was thinking how lovely it was in Burnham to remember that lonesome-looking little girl and plan for her pleasure.

She found Hazel at home and alone, as she had hoped that she would; she wanted to know more of the child before making the aunt's acquaintance. Since the family lived in New York, she hoped to be able to do much for the girl, if on further acquaintance she developed as the first interview had promised.

The first glimpse of her face as she answered Mrs. Roberts's knock suggested sadness, but it brightened instantly as she recognized the caller; and at the suggestion of a drive her eyes sparkled wonderfully. They were very noticeable eyes and proclaimed her changing moods with remarkable power. Almost instantly the joy in them faded as she said:

"I can't tell you how very much I should like to go, dear lady, but—I don't believe I can."

"Am I to be told why not?" Mrs. Roberts asked winsomely, "or is that a state secret?"

The girl laughed. "It ought to be a secret," she said, "but I believe I will tell you; it is because I have nothing suitable to wear. I mean," she went on quickly, reddening under the surprise which Mrs. Roberts could not keep from her face—she had not expected the question of dress to seriously trouble the kind of girl she had taken this one to be—"I mean that my white dress and—and my waist I have not had time to iron, and the—the other one is so warm that I could not endure it today. It is made to wear just with a jacket."

Mrs. Roberts was puzzled. Was this abject poverty, or was it ignorance? She longed to understand and to help the child.

"My dear," she said sweetly, "I know you will forgive me for being so persistent; I do want you to enjoy a drive on this lovely day. I know all about how suddenly summer wardrobes give out sometimes, especially here in the country where one brings but few clothes; but may I not suggest that any sort of a shirtwaist will do nicely for just an afternoon drive? Your morning waists, you know, of gingham, or any kind."

She stopped, uncertain what to say next, for the expressive eyes had suddenly filled with tears which the girl struggled to keep back; yet the ludicrous side of this interview also evidently presented itself, for the next second she laughed as she attempted further explanation.

"I am not wearing any kind of morning waists this summer, dear lady; they all grew too small for me and wore out. At work I just wear this." "This" was a blue-and-white-checked apron, of a coarse, sleazy material that enveloped her from head to foot. It was made rather low in the neck and with elbow sleeves; it was by no means unbecoming, and for kitchen wear was all that could be desired; but for an afternoon drive, Mrs. Roberts admitted to herself, a young girl might be pardoned for thinking it not suitable. But what unusual poverty of wardrobe it suggested for one of her appearance and manner! She must certainly have been used to a very different state of things.

As Mrs. Roberts hesitated what to say next, Hazel spoke quickly, her face crimsoning the while.

She had caught a glimpse of a man in the carriage trying to hold in check two eager horses; what must he think of her for detaining the lady so long, and what would he say to the story she would have to tell him! "I ought not to have said anything about dress, but I did so want you to understand that I would be glad to go if I could."

"I think I must have you with me, my dear," was Mrs. Roberts's answer. "I want it very much, and I have a plan to propose. My long pongee coat is in the carriage, not being used at all. May I bring it in and will you put it on with the heavy skirt? It buttons closely and will take the place of a waist nicely; then we will have our drive in spite of the unironed dresses."

She had decided to be persistent and gay; to act as though it were the commonest thing in the world for a girl to have absolutely no dress to wear.

Hazel exclaimed and demurred; she was embarrassed, she was distressed; she was almost ready to cry or to laugh hysterically, she hardly knew which; but it ended in her being gently coerced; and before many minutes she was tripping down to the carriage in a skirt of heavy brown suiting and a lovely pongee coat that covered it completely and changed her into a stylishly dressed young woman. Her simple little hat was not unbecoming; Josephine's skillful fingers had seen to that, and her gloves, fortunately, matched it well.

Just what her aunt would say when this beautiful drive was over and this beautiful coat that fitted her to perfection had been laid aside, she did not know; she resolved not to think about it, but to take the joy of it all while she had the chance. Was not this the lovely lady who had said to her: "Your Father means you to get good here, and happiness?" Was not this part of his plan?

No one who had a glimpse of Hazel's face that afternoon could have failed to see that she was getting happiness in full measure. She bubbled over with the joy of it. Every bird and flower and bit of color that she saw—and she seemed to see them all—contributed to her pleasure.

"You should be an artist," Burnham Roberts, the observant, said as he smiled indulgently at her ecstasy over a flame-colored shrub by the roadside; "perhaps you are?"

She sobered instantly. "I am nothing," she said gravely. "Nothing but an ignorant girl who must always stay ignorant now, but my father was an artist."

"Ah, that accounts for the artist soul shining out in his daughter."

"Do you mean that?" she asked eagerly. "Do you really mean that you think my love for all beautiful things in nature and in life everywhere may be because I have inherited the taste from my father?"

Burnham, who was unaccustomed to being taken seriously in any of his nice-sounding random speeches, was half embarrassed. He laughed a little as he said: "Why, yes, I suppose so. Why not? Isn't that an orthodox view of heredity, Mother?"

Then, for as much as three minutes his mother had a chance to talk, while he appeared to be giving undivided attention to his horses.

But Mrs. Roberts did not accomplish the object that she had in view that afternoon; at least not fully. Thinking it over afterwards, talking it all over with Mrs. Dennis, who also was much interested in the young girl, she admitted that she knew very little more about Hazel than she did before the drive.

"The child was so intensely happy," she said, trying to explain, "so deliriously happy, I might say, over the fresh air and sunshine and every sight and sound she saw and heard, that I had not the heart to try to pin her down to the commonplace inquiries that I wanted to make; though there is enough of the commonplace in her life. The girl is actually impoverished, apparently; I do not yet understand why."

Then she told of the long-sleeved work apron and the apparent poverty with regard to that necessity of a young woman's wardrobe; and then, under questioning, of the device resorted to to supply the deficiency. Mrs. Dennis was interested and also very much amused.

"The idea!" she said. "So you lent her your thirty-dollar pongee coat to do duty in lieu of a shirtwaist? You dear little woman! You are Flossy Shipley still, and will be to the end of the story."

"She looked lovely in it," Mrs. Roberts said thoughtfully; "I didn't know it was so pretty until I saw it on her. But, Marion, what do you suppose can be the explanation of such a state of things? People who haven't money enough for the common necessities of life do not as a rule come to summer resorts like Chautauqua."

"Unless they come to earn their daily bread," Mrs. Dennis said. "Perhaps that is the explanation; a poor relation, you know, brought along to do the drudgery."

"But 'poor relations,' even, would surely be provided with decent clothing!" said Mrs. Roberts, dismayed.

"Don't be too sure of that, Flossy dear. You have never been very conversant with how the other half lives, the moderate medium half I mean; I know about it by experience, remember; though to be sure my aunt would have gone without a new calico gown every spring of her life if she could, in order that I might have one; but she was an aunt in a thousand. I'm curious to know how you managed with the lovely pongee coat. Did the child wear it into the house and you follow her in and get it? She couldn't shed it at the carriage, of course, since she had no waist on."

"Oh, she had!" Mrs. Roberts explained eagerly. "A perfectly fresh and neat blue work apron; the child is a lady, every inch of her. She slipped the coat off in the quietest way as we turned the corner into Terrace Avenue and patted it lovingly as she laid it on the seat and said to it—not to me, mind you, but to it, 'Thank you, darling; you are beautiful, and I have worn you for two whole hours; I shall never forget you.' Wasn't that original, and pathetic? She is certainly a very interesting girl; I am quite determined to know more of her. Burnham was lovely to her, Marion; he couldn't have been more attentive if she had been a princess. He exerted himself to entertain her; and as she is not the kind of young lady to whom he is accustomed; it rather surprised me. He certainly helped splendidly to carry out his mother's wishes."

Mrs. Dennis flashed a swift half-amused glance at her friend, the thought of her heart being, "I wonder if it is really true that 'love is blind'? Doesn't she know that Burnham couldn't help being attentive to a pretty girl, if he tried ever so hard?" Aloud, she said with apparent irrelevance, "Where is Eureka this afternoon?"

Mrs. Roberts's face instantly shadowed.

"I don't know," she said. "I heard her tell her mother at dinner that she was going on a long tramp. Marion, what am I going to do about this? Isn't there *anything* that I can do? You don't think it possible that it can ever amount to something serious, do you?"

Mrs. Dennis tried to laugh; she was rather fond of Burnham, and Eureka annoyed her not a little.

"I don't know," she said. "It is impossible to surmise

what Eureka Harrison thinks about anything, or what she may do next. But I don't believe there is anything that any of us can do except to let them judiciously alone. To appear to attach importance to such a matter is often the way to produce a crisis. I have been afraid that Eurie would accomplish what she doesn't want to, just by worrying at Eureka. I really don't think you two mothers can alter things, and you ought not to borrow trouble, you know."

Mrs. Roberts sighed. "Yes," she said, "there are two of us; Eurie is just as anxious as I am to separate those two; the fact is that they are utterly unfitted for each other, and anybody can see it."

Mrs. Dennis thought—but did not say—"They are utterly unfitted to marry; either each other or *any* other until both are radically changed." But of what use to trouble Flossy with this? She would try to turn her thoughts elsewhere.

"We four mothers certainly brought our perplexities with us!" she said with a little laugh. "Burnham and Eureka keep you and Eurie busy; and there is Ruth consumed with anxiety because her grandson—whom she sometimes believes to be her son, Erskine, back again into childhood—has found some playmates of whom she does not approve. As for me, Grace's baby with his fondness for getting up an imitation of croup on the slightest provocation keeps me in nightly fear. And now, I have a letter that brings its share of anxiety. You have heard me speak of Dr. Dennis's home-missionary brother, Harlan, who has been in Utah for so long? He is so much younger than Dr. Dennis that he has always been thought of more as a son than a brother. He is a dear fellow; I have never seen him, but his letters to me always begin, 'Dear sister Marion,' though he seems like Grace's brother, instead of her uncle. Three years ago he lost his wife, and since then has been very lonesome and sad. He has two children, a boy and a girl, but of course they were away at school. And now, don't you think, after all these years he is coming east. This letter announces the probable arrival of the children and himself on these grounds in a day or two; think of it! and Dr. Dennis on the other side of the world. Some benevolent deacon who used to know Harlan's wife very well has planned it all; they are to be guests of the Presbyterian Mission House. Only think, Flossy, what responsibility for me; a girl and boy to be practically mothered! Suppose they refuse to be mothered?"

"But suppose they don't," Mrs. Roberts said, smiling. "What an opportunity for you! I could almost envy you. In any case, Marion dear, you know you 'ought not to borrow trouble.'"

Then both ladies laughed.

12

————— ❈ —————

SOME SETTLED THINGS

BURNHAM Roberts never remembered to have enjoyed a drive better than that one in which he was supposed to have sacrificed himself for the sake of his mother's protégée. Hazel, as he began to call her in his secret soul, was simply charming. When she laughed, her eyes were irresistible; when she was serious, they were heavenly. Here at last was a girl who satisfied one's ideal, and he meant to find ways to cultivate her acquaintance. Nor did it once occur to the volatile youth that he had in the course of the last six years cultivated the acquaintance of at least half a dozen other girls who were "simply charming." For the present there was but one girl in the world. The all-important question was, how should he manage to meet her again without loss of time? Fortune favored him; on the morning after the drive he came face-to-face with her as he was leaving the post office. He saw her face flush as she caught sight of him and could not know that it was because she was wearing a jacket that she knew looked too heavy for the day. He joined her at once, congratulating himself openly.

"I was just trying to plan an excuse for calling and being afraid that you did not receive calls at such an early hour. Do you?"

"Oh, no!" she said breathlessly. "I don't receive calls at all."

He raised his eyebrows at that. "Really? That sounds dreadfully inhospitable. How then are your friends to meet you?"

Hazel laughed a little. "I didn't mean quite that," she said. "I don't want to appear rude, but I am just a young girl in my aunt's family; I have no friends here, so of course—" He interrupted her.

"Are not my mother and I your friends? Do you mean that you will not count us in that list?"

"Oh, no, indeed!" she said eagerly. "Your mother has been perfectly dear; and I am so grateful to you for that lovely drive and for—but you see—" Her confusion was lovely. But he broke into the embarrassed pause.

"Very well then, that part is settled; let us understand that we are friends for all time. I understand also about the calling. If your aunt has too many friends for the close quarters that obtain in summer lodging houses in the country, so that you feel yours crowded out, we'll meet under the trees, as the squirrels do; or in my mother's sitting room at the hotel," he made haste to add as he saw her face shadow—"she will always be glad to see you. Now, about this evening; do you go to the concert?"

"No; or—yes, perhaps. What is the concert?"

"What a disloyal Chautauquan not to know the program! The concert is a choir rendering of the Sleeping Beauty. Do you turn here? You will be at home before I have time to tell you about the Sleeping Beauty. Do you know the story?"

"I never heard of it."

"Then suppose we walk toward the lake while I tell you about it? It will not detain you long; you are not in special haste this morning, are you? Haven't you so much time to spare for your friends?"

She laughed a little at the pretense of reproach in his tone; but she hesitated. There was no work really pressing just then, and nothing had been said about her quick return; but her aunt was always annoyed when she was longer in coming than her errand warranted; besides, how could she explain her absence?

"Let me persuade you," he said, almost making the turn. "It is just the morning for a walk, and you will enjoy the concert better if you get a touch of the story beforehand; you must certainly hear it tonight; part of the music is delicious."

Hazel made a sudden reckless decision and took two steps forward; he noted it and felt triumphant. Then he began to talk.

"It is an old tale of the days of the fairies. There is a beautiful princess who is the central figure; she is the lovely daughter of a great king and was destined by the good fairies to happiness; they promised all sorts of delightful things at her birth. They spun the web of her life at her cradle, and as they spun they sang:

> *We give thee beauty, we give thee power.*
> *And happy years, and that happiest hour*
> *When to a tender loving heart*
> *Another love beats counterpart.*

"They knew, you see, that the flower of real happiness blossoms at just that time. But a wicked fairy, who hated her family and plotted revenge, came to overturn all this and vowed at her cradle that:

Ere the buds of her youth are blown,
Ere a score of her years have flown,
She must wither and droop on the earth;
She must die!

"Oh!" said Hazel pitifully.

"Yes, but listen: The good fairies intervene and although they have not power to break the spell entirely they promise this:

Though the spell and its potent sway
Close her eyes and in slumber enshroud her;
Yet shall there dawn a day
When a young voice stronger and louder
Than spell of witchcraft rings through the silent
*   years—*
Then she wakes! Then she hears!

"Oh!" said Hazel again, this time with a delicious little laugh. "What lovely nonsense! Do they sing all that?"

"Yards of it; I have just given you a hint."

"Did the wicked fairy have her will?"

"Yes, indeed, for a hundred years! But she awakened. He came, the knight with the young, strong voice and said to her:

Yield thy form to my arms that enfold it,
Yield thy mouth to my life-giving kiss.

"Instantly her soul awakened; and the knight explained about the hundred years of slumber. Then this is the concluding number."

By this time they were quite near the lake, but it was deserted that morning, the program attractions being too great for even the careless ones to lose. Burnham glanced swiftly about him and finding that they were practically alone, let his fine tenor voice tell the story in song.

> Great love has guided our steps
> Has lighted our way.
> It beckons, it leads to a haven of rest.
> To a goal, to a home.
> We ask not whither, we follow its potent behest,
> We hasten, we come.

He had reason to be flattered with the effect of the song on his audience. A lovely flush overspread Hazel's face, and her breath came in little catches of surprised delight.

"The music fascinates me," she said when he stopped. "I never heard any just like it."

"You must hear it tonight," he said, making a movement toward the walk—for their momentary solitude was over. A troop of young people were rushing gaily down the hill. Burnham was glad to see them; another moment of quiet and under the spell of those lovely eyes he might have said something that could have spoiled all his plans. He contented himself now with asking:

"May I call for you this evening?"

"Oh, no!" Hazel said quickly. "No, thank you; it will not be in the least necessary. I go there often, you know; and if I am not ready when the others go, I shall not mind going alone; I am used to it."

"But I am not proposing to come because it is necessary, only because I want the pleasure of it. Why may I not call and accompany you? Is your aunt the wicked fairy who has bewitched you into not wanting any friends? If so, let me be the knight who will break the spell."

She laughed a little and flushed under his gaze. She was confused and happy and frightened.

"Oh, I want friends!" she said under her breath, and there was unconscious tragedy in her voice. "I don't think anybody in the world can want them more, but—"

"Then let me be your friend and escort. I promise to shield you carefully from all the pomps and vanities of this wicked Chautauqua; I am prepared to guard you with drawn sword if necessary; knights always wear swords, you know."

He accomplished his purpose and made her laugh again; her laugh was very charming. But his next words frightened it away.

"I am to begin, remember, by coming for you this evening at half past seven."

"Indeed, Mr. Roberts, I cannot go at all if you persist in that; my aunt, I am perfectly certain, would not approve, and I am here in her care; I have no one else in all the world."

"I won't do anything to trouble you, but please make me understand. What is there for anyone to disapprove? Can you think of anything more commonplace than my suggestion? Am I to infer that your aunt objects to all company for you? Or do you mean me to understand that I am especially obnoxious to her?"

Hazel was already ashamed of her vehemence and broke into a little laugh as she said:

"I think you must suppose me to be an idiot. All I mean is that my aunt is not accustomed to think of me as a grown person; in her eyes I am just a child who does not yet know how to behave well away from her elders. I have never had any company of my own since I came to her home, and the idea of my going out with a gentleman or receiving a call from one would be simply frightful to her. I wonder if I am at all succeeding in making you understand?"

"I think you are," he said gaily; but the gaiety was to cover a rush of very different emotions. He felt the strongest possible desire to take this girl in his arms and say:

Yield thy mouth to my life-giving kiss.

"It's all right," he added cheerfully as they mounted the hill. "I think your aunt has a touch of—the other fairy about her, but we will not undertake to break the spell rudely, lest she might consider a straitjacket necessary. But you will come to the concert tonight, will you not? I want you to hear that music. I think the south side will be the better place to secure seats, perhaps the third-aisle section. Suppose you try to find one there? If I chance to see you and can be of service, I shall be glad."

He was lifting his hat ceremoniously now, preparing to leave her at her corner. Crowds of people were passing; let them pass. All the world might make note, if they wish, of a gentleman lifting his hat to a lady in courteous good-bye.

Hazel went home in a flurry. Her aunt would be sure to make note of her long absence; what would she ask, and what would she reply?

It was better than her fears. Her aunt was absorbed and annoyed by some bills that had just come in and did not consider time. She was, however, in anything but an amiable humor. How can one be amiable who has bills to pay of unexpected magnitude, and no money with which to pay them? Her directions throughout the morning were crisper than usual, and she was harder to suit. It is true that Hazel may have called for a greater expenditure of patience than usual; she felt in a flutter of excitement; something wonderful had happened: She had a friend! "For all time," he had said. Then he meant, somehow, to see more of her. How could he? Should she go to the concert? Yes, she would. She must hear the whole of that story, despite the fact that she had nothing bright and pretty to wear, like other girls. The brown skirt and jacket did very well, though, for evenings; it was always chilly at night in the amphitheater. But should she go around to the south side? She often did, because she liked it better; still, tonight, it would look as though—Then her aunt startled her and made great scarlet waves rush over her face by saying sharply:

"Hazel, what is the matter? I have spoken to you three times without being noticed; you act as though you had been bewitched."

She did go to the concert. She was much too late to go with the others who rushed away early to secure good seats, so she went alone; but this was her own fault. Isabel offered to wait and dry the dishes if she would only hurry, and her aunt told her to pile up the dishes and leave them until morning if she wanted to. She did nothing of the kind; the dishes were washed and dried and the kitchenette put in perfect order before she left it. She was very late, she told herself, and of course no one would be looking for her to come at such an hour, but she went around to the south side, the third section from the choir. All the world had apparently done the same and no vacant seat was visible anywhere, but Burnham Roberts was. He stepped out of chaos; one moment she saw nothing of him, the next, he was moving beside her down the incline. As they neared the front, two boys, each the richer by a quarter of a dollar than he was an hour before, suddenly slipped out of the excellent seats they had been occupying and skipped away.

Despite the heavy brown suit which, being much worn in all weathers and being shoddy in the first place, was growing shabby, Hazel had never looked prettier than she did that evening. Josephine, recognizing her from the extreme north side of the amphitheater, became suddenly and anxiously aware what a very pretty girl her cousin was.

"Dangerously pretty," she said with a little sigh. Josephine was years older than she and knew something of this dangerous world.

Under the spell woven by the music and the ring in their ears of those closing words:

> Great Love has guided our steps, has lighted our
> way—
> It lives! it is here!

Those two, Hazel and her "friend," left the amphitheater together. She made no demur when he placed her hand on his arm and guided her away from the moving throngs to the quieter street where she lived. They walked rapidly, he talking pleasant commonplaces and she almost silent. Once he referred to the speed they were making.

"I am taking you home by the shortest route, in order to reach there before the 'other fairy' does, lest she be roused to action. Do you understand?" Then, without waiting for answer, "Did you like it?"

"The music? Some of it was delightful; but it was too sad. Think of it—a hundred years asleep!"

"A hundred years can be compressed, sometimes, into a single week." He left her to puzzle over what he might mean by that and asked if she liked to watch ball games. Was it possible that she had never seen a game! Then she must go tomorrow; it promised to be an exciting affair. He would like nothing better than to call for her if—then he felt the tremor of her hand on his arm and added hastily:

"Never mind, I understand; we are not sufficiently accredited as yet; I shall boldly bring my mother someday and call upon you. But at least I may secure you a seat for the game? Remember that your friend will be watching for you. Good night."

Returning, he met the woman whom he had discovered to be Hazel's aunt and mentally shook his fist at her. "Old vixen!" he muttered. "If I don't find some way soon to checkmate you, I'm not the fellow I think I am."

When her aunt and cousins reached home, Hazel was in her attic. They saw the light as they approached the house.

"I believe that child did not go out, after all!" her aunt said. Josephine considered this and decided for the present to be silent.

Hazel, in her attic, indifferent to bugs and bats and even mice, her eyes shining like stars, her cheeks very crimson, quoted softly from the cantata, words that had clung to her heart:

> *Guarded and guided by the hand of love,*
> *Such was thy past, such shall thy future be.*

She did not know what she meant by appropriating them; except that first line, that had been true of her life; she did not mean anything, only she had a friend.

It was about that time that Eureka Harrison, who had not attended the concert, turned her pillow resolutely as a token that she meant to stop thinking and go to sleep. As she did so, she told herself emphatically, "Now I have settled that, and I don't need to keep thinking it all over; I am to marry Burnham Roberts."

13

＊＋☲＊＋

FORCED INTO ARGUMENT

WITH early morning Eureka Harrison began to plan her new departure; for many months Burnham Roberts had been the one to seek and petition for her company; now she must meet him a trifle more than halfway; she must show him that she understood and appreciated his attentions. For a day or two she had scarcely seen him, but this she believed had been by her own arrangement.

At the breakfast table she challenged him to go with her to the hall to hear a remarkable woman. Those breakfast-table chats, by the way, were among the pleasantest hours of the day. Those of "Aunt Ruth's party"—as the younger ones called this gathering of the four families—who were staying at the hotel had special tables assigned to them. Eureka and her mother, as guests of Mrs. Roberts for the season, were of course at her table, and as the morning meal was most unceremonious, different members of the party straying in as suited their convenience, it often happened that Eureka and Burnham, both being laggards, breakfasted alone together. "And planned their mischief for the day," Mrs. Harrison was once heard to remark in a discouraged tone.

Eureka was well pleased that it happened thus on that particular morning.

"Have you been taking a trip to New York, or what became of you?" was her opening charge. "I haven't so much as seen you for days."

"I beg your pardon," Burnham said genially, "it is only two days since we had our latest quarrel. I have simply been pursuing the even tenor of my ways; devoted to my mother and Chautauqua, as usual. I had my mother out driving for one entire afternoon; I must do that oftener, by the way, it is better for her than so many lectures. Then I attended an excellent concert, which I believe you eschewed. Now that I think of it, you seem to be the one who should render an account; I have not seen you in any of your usual haunts."

"I have been very especially engaged with an important matter demanding solitude. I remember, now you speak of it, that I saw you out driving. Your mother had that pretty protégée of hers with her, did she not? Did you find her eyes so large as ever?"

"Larger if anything and very wide open. I never knew a child to be so observant of color and form and beauty generally; it was interesting to note her delight in what we call the commonplace. Shall I have the pleasure of preparing this orange for you?"

While he did so, he was wondering what Eureka would think of the pongee-coat episode, all the details of which he perfectly understood. He knew that he would not tell her about it; not yet—she did not know Hazel well enough to be sympathetic; but he believed that there was that in her which would make a good reliable friend when once she—

He did not finish the sentence in his thought. Eureka was talking; it was time that he gave her undivided attention.

"Well, have you promised to take her driving again this morning—don't halve that orange, please, I like it better whole—or will you go with me to hear Mrs. Wells? She is said to be well worth hearing."

"Is that designed for a pun?" he asked with the slightest perceptible shrug of his shoulders. "Who is Mrs. Wells? Does she yellercute?"

"Burnham, aren't you tired of that foolish word? It doesn't mean anything, you know; not here at least, where all the public readers are of acknowledged ability. Mrs. Wells is a lecturer."

"Oh, I think I have heard of her; a woman-suffrage ranter is she not? That is a shade worse than yell—I beg your pardon—than the average public reader."

They were not getting on; Eureka was growing vexed; she was almost tempted to ask herself—if she possibly *could*—only she would not; that matter was settled.

"Mrs. Wells speaks on Mormonism," she said drily. This time he shrugged his shoulders outright.

"Oh, *Mormonism!* Why do they let a woman come to a place like Chautauqua to maunder over that subject? What can she say that we don't know already?"

"Go and hear her and you'll discover; if all that I have heard about her is true, you know a great deal more than I fancy you do if you find that she doesn't tell you anything new."

Clearly he was not getting on with Eureka as well as usual; and he should need her help if his plans carried. Why was he irritating her in this way, anyhow? He knew nothing about the Mormons and cared nothing about them. Why not spend the morning in the hall if she chose? He pulled himself together and spoke in cheerful tones.

"Oh, I'll go and hear her if you wish and turn Mormon if you say so or do anything else this morning that your highness elects; I was never more entirely at your service."

It occurred to Eureka as she made ready for the lecture that she had not managed herself at all well that morning. If they were married people it could hardly have been worse; she had heard husbands and wives spar at each other and catch each other up in the way she had done to Burnham, but engaged people she did not believe ever had such scenes; much less those who were not yet even engaged; she ought to be ashamed of herself. Then this inconsistent creature sighed over the dreary prospect before her of interminable years of breakfast-table sparring, perhaps, after they should become husband and wife!

The hall was packed, and every outside seat was taken. Burnham was compelled to forage for chairs at a neighboring building.

"What people they are here to rush to things!" he commented as he came across the road with two chairs. Eureka's crisp reply was: "That is because they find things worth rushing to."

"She is never sweet," Burnham said to himself; and he thought of one who seemed always sweet.

The large audience was intent upon the speaker, who was a woman well fitted to command attention. No one would have thought of describing her as handsome, yet there was that in her face which attracted even the thoughtless. Perhaps it was strength of character that instantly drew one's attention; perhaps it was the conviction that here was a woman to be trusted, to be relied upon. Burnham Roberts, who might have represented the most heedless of her auditors, whispered his first thought to Eureka:

"She will never be hanged for her beauty, will she?" And was amused over the reply that she instantly flashed back at him.

"Perhaps she will for her brains."

After that they listened. The strong, clear penetrative voice fairly compelled attention; so did her use of the English language; every word seemed to be marshalled into the place that had been waiting for it, and when the speaker closed, one man standing near Burnham and Eureka must have voiced the feeling of hundreds as he exclaimed: "Every adjective that woman uses weighs a pound!"

"That is true," said Burnham, smiling, "and she knows where to place them."

"Aren't you almost inclined to think you heard something that you didn't know before?" Eureka asked mockingly as they moved slowly with the crowd.

"Well, if she is sure of her statements, she made some that deserve thinking about."

"Did she impress you as a woman who would be likely to make careless statements?"

"No, I can't say that she did; but that arraigning of the United States government was in rather bad taste, don't you think?"

"If she told the truth, why shouldn't it be arraigned?"

"Do no good."

"That will depend on how many thoughtful men were among her listeners who will go home to make their influence and their votes tell, as they have never done before."

"And also on how soon universal suffrage obtains," said an incisive voice just at their side, and Eureka welcomed and introduced Mrs. Blanchard, a class acquaintance.

"You think the women would set this thing straight at once, do you, if they could only vote?" Burnham Roberts said, good-natured sarcasm in his tones.

"Oh, we'll help as soon as we get the chance," was the cheerful reply. "Meantime, a few more women like Mrs. Wells could accomplish wonders. What did you think of her four indictments against the Mormons, Mr. Roberts?"

"Rather fierce," Burnham answered, smiling.

"Fierce? I should think so! Isn't it dreadful to have an institution flourishing in the name of religion that is traitorous to the government which tolerates it? I'm glad she was able to prove her charge by facts; so many people seem not to understand anything about that part. I thought at first that her second indictment about their being a law-breaking set was too much like the first one, but she made her point all right; and wasn't she strong on her proofs?"

"She could hardly help being," Eureka said. "An organization that flaunts its immorality in the faces of the very children, even teaching it in their catechisms, is bound to furnish abundant proof of their law-breaking propensities. I wish all the men who content themselves by calmly stating that 'polygamy is a dead issue' could have heard her this morning; they would surely be ashamed to ever say it again."

As it was not yet a week since Burnham Roberts had been guilty of making that very statement, he appreciated the thrust. He did not feel like talking about the Mormons; in truth his thoughts were elsewhere, but it seemed to be necessary to rouse himself to some word, so he said:

"Don't you consider her statement about the Mormon church throttling business absurdly overdrawn? I don't know of any legitimate business being interfered with by Mormons."

Mrs. Blanchard was roused at once.

"Oh, Mr. Roberts, that's just the trouble—you men *don't* know; if you attended missionary meetings and read up on these points, as we women do, you would know how many times business is throttled by them. You didn't hear this woman yesterday, did you? Were you there, Miss Harrison? Oh, that's too bad; she was wonderful! Some of the incidents she gave illustrated this point perfectly. Dear me! I would have illustrated it for her. I know a man living sixty miles away from Utah, who allowed his daughter to attend our mission school. He was a member of the Mormon church, you understand, and was presently called to account for his dreadful sin. He had backbone enough to say that his daughter was happy there, and he meant she should stay. He was running a little store at the time. Mr. Roberts, how long do you think it took for the Mormon power to turn every bit of patronage from that store? Just two days!"

"That is because Mormonism is so splendidly organized that they can reach their people all over the country at a few hours' notice," interposed Eureka. "It is one of the excellencies that our voters admire."

Burnham Roberts laughed; he recognized this also as a thrust at him.

"Well, that is one way in which they interfere with business. Another store was opened there by a loyal Mormon and every bit of patronage straightway went to him. The man whose business was ruined moved to another town and tried to get work by the week, or day, in some of the shops; not one of them would have him, although they were advertising for help! He had been advertised as untrustworthy; no one dared to employ him after that. He went from town to town hunting work, in vain, until he got as far as Denver. Finally he decided to make another trial in business for himself in a little place not very far from Denver; he invested all his savings in goods to stock a little store, only to find that he could not get his goods carted either by railroad or horse power! Then he harnessed his own team and resolved to get them there himself. Don't you see he had plenty of back-bone? He was determined that the Mormons should not crush him because he chose to send his daughter to a good school. He started with his load for the little town and was never heard of again! People who know all about the Mormons are perfectly aware that mysterious disappearances are not uncommon. Wasn't his legitimate business effectually throttled for him, Mr. Roberts?"

"Isolated cases do not prove anything," said that gentleman with dignity.

"Oh, 'isolated'! I told you that you did not read missionary literature. Mrs. Wells could spend every morning this week giving similar accounts of happenings that have come under her own observation. So could I, for that matter; I lived in a Mormon town once and know by personal experience what I am talking about."

"I don't care so much about the men," said Eureka. "Most of them went into it with their eyes open, or with plenty of chances to have them opened, if they cared to take the trouble; but I'm sorry for multitudes of poor victims among the women. What are their lives worth to them?"

"I know," said Mrs. Blanchard. "The 'poor *fool-ies.*' Wasn't that an original sentence? 'Always when there are fool-*ers* there are fool-*ies.*' That's a woman's rendering of Shakespeare, Mr. Roberts; expressive, isn't it?"

"The women needn't remain fooled if they don't like it," quoted Mr. Roberts, deciding to generalize, since he must needs say something. He was sorry that he said it; a storm of indignant protest rattled about his ears. When he could distinguish between exclamations, Mrs. Blanchard was saying: "Dear me! You ought to have heard Mrs. Wells yesterday; she took up that point and riddled it."

"She has riddled a good many remarks that our dear politicians are fond of making," Eureka said. "There will be no excuse for a person who comes to Chautauqua being fooled by them any longer; that is one comfort."

Eureka's tones were so caustic that Mrs. Blanchard glanced at her in surprise, while Burnham roused himself to contend.

"Now, really, I should like to understand why a woman couldn't eschew Mormonism if she chose, just as she could Methodism, or any other "ism." It may not be the easiest thing in the world to do, but if she finds herself victimized and hasn't backbone enough to get out of it, she doesn't deserve sympathy."

Mrs. Blanchard smiled calmly on him as she said: "Mrs. Wells would tell you that the first all-powerful reason is that she has all her life been a 'fool-ie' trained to it, and believes with all her heart—just because she is a fool—that her future life to all eternity depends on that one man to whom she belongs. What chance is there for such as she? Moreover, suppose she could by some miracle be freed from such shackles, enough to act, and could get away; trained as she has been, how will she support herself and her children? Where will she look for direction and help? But we need not argue about *supposed* cases. Don't you know, Mr. Roberts, the histories of those who have been brave enough to try to escape and have lived to tell their own stories? They were not lacking in courage, were they?"

"I am not arguing at all," Mr. Roberts said briskly. "I am simply being entertained. I believe you two ladies think I am a Mormon emissary sent here to spy out the land, or at the very least a Mormon sympathizer; whereas the fact is that I have not the slightest desire to join that handful of curious people and have no interest whatever in their peculiar religious actions. I am even prepared to admit that perhaps we have been too lenient of their follies and that it is time for our government to look into their teaching more carefully. Am I acquitted?"

He was smiling, but Eureka knew that he was annoyed. Mrs. Blanchard laughed and said she was glad that Mrs. Wells was converting him, and that it was quite time, for he must remember that the "handful of curious people called Mormons" now numbered considerably over a million in our own country and were increasing rapidly. At that point they reached Ramble Avenue, and to Burnham's relief she remarked that she must leave them there; so once more he and Eureka were left to themselves.

14

PUZZLING QUESTIONS

BUT they did not get on well. Eureka had been stirred to the depths of her nature by what had been revelations to her, and she felt as though she could not endure Burnham's apathy; but levity was worse. When he bent toward her and said whimsically: "Did she really think I was perhaps planning to turn Mormon and marry seven wives?" she answered coldly that she did not understand how any person with a heart could trifle over a subject so full of human misery as that; especially if he had any respect for women.

It is probably fortunate that at that moment they were again interrupted by people from the intersecting street. Among them was Mrs. Dennis and Eureka's mother.

"Were you there, Eureka?" her mother asked, as though there could be but one place to have been. "Did you ever hear anything like it! I feel as though I had been to the pit!" Before any reply could be made, Mrs. Dennis interposed.

"Eureka, may I introduce my brother? Miss Harrison, Mr. Dennis. Mr. Roberts. Don't talk Mormonism to him, though, if you want to get quieted down in time for dinner; he is a missionary from Utah and is ready to flash at the mention of the word *Mormon*."

Eureka gave the stranger a swift comprehensive glance and found him tall, pale, and uninteresting. "But I don't believe," she added to this after a moment, "that the Mormons like him a bit better than he does them."

There was still a little time before dinner, and as Burnham was sincerely anxious to get to a better understanding with Eureka, he urged that they walk on down to the shore and get refreshed; she being anxious for precisely the same thing, agreed at once. And then they quarreled outright—about the strangest thing!

It was a very small boy, one of those who were often in Eureka's train, who began the mischief by wading out into altogether too deep water and getting stuck in the mud. Ordinarily he was a plucky little chap, who knew how to get out of trouble as well as into it; but the water surging about him frightened him, so instead of making an effort to get out, he stood still and yelled. It was the dinner hour in many cottages, and that part of the shore was almost deserted, so there was no one to depend on but the two who were not far from him. Eureka, who did not realize that the chief difficulty was mud, was very much alarmed.

"Do hurry!" she exclaimed. "See how high the waves are! They will cover him before you get there. Oh, what if they should carry him away out! He would surely drown! Burnham, why are you so slow!" She whirled toward him as she spoke and was amazed to see him standing there calmly, hands in his pockets. As she turned he called out: "Come on, Willie, that's a brave boy; pull out the right foot, then the left, you can do it."

"Burnham Roberts!" Eureka almost screamed the words, "aren't you going in after him?"

"I hadn't thought of it," he said composedly. "That mud doesn't seem to be exactly suited to low shoes or to my style of trousers."

She made a gesture of disgust; the very immaculateness of his toilet down to his shining shoes and light-colored silk hose offended her.

"You can stand there and think of *clothes*," she said, "when a little child is in danger! I think you are a *coward* as well as a dude, and I'm sorry to have to own you for an acquaintance. *I* shall go after him." She was suiting her action to her word, but with a quick spring he caught her arm. "Eureka, you must not! You do not understand; really, there is no danger."

She tried to switch herself from him but he held her arm as though his hand were a vise while he tried to explain what she would not heed. At that moment there came running from a boathouse in the distance a stalwart workman who plunged his stout rubber boots into the thick black mud, fished out the boy with a single mighty stroke, and sent him yelling home. Eureka, freed from the vise, turned and walked rapidly down the shore toward the avenue that led to the hotel. Burnham followed, uncertain whether to try to speak or to keep silence. Then came an experience that, if it had been carefully arranged beforehand for effect, could not have been better planned.

A little girl had for some minutes been leisurely rowing toward them from across the lake. She looked very small to be managing a boat, but both Burnham and Eureka knew that she understood it. She was the eight-year-old daughter of a woman who washed for some of the guests at the hotel and often rowed over, quite by herself, for the clothes.

"I don't often trust the clean clothes to her," the mother explained, "because she is a frisky little thing like the rest of 'em—she's only eight—and might spatter 'em. But she can't do no mischief to dirty clothes so I let her go for 'em. O dear no! I ain't a mite afraid to have her; she's rowed a boat ever since she was two."

It happened just as Eureka, who was almost breathless with fast walking and indignation, was turning to climb the hill. The "frisky little thing" had risen for a better view of something on the farther shore—her very familiarity with the boat making her careless—and, whether she slipped on the wet floor, or turned suddenly dizzy, or how it happened, no one knew; but she pitched backward into the water. She was quite a distance from the shore, but they both heard distinctly her wild, frightened cry as she disappeared. Eureka stood still, transfixed with terror; the sturdy workman was nowhere to be seen, and there was no one else. Yes—a man was rushing down to the water's edge throwing back coat and waistcoat as he ran. Another second and he was in the water, swimming with long, masterly strokes despite his impeding clothing; she had not known that Burnham Roberts could swim like that under any circumstances. She held her breath and watched. He was making for the very spot where the child had disappeared; no, there she was! He was almost by her side! Would he reach her before she sank again? Could he save her if he did? Boats there were in plenty all along the shore; couldn't she take one and row out to them? She ran frantically down to the water's edge, only to find that the boats were securely locked. She screamed for help and waved her arms frantically, as though if people could not hear they could surely see. Very soon they did both; people were running from all directions, men, women, and children; like wildfire had gone forth that word that something had happened; and all the time Burnham Roberts was swimming with powerful strokes toward the shore, holding by one hand in that viselike grasp a little unconscious weight.

There were literally hundreds to receive them to work over the child, to assure her rescuer that she was "coming round all right," and to hurry him away in a carriage, in a dozen carriages if he had accepted all that eagerly offered. Presently Eureka saw him whirled away, looking white and exhausted. Then she turned and walked up the hill alone; she was rid of her companion without the need for rapid walking; and she had called him a *dude and a coward*.

She did not see him again until after breakfast on the following morning; then she went straight toward where he stood on the south veranda, looking bored. All the morning he had been surrounded by a crowd of young people eager to make him into a hero. He had retranslated a dozen different stories of the rescue and from out the tissue of fantastic exaggerations, picked the few simple facts; he was utterly tired of being a hero and tempted to disclaim even the desire to save a human being from drowning. He had not appeared at the breakfast table, and his mother had reported that he did not rest well during the night and had a headache; but that he assured her he was all right, and that the headache had nothing whatever to do with the exposure of the day before. No, indeed, he had not rested in the afternoon; he went to the ball game! She had never before known him to be so deeply interested in a game played by entire strangers.

To all this, Eureka had listened in silence and compunction. Had his headache to do with the unjust and unwomanly treatment he had received at her hands? She had been miserable about it ever since; she had wondered how it was possible that she could have used such language as she did; she told herself that it would be very hard indeed for him to forgive her and all the time she had no doubt but that he would; she believed that he cared enough for her to forgive anything. As she decided this, she felt a sting of compunction because she could not bring herself to care for him as he did for her.

She swept the children who were about him and who ran toward her out of her way with a word.

"No, Charlie, not this morning. Some other time, Louise. Run away now, all of you, I want to talk to Mr. Roberts." Then she turned to him. "I can't tell you how glad I am to see you out as usual after your dreadful experience yesterday. Before I ask anything about it, I want to beg you to forgive the cruel and hateful words I said; of course you know that I didn't mean them, but I can't think how I could have spoken as I did, even under wild excitement."

He was not diffusive in reply, although he said kindly that she must not let it trouble her, it was really of no consequence; sane people did not take offense at what their friends said under the pressure of strong excitement. The words were all that they should be, but someway, the manner was not Burnham's. When she tried to question him about the rescue he broke in impetuously:

"Suppose we agree to forget all about that. I have been interviewed and interrogated *ad nauseam;* the most absurd and extravagant nonsense has been talked about it. You and I know that I simply swam out and picked up a little girl who had tumbled into the lake; and that is all there is of it."

Eureka was bent on one more question.

"I won't talk about it, Burnham, if it annoys you; though I still think there is a good deal of it, but I am dreadfully anxious to understand why it was that you were so utterly indifferent to the terror of that dear little Willie Powell and then three minutes afterwards so utterly reckless of yourself for the sake of that little girl. Was it because one was a boy and the other a girl?"

He looked at her for a moment without speaking—but with a curious smile. When he spoke his voice was coldly polite.

"I beg your pardon, is it possible that you did not know that the little chap in the mud was only in danger of a whipping that he richly deserved for going in wading at that forbidden point and that the little girl would certainly have drowned if someone had not reached her speedily?"

"I did not know, I mean—I did not think—" Eureka began humbly and in some confusion, but he had turned from her with a cordial: "Good morning, Mr. Dennis," to that gentleman who was ascending the veranda steps. "Can you equal such a morning as this in Utah? To excel it would hardly be possible." Eureka felt herself dismissed.

It was all very unlike Burnham; he had evidently been more hurt by her words than he cared to own; but she felt that she had never before liked him quite so well. She decided that she must be willing to be treated coldly for a little while; he really had abundant reason for so treating her, and she must continue to show him that she was both sorry and ashamed. Had she known that Burnham's unusual manner had nothing whatever to do with her, she would have been astonished beyond measure.

The truth was that he had trials and perplexities that morning, with which he felt she could not sympathize.

Despite the advice of the physician and the entreaties of his mother, he had persisted on the afternoon before in getting out of the warm pack in which he had been placed, taking another cold bath—this time in private—and going off to the ball game, in which he was presumably so interested that he spent the entire afternoon watching it. As a matter of fact, he gave extremely little attention to the game. He occupied one of the excellent seats he had secured and sternly held the other against all intruders until the game was near its close; then he deserted both seats and walked about the grounds to see if by any possible chance the one he sought could have escaped his eye. It had been in vain; Hazel was nowhere to be seen. In the evening, instead of taking himself early to bed, as would have become a youth who had been through such an adventure in the morning, or, failing in that, instead of going down to the parlors to enjoy the reception being held there, he went off by himself, none of his intimate friends knowing whither, for the entire evening. Of course he knew that he went first and with remarkable promptness to the band concert; a function that he generally ignored. At its conclusion he had taken an apparently aimless walk about the grounds, returning late to the amphitheater, where what he called a "stupid recital" was in progress. His testimony with regard to the recital is not to be considered worth anything, because he gave his attention almost entirely to the people who went and came, or who walked very quietly around the great building. It had all been in vain. Hazel was not in the amphitheater, had not been during the evening; of that he felt certain; she was not among the promenaders outside, she did not sit on the little porch of the little cottage at the extreme end of Terrace Avenue, although the little cottage was quite dark, and she was presumably not within. He went home at last, disappointed and in doubt what effort to make next toward the accomplishment of his wish.

The perplexity remained with him on this Sunday morning. How should he contrive to meet Hazel again? Why had she disappointed him the day before? Could it be because she did not care to follow his suggestion? How should he find out? How should he secure opportunities to teach her to care? It was questions like these that were repeating themselves in his brain all the while the young people were trying to make a hero of him; all the while that Eureka was trying to make him forgive her. As yet, no answer had been given to any of them.

15

❈

ALMOST

EUREKA made another effort later. Was Burnham going to the morning service? Of course he was; no one would fail to hear the Bishop. Certainly the Bishop was to preach that day. Didn't he know that it was the baccalaureate sermon? Why, for the graduating class of course; the Shakespeare class; he to talk about being a loyal Chautauquan and not know that!

"They say it has a very large representation here. Don't you think it would be a good idea for us to join the class of 1916? It is forming now. Why, it is a four-year reading course. Where have your eyes and ears been that they haven't had so much knowledge drilled into them? Doesn't that seem a dreadfully long way to look forward? Nineteen hundred and sixteen! It seems as though one would feel *so old* by that time! But the reading circle takes my fancy; systematic reading is always so much better than the haphazard way, don't you think so? The books are wonderfully well chosen; I've been looking them up. What do you think about it?"

What Burnham Roberts thought was: "I wonder if

Hazel likes systematic reading and could be induced to join a Circle?" Aloud, he said that he had not given the matter any thought and had no opinion to express. This was disappointing; the Burnham Roberts that Eureka knew would have been likely to reply that he was ready to read the Chautauqua books, or any other books that chanced to suit her fancy.

However, he went with her to the amphitheater and watched the marching in of the multitude that represented the class circles of the years gone by, as well as the very large representation of the Shakespeare class, without making any cynical remarks. In truth, the occasion left no room for cynicism. Eureka was at first enthusiastic; then, as the long procession in college gown and cap filed down the central aisle, keeping step to the roll of the great organ, in spite of her belief that people could control all outward sign of emotion if they chose, her eyes suddenly filled with tears. It was all so vivid a reminder of college days and of the commencement week about which she had dreamed and planned and of which she had failed. There must be many girls, yes, and women and men, scattered over the earth who had wanted the college outlook and striven for it perhaps, even as she had done, and failed. It was grand in the Bishop to have conceived this plan by which already multitudes must have been inspired to seek and secure higher education, but it was grander still to have opened it to the multitudes upon whom the daily cares of life and the daily necessity for toil pressed so steadily that no regular college course was possible for them; yet here in this carefully superintended reading circle they could have a real outlook upon it all. It was glorious to him to think of it, to persist in it, to push it in spite of all the obstacles he must have encountered; in spite of the criticism and good-natured raillery that he must have had to endure—that form of discouragement was so much harder to bear than the sneering kind; for her, at least—and having had already her share of the ways in which even well-meaning people can discourage new enterprises that they did not originate, the girl made sure that the Bishop had lived through many of them.

She resolved to set in motion plans for a select Chautauqua Circle among her friends as soon as she reached home. Even if Burnham decided to spend the winter in New York—and she did not believe he would—he could easily run down one evening in a week for the circle; he would like that; it would be a definite time in which she would be sure to be at home. All this, unless he should want—but she would not think about that; there would be time enough for such plans. She was sure *she* did not want to be married yet, not for several years, perhaps. What was the need for haste? But a Chautauqua Reading Circle she would surely join without delay.

So would Burnham Roberts; almost at the same moment he settled that he would get up one in New York, early in the fall, composed of people who suited him; he was not clear as to how many members it should have, nor who all of them should be; but the name of one would be Hazel Harris.

The sermon came to Eureka as a surprise. She knew the Bishop well, by reputation; she had read his addresses, she had heard him speak informally several times; she knew that he was peculiarly happy in his use of the English language, she knew that he was capable of a very scholarly effort; she expected that an address to a "Literary and Scientific Circle" would be profound and learned in the highest degree. She even fancied she could select the text and had amused herself, as she waited in one of the small parlors for Burnham, by taking up the Bible and running over some of the majestic passages of Isaiah.

"I'm picking out the Bishop's text," she said to Erskine Burnham, who passed through the room and glanced inquiringly in her direction. "How would this do?" and she read it well.

> This is the purpose that is purposed upon the whole earth, and this is the hand that is stretched out upon all the nations; for Jehovah of hosts hath purposed and who shall annul it? His hand is stretched out and who shall turn it back?

"Wouldn't that give him scope for his powers of oratory?"

When, an hour later, the Bishop announced his text, Erskine looked over at Eureka and smiled. These were the words: "And the Lord added to them day by day those that were being saved."

What chance was here for masterly argument or brilliant display of oratory? Eureka was disappointed. When a man was capable of great things why should he choose small ones? Wait, *was* this small?

The Bishop's singularly incisive voice made every word reach her distinctly, far away, as she was among almost the outermost seats of the great amphitheater. Yet he was already leaning over the desk and talking in familiar tone as friend talks with friend, but what tremendous things he was saying!

"The message of the morning is God's word to you now and here. Will *you* be added this day to those who are being saved? The story of Pentecost is the story of the sunrise of a new day in the world's history. The tongue of fire perpetuated the ministry of Jesus through the Holy Spirit of God as light and energy in the souls of men." A "commonplace text!" Eureka had mentally called it that—she never could again. Salvation, as the preacher obliged her to look at it and think about it, was a wonderful thing!

"Salvation," said the speaker, "personal and social, national and racial, reaches out beyond the planet we live on and takes an interest in suns and stars and spheres and possible occupants of visible but, as yet by us, unexplored worlds, where all that is basest among us has been outlived or is unknown, and all that we dream at our best is beautifully and blessedly real and celestial. Celestial and yet there; commonplace and familiar, never even challenged or doubted because it is an essential feature of the heavenly civilization. Oh, for a glimpse of it! Oh, for a taste of it! We may have both. If by faith we look for it, if by love we taste, and if by *will we grasp,* we may become, each one of us, an integral part of that celestial civilization here and now.

> Today look up and see!
> Today reach out and grasp!
> Today remember Christ, and rest.

Was there any use in trying to call such thoughts, such schemes, such possibilities, *commonplace?*

"Oh, for a glimpse of it!" That, Eureka knew had been her instinctive mental exclamation, as the speaker with a few bold strokes made that other world glow before her; the world where her father lived. His next sentence had fairly stunned her: "We may have it, here and now." Her mind went off into a study of that tremendous statement.

Theoretically, she believed it; wait—did she? Why

of course! She was no infidel; she had been carefully taught. The basic truths of theology were as A. B. C. to her. Besides—there was Father. Of course it was true. Well, then—was she a fool? This was where her logic had her.

When she came back from her mental exercise, the Bishop was speaking directly to the class. What was that he was saying about love?

"Self-love is one thing, and selfishness is quite another. Self-love of the true type requires self-knowledge. What are we living for? Is it for bodily ease, and comfort and self-enjoyment, and recognition, and tributes of praise? Really, what are you living for? The development of a wholesome wide-reaching civilization, or merely success for your own narrow little self? You need to be *saved*. Selfishness accepted and never resisted is hell."

Involuntarily Eureka glanced at her companion. Burnham's face was grave, even a trifle anxious; was he listening? Did he feel himself in any sense described? Frankly she believed him to be one of the most selfish persons she had ever known. All his life, so far as she had known it, he had thought about, planned for, and indulged himself. Could he help feeling somewhat the force of the Bishop's awful words:

"Selfishness accepted and never resisted is hell?"

Then almost as though an audible voice had asked, came the question:

"What about Eureka Harrison?"

"I!" said Eureka's inner self as though answering a questioner, "I gave up everything for others. Why am I not a college girl myself, pray?"

"That is true, you made one great sacrifice for your mother; but haven't you been making her unhappy in a hundred petty ways ever since? In thousands of trifles that make up your life, have you not in a sense taken revenge for the very great sacrifice you made?" This was plain language. Eureka had never before allowed herself to speak such plain words to herself. Was the accusation in any sense true? But she must listen again. The Bishop was speaking to this Shakespeare class about its motto: "To thine own self be true."

"It is an earnest word," he was saying, "a word of wisdom; one need not be a Shakespeare in order to say it, to hear it, to adopt it, and to obey it. It is a law for every sphere in life, from the humblest miner in the lowest, narrowest levels underground, to the astronomer who mounts his observatory at night for royal converse with the remotest stars of space. And to be at your best—read Shakespeare? Oh, yes, but *follow* Christ. His words are full of light, and they burn and glow with love; and he is near us! He is today what he was on earth. Study his words and works and ways. How beautiful it would be if everyone in this class would today repeat in his inmost soul this solemn pledge:

> *Witness ye men and angels now*
> *Before the Lord we speak;*
> *To him we make our solemn vow*
> *A vow we dare not break.*
>
> *That long as life itself shall last*
> *Ourselves to Christ we yield;*
> *Nor from his cause will we depart*
> *Or ever quit the field.*

The solemnity of the words was doubly emphasized by the Bishop's rendering. Their effect on Eureka, the effect of the entire service indeed, was utterly unlike what she had expected. Accustomed all her life to religious services, familiar as she was with the very hymn that had just been repeated, she had never thought of such a thing as making its words personal.

"Ourselves to Christ we yield." How often in the choir of her father's church she had sung that line without even noticing its solemn meaning! Why should it take such hold upon her now?

For the second time, the voice of a man to whom she had never spoken, who did not know of her existence, had reached her conscience and pressed upon her the claims of Jesus Christ. What if she should heed? Suppose she should decide to say, then and there, to God, that:

> *Long as life itself shall last,*
> *Myself to Christ I yield.*

"As long as life itself" that meant forever and *forever* and FOREVER! There was no end to life. If she should, would it make a difference at once and forever? Would it make a difference that Burnham Roberts would like? She was beginning to try to recognize his claim upon her, his right to be always considered.

She glanced up at him almost timidly as, the brief after-service concluded, they joined the throngs who were surging up the aisles, chattering, many of them, like magpies unmindful of the fact that the soul of the great organ was at that moment athrob with exquisite harmonies intended for their ears; unmindful also of the fact that they had been called to stand face-to-face with a question so momentous that it concerned all their future for both worlds.

Burnham's face was grave enough, and he made no attempt to add to the ceaseless chattering going on all about them. Had he felt the power of the question that was still throbbing in her consciousness:

"Will you be added this day to those who are being saved?" The unanswered question. Would Burnham like to have her answer "yes"? Would he join her in the vow that they "dare not break"? If he had but understood it, that moment was even more solemn for him than for the girl at his side. It was his opportunity. He had never been able to influence Eureka very much in any line; but she was nearer to the most important decision in life, that day, than she had ever been before; and it happened that a word from him would have turned the scale.

But he did not speak it; he was silent, more silent than she had ever known him to be when they were alone together; nor did his face encourage conversation; it was almost moody.

His thoughts were busy, but it was not the morning service nor the momentous question that held them. It was simply "What *can* have become of that girl? How shall I manage to find out? How shall I shape things so that I can see her again?"

Eureka gave over trying to draw him into conversation, his moody, absent air irritated her; he seemed almost not to notice what she said; if he wanted to be silent and sullen, let him; she was in no mood to help him; she needed to be helped, instead; only—there was nobody to help her. Oh, well, never mind. She made a strong effort to throw off the thoughts that oppressed her. She joined some of the younger and gayer members of their group at the next corner and chatted and laughed with them merrily.

"We ought to give the more earnest heed to the things that were heard lest haply we drift away from them." Eureka simply "drifted away."

16

STORM

MEANTIME, Hazel. Trouble that seemed to her overwhelming had fallen upon her. It fell, too, through her cousin Josephine, who had always been kind and who tried, spasmodically, to plan for her pleasure. But Josephine had not moved for the purpose of making trouble; she was herself sincerely and sorely troubled.

She had not recognized the young man who had seated Hazel in the amphitheater on that memorable evening of the concert. Her calls at the great downtown store where her father was head bookkeeper were rare, but they were hardly more so than were Burnham Roberts's, although his father was a leading member of the firm and the son was supposed to be arranging to belong to it. Burnham Roberts had no objection to the money that his father's place in the business world secured for him, but he hated business—at least he thought he did—and ignored it as much as possible, comforting himself with the belief that there was time enough; someday he would "buckle down and be nothing but a clerk in a store."

Meantime, he avoided the store so successfully that even the head bookkeeper hardly knew him by sight.

But it was his appearance with Hazel that had troubled her cousin. She saw at a glance that he had the air and manner of a man of the world; where had the child picked him up? Or had they just chanced to come down the incline together? No, they were acquaintances; she became convinced of that as she watched; occasionally they exchanged words and smiles, and they left the amphitheater together.

Josephine was with one of the young women whose acquaintance she had made at the cooking school; and this lady, after taking note of the fact that her companion's glance wandered frequently to the south side of the amphitheater, asked:

"Isn't that your pretty cousin over there in front of the post? Don't you think she is very pretty?"

"Yes," said Josephine, "I think so. Do you know who is sitting beside her?"

"The man, do you mean? No, don't you? I supposed he was a friend of the family, I have seen him so often with your cousin."

She felt the little start of dismay that Josephine gave as she asked quickly, "Do you remember when and where you have seen them?"

"Why—let me see—was it yesterday? No, it was this morning; they were walking down by the lake near the pier; I noticed them particularly because they made such a handsome couple. Don't you really know him at all? Well, he's a fine-looking fellow, anyway; your cousin has shown good taste."

"You spoke of seeing them often; do you remember any other time especially?" Josephine's manner expressed such unmistakable anxiety that her companion could but respect it and try to be accurate.

"Perhaps I should not have said 'often,' I only meant several times. I saw them out driving yesterday afternoon; at least he was driving; your cousin was on the back seat with a lady."

"Are you sure it was Hazel?"

"Why, yes, I am. Don't you think she has a very distinctive face? I don't believe one would be likely to mistake anyone else for her. I had a chance to see her distinctly for they stopped at the post office and I was standing outside. I confess that I stared, especially at her lovely coat; it attracted me almost as much as her face."

"Her 'lovely coat'!" repeated Josephine, dazed.

"Yes, she had on a perfectly beautiful pongee coat, heavily embroidered; I don't think I ever saw a handsomer one. I am very fond of pongee."

Then Josephine knew that she must tell her mother! But it was no feeling of unkindness toward Hazel that made her sure of it. The child was beautiful, although her aunt did not think so; beautiful and young and ignorant of the world about which Josephine believed that she knew so much. It hardly seemed possible that a girl could be so ignorant as not to know that she must not talk and walk and drive with a strange young man, to whom she had probably not even been introduced; because—who could have introduced her to one like him? Hazel knew no one and went nowhere except on errands, and occasionally to a lecture or concert. Could it be that she was a deceitful little thing who slipped away when they thought her at home and made acquaintances where she chose? Josephine did not believe it for a moment; she believed that Hazel's beautiful eyes were true; but—oh, dear! Mother must know all this right away. She joined her mother and Isabel at the corner and went home with them in a flutter of anxiety. Perhaps Hazel ought to be looked for at once; only—how could they find her, or him, when they did not know even his name?

It was a great relief to see that light in Hazel's attic; she was safe then for the night; it would do to wait until morning; she must try to plan how best to tell the tale. She planned a great deal, lying awake for two hours to do so; but, after all, she blundered sadly.

To begin with, there could hardly have been a more inopportune time than that Saturday morning just as Mrs. Bradford had discovered that her weekly bill for eggs and butter and cream exceeded the allowance she had made for them by nearly two dollars, and that all fruits were higher priced this week than they had been before. She told Isabel sharply that she must wash out her white dress herself; they simply could not afford to have it laundered; and when Hazel spilled the hot water, she chided her with vehemence, assuring her that she acted all the time as though her mind was somewhere else.

"Dear me, I'm afraid it is!" sighed Josephine, who thought she saw her opportunity; for Hazel was just starting for the milkstand.

"Mother, I've got to tell you something very—well, *disagreeable* I guess is the word. I'm afraid Hazel doesn't know as much about how to behave as we supposed she did."

"Goodness knows I never thought she knew much about behavior, or anything else!" retorted the worried housekeeper. "What has she been doing now?" The emphasis on the "now" implied a multitude of offenses to back up this one, whatever it was.

"Did you see her last night at the amphitheater? No, you couldn't from where you sat; I was on the upper circle with Miss Carson, and Hazel was just across from me on the south side with a young man."

"With a young man!" Mrs. Bradford's tone was ominous. "What young man?"

"That's the question. Miss Carson didn't know him, and I never saw him before; but she said she had seen him with her several times."

"*Who* said she saw him with whom? You mix up your pronouns so wildly, Josephine, there is no understanding you."

"Why, Mother! it is perfectly plain what I mean. Miss Carson said she had seen that young man with Hazel a number of times; out walking, out driving, and then last night at the concert."

To say that Mrs. Bradford was astonished fails to describe the situation; she was overwhelmed with astonishment, with indignation, with dismay—and poured out so much of it in incoherent exclamations, questionings, and forebodings that Josephine regretted her rashness. She tried to smooth matters.

"Of course, Mother, it is nothing but a little heedlessness on her part; she probably met him somewhere and was pleased because he showed her a little attention."

"'Pleased!'" echoed Mrs. Bradford, and "'heedlessness!' Would one of my girls allow a strange young man to take her to places and walk about with her? I have no patience whatever with such talk as that. Hazel, come here!" This call in her most vehement tone was for the girl who, breathless with haste, stepped on the porch with her bottles of milk.

"Oh, Mother!" was Josephine's murmured protest, "let us have breakfast first." Mrs. Bradford did not even notice her.

"Come here," she repeated, "and give an account

of yourself. This is a delightful story I have been hearing about a member of my family! It seems that while I thought you safe at home, you have been traipsing through the woods and riding about, no one knows where, with a strange young man! What does it mean? It simply cannot be possible, after all the training that I have given you, that you don't know any better than to even go out driving with somebody you picked up on the streets!"

"Oh, Mother!" begged Josephine. All this sounded so unlike what she had really told her mother; she had said not a word about the woods; besides, this was no way to talk to Hazel; if Father were only here, he would know just what to say.

"Josephine," said Mrs. Bradford with severity, "I want you to be quiet; I am managing this affair, and I consider myself able to do it without help. Hazel, how long has this disgraceful thing been going on? Where did you pick up a person who is not above imposing on an ignorant girl and encouraging her to hide his existence from those who are taking care of her? Begin at the beginning and let me have the whole story."

By this time Hazel was in no state to begin anything properly. From surprised embarrassment and annoyance, she had advanced rapidly to burning indignation.

"I have no story to tell," she said, and her eyes flashed. "You have no right to speak to me in this way; I have done nothing of which I am ashamed. The young man who overtook me yesterday on my way from the post office and walked a little way with me and who was kind enough to give me a seat at the amphitheater last night is a friend of the lady who took me to her room when I was ill and was kind to me in every way."

"Oh, he is!" Mrs. Bradford, instead of being appeased, was growing more indignant every moment; for it must be admitted that Hazel's tone and manner were not conciliating. "And who is she, pray? Someone you picked up on the street, who took you home when your fit of ill temper made you sick."

"She is Mrs. Burnham of Philadelphia."

"Is she indeed! That tells me a great deal! I am sure I never heard of her before and never want to again; there are all sorts of people in Philadelphia, as you ought to have sense enough to know. The amazing thing is that you consider this a sufficient introduction to warrant all sorts of intimacies with a young man. I must say I am not only ashamed but amazed. I know your mother had peculiar ideas, but—" But then Hazel's anger blazed. Her aunt had never before heard the voice in which she spoke.

"Don't you *dare* mention my mother! I will not have her name disgraced by your talk. My mother was a lady, and you are not; or you would not say such words to a girl who has given no occasion for them. I know I am dependent on you for my bread, but I will starve rather than stand here silent and hear my mother insulted."

Her aunt advanced a step toward her and raised her voice. "Take care, Miss Impudence, don't you go any farther! Another word of this kind and out of my house you go, to earn your bread in the best way you can; I give you fair warning that I have borne from you all that I'm going to. Don't speak at *all!*" For Hazel, already ashamed of her outburst, had opened her lips—"I don't want to hear a word of any sort from you; all I ask is that you go out of my sight."

Here Isabel, who had been silent a very long time for her, interposed daringly.

"But, Mother, that isn't being fair; you ought to let Hazel explain; I am sure she can; we know that she hasn't done anything that she thought was wrong."

"Yes," chimed in Josephine, "I hadn't the least idea you would say such things to her; I thought you would just caution her to be more careful."

Mrs. Bradford controlled herself by a mighty effort and spoke with ominous quietness and coldness.

"Since when did you two discover that it was your duty to bring your mother up? What 'we all know' is that Hazel is an ignorant young girl who has had very little training about anything; and that is all I am saying to her. As a matter of course if she had known that she was disgracing herself and us, she wouldn't have done what she did. However, it is done now and we shall have to take the consequences; the only thing we can do is to look out for the future. I hope, Hazel, that at least you understand that such things must be put a stop to *at once*. So long as you are in my house you must conduct yourself in a proper manner; I will have no strange young men hanging about, meeting you on the streets and taking you nobody knows where. I wish you were safe in your uncle's care, instead of mine, this minute! Now let us see if we can possibly have some breakfast; and remember, I want no more words about this from any of you. We have had enough, in all conscience!"

Mother and daughters sat down, presently, to the belated meal and went to talking at once about the very subject that had been vetoed. They were all much excited and talked with vehemence. Mrs. Bradford, like most angry people, had said more to Hazel than she had meant and now attempted to explain the cause of her outburst.

"Of course I did not mean that Hazel was bad! She is simply a little fool; but I haven't the least doubt but that the fellow is thoroughly bad; meeting her on the streets like any loafer, planning to do so; you needn't tell me it is all accident; I know better."

"Oh, *Mother!*" from Isabel, "I don't see how you know. I met Mr. Sellers on the street last night, and he turned and walked with me; then he took me down the incline and found a seat for me. What if people should talk about me for just that?"

"Mr. Sellers is a very different person," her mother said coldly. "You have been properly introduced by people whom we know, and your mother has no objection to your talking with him. Still, I shouldn't care to have you go out driving with him until I know more about him."

This gave Josephine a new thought.

"There was a lady with Hazel when she went driving."

"Oh, there was! Why didn't you say so?"

"I didn't think of it, Mother; I was anxious for Hazel and sure that Father would think we ought to keep her with us, and I forgot all about the lady; but Miss Carson said Hazel sat on the back seat beside a lady, and this man was in front, driving."

"Why did Miss Carson need to say anything about it?" Isabel asked with an annoyed toss of her head. "For all she, or the rest of us know, the lady might have been his grandmother that he was taking out for an airing, and they might just have picked up Hazel and brought her home. I detest gossip."

Mrs. Bradford had reached the stage where it was

absolutely necessary to blame somebody; this time it was Josephine.

"You did very wrong," she said severely, "not to speak of the lady at once. As Isabel says, it would have put a different look on the whole thing. Not that I think Hazel should allow herself to be picked up on the streets by anybody who happens along, as though she were a lost article; but I am glad you see it your duty to keep her with you; that is what will have to be done in future. You have been quite too willing to shirk the responsibility thus far."

Now Josephine knew that this was unfair and that her mother had been the one who had planned that she and Isabel should be free to go without "always waiting for a third one." But she held her peace, feeling with her mother that they had all said enough on the subject. Of one thing she was very glad; that she had said not a word about the pongee coat.

17

"COMMON"

HAZEL waited for no breakfast; as soon as it was possible for her to escape, she fled to her attic and threw herself upon her cot, where the hornets and mice, if they had been at home, could have borne witness to such an outburst of tears and sobs and exclamations of indignation and distress as that attic must seldom have heard.

Mingled with her bitter indignation was an almost overwhelming sense of shame at the thought that she had appeared to others as without self-respect; as bold; as everything that her aunt included in that one hateful word *common*. Perhaps she ought not to have taken that little walk to the shore, though other girls did such things; she had met dozens of them walking and chatting with young men; still, they might have been old friends while he was a stranger; but he didn't seem so; he seemed like the kindest friend anyone could have. Was it possible that he, too, thought her "common"? Had he urged her to come to the south side of the amphitheater that evening because he knew that he could?—that she could be coaxed to do what other girls—respectable girls with fathers and mothers—would not do?

Poor Hazel! She did not believe it; she believed him to be true and noble and good; nevertheless, the thought rankled.

There was also another misery; she had broken her pledge. Aunt Sarah had been horrid, "perfectly horrid and mean!" but so had she. She had said things that ought not to have been said; they might be true—she believed that they were—but no girl pledged to strive always for the "ornament of a meek and quiet spirit" ought to have soiled her soul by speaking them.

It is good to be able to record that before that dreadful first hour in the attic was ended, this girl, so tried, so miserable, so true at heart, slipped to her knees and sobbed out her troubles and her confessions to the ear of him who has promised rest.

Nevertheless, she did not fully rest; she was young and foolish; like many an older Christian, she insisted on picking up part of the burden again and carrying it about with her.

Before noon, a kind of peace had been patched up between her aunt and herself. She had gone, with her eyes red and her face swollen and weeping, and faltered out some stumbling regrets for words that ought not to have been uttered, and her aunt had tried to be kind.

She assured her that of course she had not for a moment believed her to be intentionally bad; if she had not at once flown into a passion she would have understood that they were simply frightened at finding her so hopelessly ignorant of the world and heedless of its dangers. Why, her cousins were *appalled* at the idea of her walking and driving about with an unknown man! One thing she had certainly proved;

she was not to be trusted alone on these grounds. Hereafter she must go out with one of them, or not at all. As for the man who had insulted her, there was no question as to his badness; *men* understood about these things if some girls did not; let him come in her neighborhood if he dared! She would very soon see that he was sent about other business. If he had presumed upon the notion that Hazel had no one to protect her, he would find himself mistaken.

It cannot be said that Hazel was comforted by this interview; she came away feeling herself almost certainly "common."

As the day waned, her humiliation deepened; life had suddenly lost all its charm; she thought gloomily of the ball game which she had intended to watch; she wanted no ball game. She wanted nothing of any of them; if only she could get away and go to Mother! Oh, if she *could!* Mother would understand. She cried at intervals throughout the long day; surreptitiously in the early part of it, with absolute abandon when the work was done and she had drawn down shades and made the little annex look deserted and then gone to swelter in her attic. The rooms below were deserted; the girls, after vainly trying to persuade her to join them in going to the ball ground, offering to "do the dishes" if she would, had departed with half a dozen acquaintances, and her aunt—after urging the special features of interest at the four o'clock missionary rally, offering to wait for her if she would go, and assuring her that they would all get supper together when they came home, had finally gone away vexed, telling her as a parting message that if she preferred to sulk, rather than to act like a reasonable being, she could have that privilege.

Hazel did not sulk, but she cried as she had never

in all her troubles cried before; the utter impossibility of explaining to either aunt or cousins just how she felt weighed on her like a pall, their very kindness pressing it the more closely. By evening, when outward calm had again been achieved, eyes and face told their unmistakable tale. She went to bed as soon as she had finished the supper dishes—Josephine insisting on helping with them and chatting to her cheerfully about the wonders of the ball game. Then, "Won't you go to hear Mrs. McCoy? People say she is very good." Hazel, by this time almost too much exhausted physically to talk, could honestly say that she would rather go to bed than anywhere else in the world.

On Sunday she did not have to feign headache as an excuse to remain invisible all day; she had one that kept her a prisoner. Again they were kind; Isabel hovered over her, bathing her head with witch hazel, while Josephine tried to make the attic look less dreary; and her aunt called up from the foot of the stairs that they were to be sure and have Hazel come down and lie on her couch; it was so much cooler there. But Hazel would not; she was thankful that the day was cool and that she could honestly say the attic was comfortable, and she would not stir from it for anything. She protested earnestly and successfully against the offer of each one to stay and minister to her; she would not have them lose the baccalaureate sermon for the world! She drew a long sigh of relief when at last they departed and fought her way alone through a day of physical and mental pain; she was almost glad when her head ached so hard that she could neither think nor cry anymore.

The next morning, despite the headache which still continued, though in a subdued form, Hazel plunged into work with an energy that augured well for

Isabel's white dress which she had offered to launder and persisted in undertaking; in truth, she added to the regular Monday routine all the extras she could, with a half-frightened feeling that it was only by working to exhaustion that she could manage to live. By Tuesday morning the girl looked so white and worn and had such heavy black rings under her eyes that Josephine resolved to interfere.

"Mother," she began with firmness, "don't you think it is going to be impossible to keep Hazel in this little tucked-up house all the time unless she goes out with us? A girl of spirit would be sure to resent such a thing anyway; she wants to feel free to go and come when she likes, of course, as the rest of us do. I think it is all nonsense about not trusting her; now that she understands, she will be careful enough; and, anyhow, she does as she is told wonderfully well."

Mrs. Bradford looked annoyed, as she generally did when her daughters called her ways in question and told what they thought; but before she could reply, Isabel, more diplomatic than her sister, put in her word.

"She looks *dreadful* this morning! as though she had had a fit of sickness, or was going to; we'll have her sick on our hands, next, and Father flying up here to attend to us all. Wouldn't it be horrid to have somebody real sick in a little tucked-up place like this!"

Then Josephine added, "Do, Mother, send her on an errand somewhere. The air is delicious, just a walk in it will do her good; she won't go out with us; I tried to get her to go to the class with me this morning, but I couldn't."

Mrs. Bradford felt like saying that if the silly girl chose to be so obstinate she might stay at home forever; but that reference to Mr. Bradford and his anxieties checked her; besides, the child really looked miserable; what if she should sulk herself into genuine illness? On the whole, Mrs. Bradford decided to ignore former commands and began as soon as Hazel entered with a fresh supply of milk.

"Hazel, if you are through your breakfast, I wish you would run to the office with those letters on my table. I want your uncle's to go by the early mail; you'll have to get me a quarter's worth of stamps, too, and put some on the letters; I'm entirely out. You'll find a quarter in my purse in the left-hand drawer."

In this way it came about that Burnham Roberts moodily waiting for change at the money-order window gave a sudden exclamation and, forgetting his change, rushed over to the window where Hazel was waiting for stamps; he had almost given up the hope of meeting her by any of the ordinary ways. There was unmistakable eagerness in his greeting.

"Good morning. Where have you been for this long time? Why did you go back on me in such cruel fashion when I begged you to let me show you the ball game? And why weren't you out all day Sunday? You have been ill!" he added hastily and anxiously as she turned startled eyes upon him.

She glanced about her nervously. For all that she knew, she might be doing something very "common" at this moment; who was there on the watch to make a note of it? She felt as though she ought to rush away without a word; but the postage stamps must be waited for, and there were several others to be served before her.

"I could not come," she said, her voice low and tremulous. "And I must not talk with you. Oh, no," replying to another anxious question—"I am not ill, I am only—miserable."

"What is it?" he asked with increasing earnestness and increasing gentleness. "What has happened? Something I see that troubles you very much. Am I in any way to blame? What can I do? Are you waiting for letter stamps? I have some; let me stamp and mail those letters, then we will walk to some quiet place where you can tell me all about it."

She held to the letters and spoke almost as if in terror.

"No! Oh, no! Indeed I must *not!* I cannot walk with you anymore, nor talk with you; I must go at once; my aunt is—Oh, Mr. Roberts, *please!* I cannot tell you anything."

She did not mean to; afterwards, she did not understand how it was that she had. He was not insistent; he did not try to take the letters nor to do anything contrary to her wish; but he questioned her gently, ingeniously, while he was taking the stamps from her trembling fingers and affixing them to her letters; she was sure that she did not tell him much, not anything like the whole dreadful story; yet he seemed to understand. When, after a very few minutes he held open the door for her to pass, himself remaining behind, all he said was:

"I shall see you soon; good-bye until then."

To himself he said as he stood looking after the girl: "The old cat! The insufferable old cat! If I don't get even with you, my name is not Burnham Roberts." It is quite safe to infer that he was not speaking of Hazel! Before noon he did what he had done all his life when he reached a place of straits and was not sure which way to turn, went in search of his mother. He chose his words with diplomacy.

"Mommy, do you know that you and I have succeeded in getting your little friend into a sea of trouble? It seems that it is not safe, in this hotbed of gossip, to bestow ordinary courtesies on acquaintances."

They were in his mother's dressing room, and she turned wondering eyes on him from the mirror before which she was arranging her hair.

"What do you mean, Burnham? Which of my friends is in trouble?"

"The latest one," he said lightly. "The little girl we took driving; afterwards I had the audacity to provide a seat for her in the amphitheater; moreover, I met her on the street and walked a few squares with her; and it seems her aunt is a person of very limited brains and large imagination. She chooses to think that her niece has not only made some objectionable acquaintances, but has been too familiar with them; and the child is now practically a prisoner in that two-penny annex where we found her."

"The idea!" said Mrs. Roberts. "The poor child! And I was just planning a way to have her with us for part of tomorrow so as to give her a better chance to see the procession and all the other functions."

"Glad to hear it," said her son, speaking gaily. "I have a great desire to see that remarkable aunt meet her match; and experience tells me that what Mrs. Evan Roberts plans she will be likely to carry out, regardless of ignorant persons who think they can hinder."

What mother but would be pleased with such a word from her son? Mrs. Roberts smiled and knew that she would certainly try to carry out her plans.

It was this chain of events that caused Mrs. Bradford to be flying about her room that afternoon in frantic haste to make certain changes in her toilet that she had not meant to make so early.

A little girl rooming in the cottage of which Mrs.

Bradford's rooms were an annex had heard and answered a knock at the side porch door and carried to
that lady a card that she had long coveted, bearing
engraved on it the name: "Mrs. Evan Roberts." Mrs.
Bradford knew that it would forever hereafter grace
her parlor table. She was practically alone in the house;
her daughters were away for the afternoon, and Hazel
had retired to her attic, where knocks at lower doors
were not heard; so the hostess arrived at last on the
side porch, where in pleasant weather her callers were
received, breathless from haste and profuse with apol-
ogies for keeping her guest waiting. This gave the
caller time to recover from her surprise and readjust
her possible program for the interview. Behold, the
obnoxious aunt that her son had deftly challenged her
to conquer was the wife of her husband's head bookkeeper! She had met the lady before and believed that
she understood something of her character. Her hasty
mental comment was: "That poor child! Now I understand something that puzzled me."

Rapidly she reconstructed her mode of approach
and presently broke in upon Mrs. Bradford's rapture
over receiving a call at last from her "dear friend" with
a quiet: "Part of my errand this afternoon was to see
your niece, whom I met a few days ago. Is she at home,
and may I have the pleasure of a little visit with her?"

Then was Mrs. Bradford all but overwhelmed. So
that sly girl had actually come in contact with Mrs.
Evan Roberts and said not a word about it! When had
they met, and how? Had Mrs. Roberts heard of the
gossip that was no doubt afloat? If so, how should she
find out how much, or how little had been heard and
what attitude about it should she take with the great
lady? She was visibly disturbed; and her guest, pitying
her embarrassment, essayed to explain.

18

DILEMMAS

"I PRESUME she has told you of making the acquaintance of my dear friend Mrs. Burnham, who brought her home from the shore the day she was not feeling well? It was through Mrs. Burnham that I met her. I became interested in her at once; one cannot help being interested in young girls. Soon afterwards, I called; and finding her at home alone, carried her with me for a little drive into the country. I hope you have forgiven me for running away with a member of your family?"

She was aiming to put her hostess at ease, but had simply added astonishment to her embarrassment. So this was the lady in the back seat with Hazel when she was seen driving out with a strange young man! If Mrs. Bradford had only known! What mattered it who the young man was, since he was with Mrs. Evan Roberts? Still, despite a little flurry of indignation, Mrs. Bradford was relieved. Part of her annoyance over Hazel's supposed departures from the ways of propriety was born of genuine anxiety for the girl; she honestly believed that Hazel in her ignorance had fallen a prey to the wiles of a bad man; to find that he was a man for whom Mrs. Evan Roberts was ready to vouch was a very great relief; and to realize that it was Mrs. Roberts who had invited Hazel to drive—of course because she knew her to be *her* niece, was a joy almost too great to be believed. Having been genuinely disturbed, the relief brought her to the verge of tears and bewildering exclamations.

"Oh, my dear Mrs. Roberts, how shall I tell you what a load you have taken from my heart! I have been *so* distressed and *so* uncertain what steps to take; being away from my husband with the responsibility thrown on me, of course I felt it all the more. You know how necessary it is for a young girl to see to it that her good name is kept intact, and my poor niece had not, I am sorry to say, the kind of early training that would make her careful. When I heard that she had been out driving with a young man, a total stranger, whose *name,* even, I was unable to discover, you may judge how I felt. The child is naturally so secretive that she did not even mention the drive to me, much less your name; had I for a single moment supposed you to be connected with it, I should have understood, of course, and all my anxieties would have been over; as it is, I am sure you can realize what I have suffered, for of course you know what gossip is."

Mrs. Roberts was not sure of any such thing; certain of this woman's phrases bewildered her.

"Do you mean me to understand," she asked quietly, "that your niece has been the subject of unpleasant gossip, and that my son with whom I was driving out that afternoon has been the innocent cause?"

"Why, you see," began Mrs. Bradford, embarrassed again as she saw to what such an understanding might lead. "I hadn't the remotest idea as I told you that *your* name was associated with it in any way; Hazel told me nothing; she is by nature so secretive that there seems to be no use in trying to win her confidence; I have to depend upon others; and this is what came to me."

Here she leaned forward and dropping into undertone gave an elaborate account of Hazel's supposed indiscretions, and the distress of her aunt and cousins.

"I am sorry, indeed," said Mrs. Roberts when the story was concluded, "that my effort to give pleasure to a little girl whose face and manner I fancied should have led to unpleasant comments. I shall have to confess that it all seems very simple and commonplace to me. The instincts of gentlemen prompt certain attentions to ladies of their acquaintance, of course, but such do not as a rule furnish food for gossip. Still, I can see how you as a guardian felt the need for being even more than careful. Our misfortune was in not having met any other members of the family on the day that I called for your niece to drive with me."

"Yes, indeed," began Mrs. Bradford eagerly. "If I had only known"—She launched forth on an earnest reiteration of her ignorance of the Roberts name as associated with the matter and the potency of it, if she had but known; to all of which Mrs. Roberts gave slight heed; her mind being busy with the problem of how, under the circumstances, she could best proceed with her scheme. Mrs. Bradford, too, was thinking, almost as fast as she talked. The problem with her was how further to present her niece's story to this woman who represented power. If Mr. Bradford could secure an addition to his salary, a large addition, because of the coming of another member into his family to be fed and clothed, it would be what she, Mrs. Bradford, had long believed ought to be done. Why should she not, having an unprecedented opportunity, talk from that standpoint? The diplomatist decided to undertake it.

Since Mrs. Roberts was so interested in Hazel it was right that she should know all about her. The poor child was left penniless and destitute; she might almost say utterly destitute; she had not even decent clothing when she came to them more than a year ago after the death of both her parents. There had barely been money enough scraped together to pay her traveling expenses from the Pacific coast. The child's father was—well, he was a painter; Mrs. Roberts knew what improvident people they generally were. Oh, no, not a *house* painter, no indeed! If he had been that, he could probably have made a decent living for his family. He called himself an artist, and really sold a good many pictures at one time; but they traveled a great deal, always taking the poor child with them and wasting their money and her opportunities, for while she had been all over the world, one might say, she had never stayed long enough in one place to be taught anything useful. When the father died, there were debts that swallowed up what little they had. Oh, it was a distressing tale, and what they had been through, Mrs. Bradford would not harrow the soul of her guest by trying to describe. Suffice it to say that they sent for the girl, of course, and helped her to get to them and were doing the best for her that they could; but Mrs. Roberts knew how expensive living in New York was for poor people, and the truth was that since Hazel's coming it had been hard work sometimes to make ends meet. When she, Mrs. Bradford, had planned for this outing in the country, she had done it at infinite sacrifice chiefly on Mr. Bradford's account; he did so need a complete change; but behold he had not been able to come at all! It was wonderful what difference it made to have one more to feed and clothe; to say nothing of traveling expenses. Still, Mr. Bradford had borne it all with cheerfulness. Hazel was the child of his half brother only, and they had been separated when quite young, but he felt that he must treat her just as he did his own; and they were doing it; although of course it was at the expense of sacrifice. And there was nothing but sacrifice, so far; for Hazel had not been trained to helpfulness in any line; even about the duties of a quiet home. Mrs. Roberts, if she was at all interested in such matters, would be amazed to see how ignorant a young girl could be; she was trying to teach her, of course, what all girls should know, but it was a hindrance, rather than help; still, they were not working for reward, and they meant to do their little best for her.

It was a masterly plea, and to some of it Mrs. Roberts had listened with interest; even asking questions to draw out further details, as she began to see how the story would further her own plans; but her response was not in line with the narrator's hopes.

"I am glad you have told me this," she said when Mrs. Bradford at last reached a period, "because it opens the way for a little plan of mine that may be a temporary help to us both. We have in our party this summer a number of little children, four grandchildren of mine and four or five others belonging to very dear friends; they all play together, and we have been looking for a suitable person to take direction of their plays and walks for two or three hours each day. Would you be willing to lend us your niece for this purpose during the remainder of your stay on the grounds, provided of course that she is willing to come?"

Without waiting for reply, she hastened to add particulars.

"Although we should want only two or, at most, three hours of help each day, we should want the time divided in such a way that the only convenient plan would be to have her remain with us so as to be within call when needed; it would therefore be right to pay for more than the two or three hours of service; if you will lend her to me for the next few weeks, I will give her room and board and ten dollars a week. That will enable her to furnish a few trifles for her own wardrobe; girls always like that, you know."

Then was Mrs. Bradford in a dilemma. What was she to say? She had already carefully explained that Hazel was rather a hindrance than a help to her, so excuses of that kind were cut off. Moreover, she was aware that ten dollars a week was very unusual payment for the service required, and none knew better than she how many "trifles" it could be made to buy; but—and here—the lady being at her wits' end, determined to flee the exact truth.

"That is certainly a very generous offer, but I am afraid, my dear Mrs. Roberts, that my husband's peculiar ideas will prevent its acceptance. For a plain businessman, I shall have to confess that he has some sentimental and expensive ideas. Loyalty to his brother—although he was only a half brother—has taken hold of him to such an extent that he simply will not hear of Hazel's being set at anything that we would not plan for our own daughters; so the idea of her going out to any sort of service had simply to be abandoned. Personally I believe that it is the worker who dignifies the work; and that whatever a truly self-respecting person is willing to do will not in any true sense injure her, but one cannot run contrary to the prejudices of one's husband, you know."

How amazed would Mrs. Bradford's daughters have

been had they heard these lofty deliverances from her lips! Yet Mrs. Bradford believed that she believed them. Her caller smiled indulgently; she had recognized a quotation from one of the leading speakers at the Woman's Club.

"It is an interesting subject for discussion," she said, "but fortunately we do not have to enter into it now; we have simply to remember that we are at Chautauqua, where peculiar conditions prevail; the waiters at many of the large boardinghouses, you know, are college girls and boys, who know that they do not in any way imperil their social positions by taking up this summer work; the word *servant* is not thought of in their connection. Not that it isn't a good word; I would be honored in hearing it applied to myself—in the same way that Paul used it." The last phrase was added in response to Mrs. Bradford's look of bewilderment; but it did not especially enlighten her; the poor lady was too busy securing her social position to have time for great familiarity with Paul's letters.

"That is the trouble," she murmured, her mind still on the word *servant* in the sense that it was familiar to her—"It is a word that *sticks;* and some people, as you say, are foolish, and so—"

Mrs. Roberts interrupted.

"I mean, of course, to include your niece as a member of my family; we have a family table at the hotel, where she would have a seat with us."

Mrs. Bradford's face cleared, and her heart experienced a sharp twinge of envy. What an opportunity this might be for Josephine or Isabel! She could hear herself explaining to her few Chautauqua acquaintances:

"My daughter has gone to spend a few days with our dear friend Mrs. Roberts at the Atheneum. Mrs.

Evan Roberts, you know, of New York. They are in straits of course about help—such people always are—and as my daughter is passionately fond of children, she has offered to keep the younger ones of their party in sight when they go to walk and see that they don't get drowned or run over; it gives her walks a definite object, you know; she was very glad to be able to help them out." It sounded well, she resolved to venture.

"That is really a very tempting offer, dear Mrs. Roberts, for a girl who needs to earn money; if Hazel, who I am sorry to say has inherited from her mother some false ideas, should be too proud to accept it, I am sure that either of my daughters would be glad to help you; they are both delightful with children and are so anxious to help their father with his heavy financial burdens that I am in constant fear lest they will do something rash that would bring in a little money; it would really be a relief to have one of them safe with you for a few days."

It was well done, but Mrs. Roberts was not caught.

"Such desires are a credit to your daughters," she said kindly, "but my youngest grandchild has fallen in love with your niece, and as she is a shy little creature, slow to make acquaintance, I do not think I shall try for anyone else during this short time if Hazel will not come to us; may I see her, Mrs. Bradford?"

Mrs. Bradford decided to try the truth again.

"I will see if she is in; but, dear Mrs. Roberts, I am afraid she could not go to the hotel just now, even if she wanted to; to be entirely frank, her wardrobe is not in condition to leave home. I have had so many expenses and such unexpected ones since coming here, that the ready-made garments suitable for the country which I intended to buy for her as soon as we reached the grounds have had to wait until my husband can send us another remittance."

Even that did not silence Mrs. Roberts. She arose as she spoke.

"That need not trouble you if Hazel is willing; I shall be glad to advance a portion of her salary and let her make the necessary purchases at once. One comfort in being in the country lies, I think, in the fact that we need only simple, easily laundered garments. It happens that my daughter is going to Jamestown tomorrow afternoon, and she would be glad to undertake any commissions. She is an excellent shopper; I depend on her for my own needs. May I see Miss Hazel a moment?"

"'Miss Hazel' indeed!" muttered Mrs. Bradford as she toiled up the steep and narrow stairs in search of her niece.

19

"WE'LL DO IT TOGETHER"

HOWEVER, before she reached the top stair, she had decided that, perhaps, under the circumstances, this was the best that could have happened. The Roberts family would certainly not feel at liberty to spend very much of the "salary" on clothes, and a few clothes Hazel must have at once; the girls were simply insistent about that. The more she thought of it, the more she felt that it might be "providential"—Mrs. Bradford was never quite sure on that point—if there was gossip afloat, it would be a great thing to have the protection of Mrs. Evan Roberts.

"Dear Mrs. Roberts has taken such a fancy to my niece that we are really almost jealous! She is staying with them now, helping a little in the care of the children—in the interval between nurses, you know—oh, she is well acquainted with them; she has been out driving with the family." She heard herself explaining to the curious after some such fashion; perhaps to those who had tried to gossip; she liked the sound of it. Moreover, what an entering wedge to intimacy with the Roberts family it might be, later, to have Hazel so well acquainted with them! She would tell her that she would better accept the offer.

It was her full intention to superintend the interview between Mrs. Roberts and her niece, but possibly "Providence" arranged otherwise. It appeared that the owner of the cottage had been visiting her attic and was waiting at that moment to have an interview with her tenant about an important matter. Hazel had already started to summon her aunt for the purpose and met her at the head of the stairs. There was just time to explain hurriedly the nature of Mrs. Roberts's errand and to urge acceptance on the ground that the "salary" would relieve her uncle, at least a little, in his difficult task of supporting them all, when the lady appeared and claimed her attention. Hazel whisked past them and flew down those narrow and treacherous stairs like a winged creature.

Could Mrs. Bradford have heard the opening words of that interview below stairs she would have been less certain of the "providential" element.

"Dear child, what *have* you been doing to yourself? You look positively ill!"

"Oh, I'm not ill; I've been having a perfectly terrible time and have cried ever so much; that is what is the matter with my eyes."

Then Mrs. Roberts, watch in hand, said tenderly:

"Poor little girl! I want to hear all about that 'perfectly terrible time' as soon as I can; but just now I must talk very fast; I am late for an appointment. Has your aunt told you that I want to run away with you for a little? Will you come to us, dear, and help us with the children for a few days?"

Hazel's tear-swollen eyes flashed joy at that, and to cover emotion that evidently lay near the surface, she clasped her hands in an extravagance of delight, mur-

muring in tragic tones: "Oh, Mrs. Roberts! will I spend a few days in heaven?"

Mrs. Roberts laughed appreciatively. "The Atheneum is far from being heaven, dear, although it is a very good hotel. Then I may send for you this evening, may I not? Your aunt and I have made all the arrangements about that important matter of clothes, so they need not delay you, and there are special reasons why I want you for tomorrow. Now I really must run; I have quite overstayed the time that was at my disposal, and it is shocking in me to be late." Then, because she was a little woman, she stood on tiptoe to kiss Hazel's glowing cheek as she said: "You and I will have some quiet talks together, dear."

It was early on the following morning that a number of guests at the hotel were gathered on one of the verandas waiting for the summons to breakfast and watching the gambols of a group of children on the lawn. Little white-robed fairies flitting about a central figure—a young girl in a freshly laundered white dress that had become too small for her and was worn and darned in several places. But the defects were skillfully hiding under a ribbon here and a flower there, and the whole effect was of girlish grace and winsomeness. She sat on a rustic seat under a great tree and was deftly weaving a flower wreath for one of the children who waited to be crowned. Other babies were clamoring for like service.

"One at a time," the girl said brightly. "There shall be a wreath for each of you before the day is done, but we must crown Marjorie first, because she is to be a flower girl, you know."

"And me next," piped up a shrill voice, "because I'm to sing at the concert."

"Oh, yes, of course. Our four singers must be

crowned. Sing a verse of your song for me while I work."

Instantly they formed in line, the four important ones who had part in the children's cantata to be given that afternoon, and their shrill little voices rang out in song.

The sun was shining on the sea,
Shining with all his might;
He did his very best to make
The billows smooth and bright.
And this was odd, because it was
The middle of the night!

"It's an awfully silly song!" one singer paused to criticize, "'cause the sun doesn't shine at all in the night."

"The moon does," shouted the little one standing next. "Let's sing the moon verse." Forthwith they sang:

The moon was shining sulkily
Because she thought the sun
Had got no business to be there
After the day was done—
"It's very rude of him," she said,
"To come and spoil the fun!"

The sea was wet as wet could be!
The sands were dry as dry!
You couldn't see a cloud! because
No cloud was in the sky.
No birds were flying overhead—
There were no birds to fly!

"What utter nonsense to teach children!" exclaimed Eureka Harrison, who was among the company on the veranda.

"So it is," admitted a lady standing near her. "But it is from the cantata that is to be given this afternoon; Lewis Carroll's absurd story of 'The Walrus and the Carpenter,' you know. Have you heard it? It's ridiculously funny and charming. How well those children sing it! Who is the girl who is training them?"

"Her name is Hazel Harris," Eureka said briefly. Then a lady at her elbow volunteered information.

"She is a new nurse girl, I think; at least I know that some of the mothers have been looking for help, and she has been around with those children all the morning. She is very pretty, isn't she, and graceful?"

At that moment Burnham Roberts left the post against which he was leaning and moved to the side of the one who had first questioned.

"I beg your pardon, Miss Woodbury," he said. "Did I hear you asking about the young lady on the lawn with the children? She is Miss Harris of New York, a friend of my mother; she has come to help us look after those little terrors down there for a few days in the absence of their nurse."

When he reached Eureka's side a moment afterwards he had a word for her ear alone.

"I happen to know that my mother is anxious that Miss Harris shall not be mistaken for an ordinary nurse girl because she is with the children. Of course you will help us in correcting any such absurd impression."

"I shall not go around telling it, if that is what you mean," she answered coldly. "Though I fail to see what particular harm such an impression could do."

"It is not true," he said, speaking with more sharpness than the occasion seemed to her to require, "falseness always does harm." Then their attention was diverted to the scene on the lawn. Other children had arrived and were trying to get close to Miss Harris, to the discomfort of one small boy who was shouting fiercely to another a trifle older than himself.

"You keep away! You can't have her."

"I can too!"

"You can't *have her*, not one teeny-tawnty! She's ours!"

"She ain't either!"

"She is too! She belongs to just us nine; Mamma said so."

"Teddy!" called Burnham Roberts in a tone of authority. "Hold on there, little chap; don't be rude."

"Well, but—Uncle Burnham, Miss Harris is just *ours;* Mamma said so; and Grandma did too."

"That's all right, Teddy, hold on to *her* forever; but don't forget that you are a gentleman."

His next words were for Eureka in complacent tones: "That mother of mine is a genius." He was still gazing down upon the ever-moving group below; Eureka's eyes followed his; so far as she could discover, no "mother" was in sight.

"I don't feel disposed to challenge the statement," she said. "But I fail to see the connection."

He laughed cheerfully. "I was thinking of Miss Harris and the masterly way in which my mother accomplished the impossible. Do you know that the child is the victim of a belligerent and otherwise objectionable aunt, who was making life miserable for her? But yesterday my mother slighted down upon them like a visitor from another world and spirited the child away without commotion or jar of any sort; without even antagonizing the aunt; she created, while she talked with her, a field of usefulness for the niece that served as an excuse and accomplished it all within an hour's time. Isn't that evidence of genius?"

"It is evidence of idiocy," muttered Eureka. But not until she had turned away from Burnham and had only herself for a listener. Pursuing the same train of thought an hour later, she gave a less harsh version of it to Mrs. Dennis.

"With all due deference to Aunt Flossy's loveliness and general fascinations, don't you think she is sometimes a bit of a goose?"

"Flossy!" said Mrs. Dennis, surprised. "I haven't had such a thought for a great many years; on the contrary, I think her a wonderfully wise little woman, as a rule. What has she done to suggest such a dreadful idea?"

"Oh, I don't mean anything very dreadful," Eureka said with a little laugh. "I agree with you 'as a rule'; I'm as fond of Aunt Flossy as any person can be; but all the same, I think she has been rather foolish in bringing that Harris girl here. She must know as well as we do that her son simply *can't* resist the charm of a new and pretty face; and when kittenish manners are added, as they are in this case, he is hopeless—for a few hours. Why doesn't she protect the girl from the inevitable, if she really wants to help her? That's what I don't understand."

Mrs. Dennis gave Eureka's face, that was only partially turned toward her, a sudden searching look before she made any response. Then she said:

"You are thinking only of the child! You have no fear of the effect on Burnham?"

Eureka drew herself up, almost as though the question were personal.

"Not the slightest," she said, turning bright, keen eyes fully upon the questioner. "Aunt Marion, how can you possibly ask such a question when you know him so well! There was never a man better able to take care of himself than Burnham Roberts. But that makes one all the more anxious for the girl. *He* simply doesn't mean anything at all; but how is she to know that before it is too late for her happiness?"

They were interrupted before other words could be spoken; but Mrs. Dennis, who a little later was waiting for her party in one of the small reception rooms and thinking over Eureka's outburst, began unconsciously to hum the words of the children's moon verse:

> *The moon was shining sulkily*
> *Because she thought the sun*
> *Had got no business to be there*
> *After the day was done.*
> *"It's very rude of her," she said,*
> *"To come and spoil the fun!"*

The only other occupant of the room was her brother-in-law, the missionary from Utah. He lowered the morning paper at which he was glancing and looked at her curiously.

"Has 'much music' gone to your brain?" he asked. "Else why this remarkable selection?"

She laughed shamefacedly. "I must have been thinking aloud," she said. "I didn't realize that I was singing. It is the children's 'moon song,' and there is a great deal of human nature in it; I have just been having an interview with the moon while she was acting that very part and didn't know it."

By this time Burnham Roberts had departed with his mother and Hazel to secure the best possible position for viewing the morning's doings. The great day of the Chautauqua season, known to the initiated as "Recognition Day" had arrived.

"But I am to stay with the children!" Hazel had

said, her eyes wide with surprise as immediately after breakfast Mrs. Roberts made her acquainted with the program.

"Not today," was the smiling answer. "The children's mothers are anxious that you should see the sights this morning. They think you may not have an opportunity again to see so unique a procession. The children will be well cared for; their Aunt Eureka says that all she wants of the day is Earl Barnes's address, so she has engaged to keep them within calling distance until Norah is at liberty."

"That is precisely like you," had been Burnham Roberts's undertone comment to Eureka when he heard of this arrangement. "You can always be relied upon for doing the unexpected and the thoroughly kind and unselfish thing. We'll do it together this time; I'm going to give the little girl the day of her life."

"You are going to begin the misery of her life!" Eureka thought but did not say. She watched the three move gaily down the hill to the time of the chiming bells—Mrs. Roberts being apparently as carefree and ready for pleasure as was the young girl beside her—watched them with gloomy eyes. Why didn't that little mother see what she was doing? the "time of her life," indeed! If somebody could only warn the poor girl.

"Instead of which I offered to help, so that we could 'do it together!'" The laugh with which the soliloquy closed had in it a touch of bitterness. This girl was by no means certain that she relished the lifelong program that she believed was mapped out for herself, yet her uppermost thought that morning was pity for the "little idiot" who was marching gaily to her doom.

20

"Sing Paeans over the Past"

THEY were right about Hazel; she had never before seen, never imagined, a prettier sight than that procession led by one hundred little girls robed in white, wreathed in flowers, and with baskets of flowers in their tiny hands. They were so fascinating that for a time she had eyes only for them. Burnham had made a shortcut ahead of the main procession, which brought them presently within view of the golden gate and the evergreen arches; this was Hazel's first sight of them, and her questions came rapidly. Burnham Roberts, whose first act had been to find a seat for his mother within full view of the Hall and with several of her friends, had returned to Hazel, bristling with information. He had taken the utmost pains to make ready for those questions.

"Those are all members of the Shakespeare class, notice the wild roses!" "Yes, all who wear that emblem; it's the class of 1912, you understand." "They are the ones who are to pass *through* the golden gate, not around it." "Yes, only they, with the exception of a few belated ones who, in the years gone by, did not reach here to go with their class. Only one passage through that gateway; so you see it is a golden day in life's history; a little like a wedding day, isn't it? the marriage service standing for the entrance into a new name and home."

"Or like the gateway to heaven," Hazel said, her lips parted in eager delight and her cheeks aglow. "We pass through that gateway but once, you know."

He felt no disposition to laugh or to make a semisarcastic remark such as Eureka would surely have received had her spoken thought run in any such channel. It seemed an entirely simple and natural thing for this young girl to refer to that one event, which by common consent had been tabooed in polite society as not the gloomy and dreaded end of life but the gateway to home. Was she different in this, as in everything else, from other girls?

"Oh, they are singing!" said Hazel. "What is it? The tune is lovely." As they sang, they marched. The multitude representing the class of 1912 passed through the golden gate with quick, triumphant tread, passed under the first and second arches, while the little flower girls, massed on either side of the walk, literally lined their pathway with flowers.

"How lovely!" said Hazel again. "How *perfectly lovely!* I *wish* I could hear the words that the choir is singing!"

Her companion thrust a hand into some pocket and produced therefrom a printed program of the day's exercises, pointing to the song that was ringing through the flower-perfumed air.

A SONG OF TODAY

Sing peace over the past!
We bury the dead years tenderly,

To find them again in eternity
All safe in the circle vast.
Sing paeans over the past.

Farewell, farewell to the Old!
Beneath the arches and one by one
From sun to shade, and from shade to sun,
We pass, and the years are told—
Farewell, farewell to the Old.

And hail, all hail to the New!
The future lies like a world newborn
All steeped in sunshine and mists of morn,
And arched with a cloudless blue,
All hail, all hail to the New!

Arise, and conquer the land!
Not one shall fail in the march of life,
Not one shall fall in the hour of strife
Who trusts in the Lord's right hand;
Arise and conquer the land!

The Lord shall sever the sea!
And open a way in the wilderness
To faith that follows, to feet that press
On, into the great to be!
The Lord shall sever the sea.

Burnham watched the girl as she read the words; they were moving forward with the crowds, keeping time instinctively to the music, but she read every word.

"Aren't they wonderful!" she said as the last note of the song died away. "I feel as though I had never before heard such words."

"It is poetry, all right," Burnham said. "There are a number by the same writer in the book used here.

Copyrighted, you see; evidently written for the occasion, and all with the ring of true poetry."

"Lathbury," read Hazel, referring to her program. "M. A. Lathbury, I must remember that name; I want to read every line that writer ever wrote.

> *The Lord shall sever the sea,*
> *And open a way in the wilderness!*

"I am afraid, Mr. Roberts, you will think me almost sacrilegious, but do you know, I can't help feeling that that is just what he had done for me? You will not understand it, of course, but oh—I *was* in the wilderness! and there didn't seem any way out. He *must* have done it."

Burnham Roberts had no reply; tears were shining in the eyes of the young enthusiast; he feared that she could not see his look of sympathy, but the words he wanted to speak he knew were not suited for that time and place.

"Watch the class filing into the hall," he said, trying to speak in a commonplace tone. "See what a large representation they have here; they are from all over the country. I am told that there are twenty-five states represented by this one class. That means a pretty wide-reaching influence, doesn't it?"

"Who are the ones who were already seated before the class arrived?" Hazel questioned. They had reached the hall by that time and were standing where they could command a full view.

"They are all members of the C.L.S.C. Haven't you seen and heard those cabalistic letters everywhere for the last few days? They represent the one great Reading Circle of which all these people are members; the graduates of the years past, and the would-be graduates of the years to come. Notice the class flowers, especially the pansies, that's the aggressive class this year, the Eighty-sevens; that is their banner in the corner nearest you, the one with a pansy on it; they think it the handsomest banner here, and I'm not sure but they're right."

"'Neglect not the gift that is in thee,'" read Hazel from the banner.

"Yes, that's their class motto. They certainly are not neglecting it this year! They are everywhere in evidence. It is an anniversary with them of—of 1887 to 1912—why, the twenty-fifth, of course! Ah, that's the reason they are so aggressive. They even have a class breakfast tomorrow morning! Stebbins is in a flutter of preparation for it; he is my college friend I told you of, and it's his class."

"Do college men belong to these classes?"

"Oh, yes, indeed, and college women, scores of them. Stebbins is enthusiastic over the whole thing. He says the books represent modern thought and recent scientific conclusions and all the rest of it in the best possible language, and besides being well worth reading for themselves, the scheme affords boundless opportunities for helping others; Stebbins is a great fellow for helping."

Hazel was gazing about her while she questioned and listened, intensely interested in everything.

"There is an army of people wearing oak leaves," she said. "No flower at all, just a leaf. What can that mean?"

"They are the undergraduates, whose honors are yet to come; the 1913 you see, and all the rest of them. The class of 1916 is forming here this season; it is a four-year course, you understand. You and I ought to join that class, Hazel, and go through the golden gate in four years from now. Shall we?"

There was a heightened color on the girl's face; he had never before called her "Hazel," but of course he would, now that she was in his mother's employ; she fell in promptly with what she believed to be his mood.

"I think so," she said gaily. "I have already been made 'Queen Wilhelmina' this morning, and Marjorie has arranged that this afternoon I am to be Tennyson's 'Maud'; fancy that little mouse knowing Tennyson's 'Maud'!—so you see I am prepared to play anything today. There are my cousins wearing oak leaves!"

"Indeed!" said Burnham. "Kindly point them out to me; where are they sitting? They must have joined the class of 1916. Does that make you more, or less willing to do so? I mean—are your cousins as pronounced in their views as your aunt seems to be?"

Hazel was glad that she need make no reply; she was not sure just how she felt toward her cousins; now that she was away from them she realized more than she had before that they had tried to be kind; that often her own dreariness had pushed from herself little kindnesses that they were ready to offer; and that even her aunt had perhaps been more often solicitous for her real good than she had received credit for being. The question that was beginning to haunt Hazel was, could she cultivate a different feeling for these her only relatives, a feeling that would last when that sorrowful day arrived in which she must return to them? Of course Mr. Roberts could not understand any of this and must not hear about it; she was glad that the great assembly had again burst into song.

Burnham, in answer to her questioning eyes, quietly pointed out the words on the program.

> *A sound is thrilling through the trees*
> *And vibrant through the air;*
> *Ten thousand hearts turn hitherward*
> *And greet us from afar.*
> *And through the happy tide of song*
> *That blends our hearts in one,*
> *The voices of the absent, flow*
> *In tender undertone.*
>
> *Fair Wisdom builds her temple here*
> *Her seven-pillared dome;*
> *Toward all the lands she spreads her hands*
> *And greets her children home.*
> *Not all may gather at her shrine*
> *To sing of victories won,*
> *Their names are graven on her walls—*
> *God bless them, every one.*

Hazel's eyes were shining through a mist of tears.

"It is all so beautiful!" she said, responding to her companion's sympathetic and enquiring glance. "It must come home to the hearts of so many hungry people! They are middle-aged, a good many of them; they are having things that they missed in their youth. Besides, there must be people at home, perhaps older than these, who are part of the same circle and included in the prayer: 'God bless them, every one.' Don't you think that this touching poem is very nearly the most beautiful thing that the Bishop has done in his long, beautiful life?"

It was much the same thought that Eureka had expressed but a short time before, when Burnham

Roberts had listened with an amused smile and a disposition to rally her upon her "streak of sentimentality." He felt no such desire now; on the contrary, it seemed to him a happy and expressive way of voicing his own feeling. There was no time for response; the Bishop was speaking.

> Members of the Chautauqua Literary and Scientific Circle, Representatives of the Class of 1912, Dearly beloved: You have finished the appointed course of reading; you have been admitted to the Grove; you have passed under the arches dedicated to history, literature, science, and faith; you have been admitted to the Hall in the Grove; and now, as Chancellor of the Chautauqua Institution, I greet you and announce that you are approved graduates of the C.L.S.C. and entitled to membership in the Society of the Hall in the Grove: "The Lord bless thee, and keep thee: The Lord make his face to shine upon thee, and be gracious unto thee: The Lord lift up his countenance upon thee, and give thee peace."

Following this official recognition came the C.L.S.C. flag, with its painting of the Hall as it was in the early days, and its Chautauqua emblems, the open Bible and the cross of Christ. During the giving of certain class notices, Burnham Roberts fell to whispering.

"That man who described the flag and explained the tablets has been here ever since there was a Chautauqua. My mother met him here when she and her three friends came as girls. You know which ones I mean, do you not? We call them the 'Four Girls.'

They had some unique experiences here, and some impressions were made that have lasted. This man was one of the teachers and lecturers at that time; my mother remembers him perfectly; some of his teachings she says she is living by."

"They must have been wonderful teachings!" murmured Hazel. The feeling that she had for this young man's mother she could not have put into words. "And here he is teaching yet!" she added. "He looks and speaks as though this class might expect him to attend their twenty-fifth anniversary."

"He is Dr. Jesse Lyman Hurlburt," explained Burnham in his capacity of general informer.

"Oh, I *know* him," whispered back his audience, "I shall remember him forever. One night, only a few weeks ago—but it seems like ages—I was passing this very hall, and this man was talking. I was—oh, so miserable! and do you know his voice reached me just in time! He will never know it here, but I shall tell him about it someday, when I meet him in heaven—what he saved me from that night."

Then they had to listen again, for the Bishop was dedicating the class tablets.

"This mosaic tablet as a memorial of the class of 1912 we hereby place in this hall as a part of its lasting pavement and as a feature of its decoration. May they whose feet tread this pavement stand firmly on the Rock of Ages and dwell forever within the walls of the eternal 'city which hath foundations, whose builder and maker is God.'"

"He never forgets the foundation," Hazel said, and her companion, whose natural tendency it would have been to ask in cynical tones "What foundation?" had no reply to make. This simple, sincere girl seemed to take earnestness for granted.

They were moving now with the throngs in the direction of the amphitheater, and Mrs. Roberts, having been carried off with "Aunt Ruth" in Erskine Burnham's carriage, the young man was able to give undivided attention to his companion; but he had no words to speak. There was a tender light in the girl's eyes and an assured something on her face that held him silent and puzzled. Why had those few words of dedication so moved her? Was she so constituted that any reference to a future unknown world, couched in beautiful language, set her heart athrob with something that seemed like both hope and desire? He felt that he wanted to make *this* world such a happy place for her that there would be no room in her heart for that other one; but he had a miserable feeling that he should fail. She interrupted his thoughts; she had not even noticed his silence.

"Isn't it a blessed thing," she said earnestly, "that a place like Chautauqua was developed and is being sustained by a man whose feet are set firmly on that 'Rock of Ages'? It might so easily have developed into a mere place of amusement; or into a mere gathering of scholars for literary and scientific studies; but he went deeper and planted it on the only lasting Rock; I am *so* glad!"

He tried to smile at her enthusiasm and to rally her.

"You use that word *mere* in rather startling connections. 'A *mere* gathering of scholars,' There are multitudes, you know, who consider *that* the great foundation; and there are those who contend that Chautauqua, today, stands for just that—with a little taffy interspersed in the way of amusement."

"But it is not true," she said earnestly. "You and I know it is not; everyone who has been here this year knows better. That open Bible on the banner and that cross of Christ are its foundation stones; and I am glad, *glad!*"

Burnham Roberts took his seat beside her in the amphitheater, uncomfortably conscious that she knew on what Rock her feet were planted, and that a great gulf separated them.

21

◆═◆═◆

MAIDEN EFFORTS

THE day began like many Chautauqua days during the season of 1912. Rain through the night, brilliant sunshine in the early morning, every leaf and blade of grass and tiny wildflower a-sparkle with diamonds, and the air like wine. In all soberness there was nothing about the beautiful day different from a thousand other beautiful days gone into the unwritten past; yet great things happened on that day. Is it not probable that really great things happen on every day?

Mrs. Bradford, as she locked the door of her kitchenette—resolved to put her responsibilities and anxieties all aside for once and have as good a day as she could find—had not the least idea that its happenings would influence all her future.

Mrs. Bradford missed her husband's niece; she was amazed to discover how much. Who would have imagined that the girl whom she had honestly supposed idled away most of her time, really managed to accomplish so many things that, left undone, were missed! Had she realized it, she would almost have kept Hazel with her; perhaps she ought to have done so, anyway. Josephine worried about her; she had seen her cousin several times in company with "that Roberts fellow" and was afraid that it would "turn her head." But Mrs. Bradford did not know how she could be expected to help it if it did. She heard herself explaining to her husband that the child couldn't always be kept in a bandbox, and if she did not know any better than to have her head turned because the son of her employer was kind to her, the sooner she learned by experience the folly of such ideas, the better. Then Mrs. Bradford, seeing in mental vision her husband's troubled face, sighed, but resolved to wash her hands of it all for this one day, at least, and enjoy herself.

She was on her way to the Women's Club. Now the Women's Club of Chautauqua is an organization that had been a revelation to Mrs. Bradford. She had not discovered it early; that is, she had not known that regardless of her not being a member of a club of any sort, its daily meetings were open to her. Also, it was a recent discovery that this was not simply a literary meeting.

Local literary organizations such as she might have joined Mrs. Bradford had carefully steered clear of, because she belonged to that not small company of people who, being aware that they are not in the least literary and could not take part acceptably in any program calling for that kind of knowledge, yet are by no means willing to have other people discover this fact. The only safety for such persons lies in their having sneers for all club gatherings of every sort and being superior to those who thus "waste" their time and neglect their homes. But one fortunate day, just after it had been drilled into her brain that the daily meetings of the Chautauqua Women's Club were open to all women, the booklet announcing the topics for the season fell into Mrs. Bradford's hands, and she made other discoveries.

"Why, dear me! They talk about 'Up-to-date Housekeeping' and 'Luncheons for School Children' and 'Overdress in High Schools' and 'Labor-Saving Devices'! I know as much about such things as anybody. I mean to go." And forthwith she went.

One topic in particular, "Hospitality on a Small Income," caught her earnest attention. It was a sore subject with her. Perhaps nothing in her experience as the mother of growing daughters had troubled her more than the belief that she could not afford to entertain their friends. Even the small circle of young people with whom they had as schoolgirls felt at home—and by whom they had occasionally been invited to evening gatherings—Mrs. Bradford knew her girls had never heartily enjoyed, because their mother was sure they could never return such courtesies. "We can no more give a party," she had drilled into them, "than we can fly! And you can't go often to such places without feeling mean, unless you make some return." So the Bradford girls, this poor mother knew, had grown up feeling always on the outside of things. They were "always trying to hang on where they didn't belong," was the way that Josephine in cynical moments had described it, and Isabel had responded drearily:

"The trouble is we don't belong anywhere; one has to hang on to something."

At the Chautauqua Club this mother had learned that hospitality was a matter of the heart rather than the pocketbook. She had listened to the words of sweet-faced, simply dressed, cultured women, who spoke of their plain homes and limited means, not as though they were things to be blushed over and hidden as much as possible, but to be looked upon as incidental and secondary matters. Such women described, by invitation, in minute detail, their ways of entertaining their friends, without elegant china, and cut glass and damask; without expensive luxuries of any sort, and with such service as the astonished lady listening knew that she herself could command. Spoke of it all in its simplicity, quite as a matter of course.

To say that Mrs. Bradford was astonished is to put it mildly. She was all but overwhelmed with the simplicity of the revelations and the matter-of-course way in which they were given and received. Hospitality among what she was pleased to call "refined" people had meant to her plate and napery and trained service such as she could not command, and costly luxuries for the palate, such as she could never serve.

"'Thin slices of good bread and butter and a cup of good tea or coffee' indeed! Who couldn't furnish such commonplaces, even in abundance, once in a while!" She thought of the day that Josephine had wanted to entertain nine girls and boys of her high-school class and been denied; thought of it and sighed; if she had but known!

She was learning other lessons at that same club; lessons that she could not have described, that she did not realize she was learning. The fact was that she was in a changed atmosphere; breathing a moral air that was altogether new to her, getting new conceptions as to relative values, and it was all acting like a tonic on her whole mental system.

New valuations of common things, new ways of looking upon daily toils and cares; new ideas of that word *home;* new conceptions of motherhood; views of possibilities for one's children within reach of every true mother; possibilities that had actually nothing to do with limited purse, or even with environment! In short, what Mrs. Roberts had smiled over as only a parrotlike quotation from a prominent club woman, represented ideas that were beginning to filter through Mrs. Bradford's mind, making ready to absorb the poisonous germs that had long found lodgment there.

This morning was the closing meeting of the club for the season, and Mrs. Bradford, who was just beginning to realize what it had been to her, was in an unusually susceptible frame of mind.

All about her were women, middle-aged, and more than middle-aged, as well as younger ones, rising to say in few words, yet with evident feeling, how much the Women's Club had meant to them that season. One said that she was going home to organize a work among young girls, like unto that of which she had heard this summer. Another planned to have a children's play hour patterned, on a small scale, like those which had been described in the club; it was to be opened in their own backyard and was destined especially for five neglected little boys who lived in a nearby alley, and who had heretofore not been allowed to put so much as their noses through her fence. Another said that she had discovered here how she could use her parlor and her son's love of music and her daughter's talent for recitation in a way to win souls, and she was going home to work it up. Mrs. Bradford, who had done much talking in her own home circle, and who was a woman of force and energy in her own small world, dominating to a large extent husband's and children's home life, had never spoken a word in what may be called public; but this morning she was strangely moved; why should she not let those who had influenced her know it? They had spoken to her, those women about her, quite as though she were one with them. Earlier in the meeting a woman seated back of her had leaned forward to whisper:

"Don't you think it would be nice for us to emphasize our appreciation of our president's reappointment for another year by a rising vote? Of course the management appoints her, but we want her to understand that we wouldn't have any other president for anything in the world. Don't you feel so?"

And Mrs. Bradford, who had never had a president of any sort to call hers, answered heartily, "Oh, yes, indeed!"

"Then, if I make a motion to that effect will you second it?"

In a flutter of surprise, she had whispered back that she would; and heard herself say, a little later, in a voice that did not sound like hers, "I second the motion," whereupon that entire assembly had risen, as one woman, to respond to the resolution with clapping of hands. Mrs. Bradford was one of them! Her voice had helped to bring about this demonstration; this multitude of refined, cultured women who had evidently enjoyed advantages that she had not, smiled upon her, chatted with her, and asked her opinion. They had talked about home and school and books and work and church and state and life generally and said almost nothing about money; how could it help but drop from the high pedestal where this woman's false views of life had placed it?

Oh, she was not one who would ever despise money; there was really no danger of that; but it was beginning to be more hopeful that money might hereafter take its rightful place in her thought as one of the means toward an end, instead of the end to be sought at any cost. She studied the faces intently that morning of the women whom she could see; they had ideals, those women, she had heard many of them speak; they had homes to plan for, and husbands and children, so had she; but in what different ways they were living for them! She looked at the fair, pure face of the president whose words had more than once come home to her with force, as no other woman's ever had. A sudden resolve came to her, taking hold of her vigorous nature with a strength that made her sure she would abide by it. She rose up and spoke out her thought.

"I am going back to be a better woman and make a better home." To her astonishment, almost to her dismay, that entire assembly broke into applause. As soon as the hour was closed they gathered about her, those friendly women, clasping her hand and speaking cordial words.

"You made the address of the morning," one said. "Struck the keynote," said another. "I think as much!" from a third. "She gave us our marching orders; we must all get into line; after such privileges we dare not do less."

Mrs. Bradford's maiden effort received like that! She must live up to it; she wanted to.

She looked again at the gracious president clasping hands with the swarms of women gathering about her, speaking sweet, strong, tender words; fitting each to the other's need in a way that seemed wonderful. Mrs. Bradford had never stood near enough to her to take her hand. She had wanted to be introduced, to be able to say afterwards: "Oh, yes, I met the president of the Women's Club; she is the Bishop's sister-in-law, you know." The phrase somehow seemed to her to bring her into intimate acquaintance with the Bishop. On this morning she thought of none of these ambitions; she wanted to get the clasp of this woman's hand because she knew that she had been helped by her. She pressed forward with the others and waited. Presently their hands met, and the bright, tender eyes rested on her face for a moment.

"God bless you and guide you," said the low, clear voice; and as Mrs. Bradford passed on, to make room for others, she felt that she had received a benediction.

Josephine was crossing the park, coming rapidly with swift steps and a manner that expressed a decision reached. She saw her mother in the distance and came straight towards her; she was very glad of the meeting; the conflict that she was sure would have to be met would be better begun out of doors.

"I was coming in search of you," she said. "Are you going home? I'll turn and walk with you; I want to have a talk. I've just come from the cooking school. Did you ever hear of cooking things in paper bags?

"Yes, just *bags,* instead of dishes. You put the things in the bag, pin them up, and put the bag in the oven, just as you would a pan or basin, and they cook beautifully."

"What kind of things?"

"Why, almost all kinds; meats, and peas, and beans; oh, and apples; the apples were delicious baked in bags; we had some."

"But what's the object?"

"Oh, you keep the flavor in the food instead of in the air; roast meat, she says, is as fine again cooked in a bag; and it cooks quicker, too."

"But you couldn't have any gravy."

"Yes, you could; the juices stay right there in the bag, and you pour them out and make your gravy."

"Out of a paper bag? I don't believe it," said Mrs. Bradford, the outspoken.

"Oh, but it does; we saw her do it. You ought to go to the cooking school. There's to be a public lecture this afternoon on 'Frozen Dishes.' I wish you would go and take notes for me; you'll get ever so many hints that we can use at home, and I can't be there because I am to meet one of the teachers at the same hour for a business talk. Will you go, Mother?"

It was a descent from Mrs. Bradford's place of feeling. And yet—was it perhaps possible that a better home might somehow include "frozen dishes"? At least it was the new plane on which she was thinking that made this mother respond meekly that she would go.

"That's what I want to do now," continued Josephine, too much absorbed in her own train of thought to notice her mother's quiet mood—"I want to have a business talk. Mother, since I came here I've changed all my plans. I used to think that I should make my living either in dressmaking or millinery; but I've decided that my talent lies in cooking."

"In cooking!" gasped the mother.

"Yes," Josephine said resolutely. "I was always fond of fussing in the pantry, you remember, only we never could afford to use butter and eggs and things; but I've learned how to make money out of them; I'm going to cook for other people."

"Josephine!"

"I *am*, Mother, listen; I've got it all planned."

22

NEW DEPARTURES

SHE talked fast, determined that her mother should have no chance to make comments until the plan was before her.

"I'm going to begin on a very small scale, out in some of the suburbs where rents are cheap. I'll rent a little speck of a room and a gas plate, or something of that kind and make—first I think I'll make some delightful cookies, such as will melt in your mouth; I've learned how, and I'll sell them for ten cents a dozen; when people find out how good they are, they will want dozens and dozens of them. Then I'll add tea cakes or velvet sponge cake; and, by and by, bread—oh, I can make such beautiful bread! Of course it will take time to work up a business, but I've talked with the teachers about it; and they say it can be done; they think the time is ripe for just such efforts in a good many places. After a while people will begin to say:

"'How do you make such excellent bread? I wish our cook knew how to do it.' Then I shall say: 'Send your cooks to me, or, better still, your daughters, and

I will teach them.' In a little while I shall have a nice class started. You see, I really have learned how to do a good many things; and the beauty of it is, I can go into the practice class in the university domestic-science department and keep on learning, all the while I am teaching. Of course I haven't everything thought out yet, but I know enough about it to be sure that I can accomplish something."

This was by no means the usual Josephine; speaking with calm, judicial, and often semisarcastic manner. She was simply an eager girl racing over her pauses and being anxious chiefly to keep back as long as possible the flood of dismayed opposition which she expected. She was unprepared for Mrs. Bradford's silence and was almost overwhelmed by her first remark.

"I don't see why you need go to the suburbs or rent a room; our kitchen is large enough for first experiments; and we have an excellent range, you know. It would be much easier to find customers among acquaintances, I should think."

"Why, Mother!" was Josephine's exclamation; and again, after a moment's pause, "Why, *Mother!*" in jubilant tones. "You almost take my breath away! I expected to have to argue with you for a week and then not convince you. But, you see, I felt that I had got to do something that might grow into a little help for Father. The teachers here are so nice and kind; they have given me ever so many hints. Do you really mean that you will let me work in the kitchen, and talk about it to the girls, and sell them things? What has happened?" But Mrs. Bradford did not choose to tell what had happened; she was not certain that she could. Neither did she care to tell what she had heard one morning at the club about a girl in Ohio who did this very thing—aided and abetted by her mother— and made of it a splendid success. She meant to help Josephine all she could; but it would be just as well for the child to discover it by her acts.

Isabel stood on the side porch, waiting for them to come up. "I've been watching for you," was her greeting. "I went over to the hall to meet you, and then missed you, after all. I came by a shortcut. Mother, I want you to go to class with me this morning and meet the teacher; I told her I was going to bring you; she is lovely."

Josephine laughed. "You are being beset on all sides," she said gleefully. "Go on, Mother, and frivol with your youngest, while the staid oldest daughter remains at home and gets you up such a dinner that you will never want to go to a boardinghouse again."

"'Chautauqua Department of Health and Self-Expression,'" read Mrs. Bradford from the circular that Isabel thrust into her hand. "'Exercise that rests.' I wonder what kind it can be? I'm sure I have exercise enough, but I must say I don't feel especially rested. Why in the world do you want me to go and look on at those idiots twisting their bodies into all sorts of shapes? Look at this one trying to reach her toes without tipping over! I must say I have no patience with women who make fools of themselves taking such exercises. It is bad enough for silly girls to waste their time and money in that way."

However, she had turned from her doorway and was allowing the eager Isabel to pilot her down the avenue toward the School of Expressions. She continued to read as she walked and to make comments. "'It is not the work we do, but the energy we waste when not working that exhausts us.' Humph, much she knows about it! I never waste any energy."

Yet perhaps there was never a woman who wasted more than did Mrs. Bradford. The trouble with her, as with many another, was that she did not know herself. She read on: "'Learn to relax, to let go—physically and mentally—to untie the fuss and worry knots.' Yes, I wonder how? It's easy enough to talk!" But the tone was less scornful; there was even a touch of wistfulness in it. The poor woman suspected that "fuss and worry knots" were all over her face; those words just described it; she had done so much fussing and worrying all her life! And it seemed necessary to continue doing it; how else were they to live?

Isabel caught at the wistful tone and answered it.

"You wait, Mother, she will tell you how; she says she has been doing it a good many years and has rested more tired women than she can count."

But the pretty creature who presently broke on their vision arrayed in a perfect fitting white gown, with masses of beautiful hair arranged in graceful coils about a shapely head; with a glow of brilliant color on cheeks and lips; with eyes that were bright with the joy of living; and tingling with energy to her very fingertips, yet expressing ease and grace in every movement; she looked too fair and glad a creature to know anything about real fatigue or worry. Mrs. Bradford's skepticism returned. She curled her lip and murmured:

"I wonder if that is the boasted teacher! She's too young to know how to teach anybody anything."

Isabel laughed. "Just wait," she said. And it was a fact that as soon as the teacher began to talk, to explain, to answer with ready comprehension and sympathy the volley of questions poured at her, to move that supple body of hers that seemed to have no more weight in it than a cork and did her instant bidding with an unfailing ease and grace, Mrs. Bradford discovered what every member of the large class had done, that here was one body that was a willing servant; instead of a tyrant demanding from the jaded spirit impossibilities. It was impossible to imagine either lassitude or utter absolute fatigue in connection with her. Moreover she could show others how to make aching muscles and throbbing nerves own a master.

"You want to learn how to get a good, healthy 'tired' that will make rest a joy, and work that follows it a pleasure"; she said brightly, as if that was a very ordinary lesson easily mastered. Mrs. Bradford, from listening with an air of endurance as one who had been smuggled in against her will, grew interested, grew absorbed in the genial flow of talk that was not a lecture, nor a lesson, and yet was distinctly both. When she came to herself and found herself standing with the others trying to reach her toes without tipping over—the precise effort that she had so sharply criticized, she did not know whether to be ashamed and indignant at somebody or to laugh. But fun got the upper hand, and she joined in the hearty laugh that was going the rounds at the expense of them all. After that, she forgot that it was a class and a lesson and that she was a middle-aged woman with dignity to sustain; for a full half hour she did that excellent thing for such women as she—forgot Mrs. Bradford entirely.

"Isn't she lovely?" Isabel began the moment they were on the street. "She lives in New York, don't you think; teaches there, you know. I can go right on with the lessons after we get home."

But this indiscreet remark brought one of the "fuss knots" promptly back to Mrs. Bradford's face.

"You talk as though we were made of money," she

began sharply. But Isabel was serene and quick to speak.

"No, I don't, Mother; I'm talking of a way to make some. That's the beauty of it all. She is going to recommend me and give me special lessons and all that; you should hear her praise your daughter, ma'am; you'd be proud of her. I'm her star pupil, and she's going to help me get up a class of young girls in our neighborhood; and I'm to go out with her twice a week to one of the suburbs and help with a class of beginners. Oh, I *know* I can work it up! She says I can; she says I'm just the one. I'm going back home to earn my own living, not only, but to help earn yours, and give you a chance to get rid of some of the 'worry knots,' Mother, see if I don't."

Mrs. Bradford laughed outright, a merry laugh such as she had not in years relaxed sufficiently to give. The comic side of this strange morning was getting possession of her.

"Between you and Josephine," she said, "I don't see that there will be anything for me to do hereafter but try to stand on one foot and swing the other and eat cookies."

"Cookies!" repeated Isabel. "Oh, has Josephine told you? And you don't mind? You are willing for us both to take hold of this work and earn money by it? You darling mother! If we weren't on the street I'd kiss you this minute! You can't think how we have wanted to do something to help you and Father before you worked yourselves to death for us. We both felt disgraced to settle down at home and do nothing; we've felt it for ever so long, but we couldn't plan anything to do that you were willing to hear us even mention; and so we just kept on being unhappy, growing sharp and hateful sometimes, and not seeing any way out.

But after we came here—it's in the air, somehow—we knew that we couldn't live in that way anymore, and we thought we should both have to go away from home and get work to do, so you wouldn't feel disgraced; but now these plans have come up; and we both feel sure we can carry them out, and you don't feel badly about it, do you? You will be glad to have us doing things that will help others, as well as ourselves, won't you? Doesn't it all look different to you? Oh, I know it does; I can see it on your face, and I'm just as happy as I can be."

"Josephine," said her sister in the privacy of their sleeping room that night, while Mrs. Bradford lingered in the kitchenette, "what has happened to Mother?"

"I don't know," was the answer. "Something has; she is different."

But Eureka Harrison's day had no such triumph in its closing. The truth was that Eureka was having a succession of unsatisfactory days. All the more unsatisfactory, perhaps, because she believed that she understood the situation and felt that there was nothing for it at present but to endure. Of Burnham Roberts she was seeing almost nothing and understood the reason. Burnham was in the midst of one of his "infatuations," the most pronounced of any since he and she became intimate friends; and his mother, who still had more influence over him than any other save Eureka herself, seemed to be blind and deaf. She had herself created the situation by bringing "that girl" to the hotel, where all sorts of intervals with her at all hours of the day were possible; yet the mother seemed to be looking on serenely, even helping on the intimacy by removing from their path what could easily have been made into obstacles. It was unaccountable, unless she hoped by such management to help the young man to recover more rapidly from his absurd fancy on the principle that "familiarity breeds contempt." In that case, she must know by this time that she was not succeeding. As for her own influence, Eureka instinctively drew herself up with a haughty gesture when she thought of it and told herself that whatever happened she should not interfere. If Burnham had, before this, spoken to her the decisive word that would make their engagement formal, she would undertake to remind him that such glaring lapses into admiration of pretty faces were beneath his dignity, as well as insulting to her. But as matters now stood between them, it would simply be an added humiliation to appear to notice it at all. She could not even comfort herself with the thought of paying him back in some way for all this humiliation when the ordeal was over, for she was tired of the position which she now occupied; anxious to get through with it and begin to get used to being engaged. Therefore she realized that she would have to be nice to Burnham as soon as he gave her a chance, because he really had not yet forgiven her for that trying day at the lake and the horrid words she had spoken. It was entirely possible that those words were the cause of this present humiliation; perhaps Burnham was simply taking revenge for having been called "a dude and a coward." She could hardly blame him; only she would like to tell him that he ought to be man enough not to make that poor silly little girl his victim.

Throughout her thought about it, Eureka kept her anxiety for the girl uppermost; despite the fact that she thought of her as a silly moth hovering around a dangerous light, she could not help seeing that the light was more to blame than the moth. Burnham openly and unhesitatingly sought the girl. He asked for her without a shade of embarrassment; followed the train when he found she was out with the children for a walk; or boldly planned a trip with them that as a matter of necessity included her. It is true that he had always given more or less attention to the children, and they were fond of him; so that his attentions to them seemed unusual to no one but Eureka.

It was in the early afternoon of one of her dissatisfied days that Eureka, having let all the various members of her party go their several ways without her, wandered out by herself in search of relief. Her life had never seemed to her more insane and purposeless than it had since that day when she called her problem settled because she had decided to marry Burnham Roberts and compel him to make the most of himself while she gave her mother the life of luxury and freedom from sordid cares that she ought to have. But whatever the future might bring to her of peace and the sense of well-doing, the transition period was certainly not pleasant. It took resolution to keep her from admitting to herself that she was tired of it all before it had begun.

Her wanderings brought her, in due time, to the neighborhood of the hall, where a meeting of some sort was in progress, evidenced by a crowd. Moved by that natural impulse to try to get into a place that seems to be already over-full, she elbowed and wedged her way back of the platform to one of the pillars, and leaning against it for support determined to listen for a few minutes. A woman was talking.

23

"Where Two or Three"

"WE SHALL get quick results from the mountaineers," she was saying. "And that is a matter worthy of consideration when there are multitudes to be reached. Here are a dozen men struggling in the water; which of them shall you pull out first? Why, other things being equal, the man who can help save the others, of course; these mountaineers will help every time."

Eureka was in line with the speaker, who was a woman no older than herself. Their eyes met at the moment, and the newcomer flashed a sympathetic response for the bright bit of logic just presented and listened. The girl was drawing a word picture of an old man coming on foot sixty-five miles over the mountains to beg the missionary teachers to come out to his place and start a school. "'Many a time,' he told them, 'I've plodded fifteen miles up our hill and looked over at this mountain and wondered if anybody would come over to us and learn my girls, before they got growed up and fixed, and it was too late.'"

The quick tears dimmed Eureka's eyes. There were

girls, then, longing for education, who had missed far more than she had; girls whose fathers were eager, but powerless. What a thing it would be to teach such hungry minds as those!

Now the audience laughed heartily. The speaker showed her power in quickly changing the emotions of her hearers by a vivid recital of facts. She was sketching the dreary cabin home of an isolated mountain woman, who showed off with pride her eight children ranged in a giggling row before the visitor.

"'Yes, there's a right smart passel of 'em, and they've got mighty nice names. This one's 'Lizabeth, and this here one is Virginia; and the next is Reno; then there's Naomi who had ought to come next, but she's dead. The last one down there at the foot has got the prettiest name of all; I named her Castoria. I ain't got nothin' but names to give 'em, so I done the best I could.'"

Eureka laughed with the rest. The story was certainly funny, but the skillful narrator sketched vividly the pathetic side when she imitated the tone of that mother who had done her best; "Names is all I got to give 'em." The girl by the post who was often lonely, even among her friends, felt her heart swell with sympathy for the struggling soul. For the second time that afternoon the impulse swept over her to take hold somewhere at the world's work for others. "If it were not for Mother," she told herself, "I would go among those mountaineers and hunt up some of the isolated cabins and get hold of these women and help them save their girls and boys. I wonder if they would have me when I'm not even a church member. I suppose that girl is a home missionary. But dear me! I could bring some hope into the lives of those poor creatures, even if I couldn't preach to them."

Then she listened again. This time it was a story of one of the local preachers; poor, uncouth, illiterate, yet with what the speaker called "the root of the matter" within his soul.

"He doesn't approve," she said, "of having suppers and fairs and fetes and bazaars and all those modern devices for raising money for the benefit of the church. He has heard no talk on that subject and is not able to argue about it; but by some process that he cannot explain, it has, he says, been borne in upon him that 'them kind of things don't fit.'"

"The young people of his congregation wanted to get up a strawberry festival to help pay for a church clock; they came to get his help, but he shook his puzzled head and said: 'I can't do that, nohow, chil'ren, not for the church. It's borne in upon me that strawberry festivals ain't the right thing. Not that there's any harm in strawberries, nor in eatin' of 'em—his tone growing more and more puzzled—'but ye see—ye see, it's like Peter that time warmin' hisself by the fire, and Jesus at the other end of the room lookin' on. Remember? Not that there's any harm in fire, or in warmin' of yourself'—a pause, the fingers of both hands plunged into his shock of grizzly hair until each hair seemed to stand erect in the man's effort to understand his own logic. Then a light broke over his face. "I'll tell you chil'ren what's the matter; you see, it was the *wrong fire*.'"

The audience roared. Eureka joined heartily in the laugh, yet she was in sympathy with the native pastor. Her father had been one of those who did not approve of eating and drinking "for the benefit of the church." What a pleasure it would be to sit down beside that troubled man and help him to get a clear grasp of his own thoughts! While the speaker went on to tell of his prayer for certain members of his church:

"'Lord, we've got some members here that need a lot of bracin' up on the *leanin'* side.'" One listener was distinctly wishing herself a home missionary. "If it were not for *Mother*," she told herself wistfully; as though that were the only obstacle!

Her mother was there, listening to the stories; moved by them to laughter and, like her daughter, almost to tears.

Eureka joined them at the close, her mother and Mrs. Dennis, and committed herself to walking with them before she discovered that Mr. Dennis, the missionary from Utah, was of their party.

"Were you at the meeting?" her mother asked in surprise. "I did not know you came to missionary meetings. It was good, wasn't it?"

"Very good," Eureka said emphatically. "Those women are doing things that are worthwhile." She dropped behind when they reached the sidewalk, and Mr. Dennis did the same, leaving the elder ladies to go on together.

"Then you are interested in home missions?" he said cordially. "I am always especially glad to find young women who realize what a tremendous work is waiting to be done in our own country. Not that I am not heart and soul in sympathy with foreign missions also; it is merely a case of 'These ought ye to have done, and not to have left the other undone.' But you should study the work in Utah; that's the great opportunity. Of course every missionary thinks his field the most important," he added, laughing, "but I know mine is. Are you a teacher? No? I thought you might possibly be one of the army planning for Utah in 1913. The N.E.A. goes there, you remember."

But Eureka did not remember, as he saw by her face.

"The National Educational Association, you know. Utah has been reaching after that for five years, and has finally succeeded. I tremble when I think of the multitude of the uninformed who will go there to be hoodwinked. Courted and feasted and fluttered and rushed about in fine automobiles to see fine views and be told fine stories and sent home to say: 'Why, the Mormons are all right. What do those home missionaries mean by making such a fuss about them?'"

Eureka's laugh was a trifle scornful as she said:

"You are not giving our teachers credit for much penetration."

"Oh, it isn't for lack of brains that they will be misled; they are busy people; they have to study chiefly in line with their work; they haven't taken time to study up the Mormon question in detail, and there are those among the Mormon authorities who 'live and move and have their being' for the sole purpose of hoodwinking eastern travelers. They have planned, if possible, to deceive the very elect; and they'll do it, too, in some cases. They understand the 'angel of light' business better than any other people in the world."

Ever since Eureka had listened to Mrs. Wells, her soul had been aflame with righteous indignation over the whole Mormon scheme.

Here was one who knew things and could give proofs that he did; who had made the whole horrid subject a careful study for years; it was a chance to learn. They sat on the hotel veranda until the dinner bell interrupted them, she bristling with questions, and he prompt and eager with his answers.

"He is a very interesting man," she told her mother that evening. "He knows things and knows how to talk about them. There is some sense in conversing with a person like him."

Mrs. Harrison made no reply, although she had evidently been pleased that Eureka had chosen to carry on a conversation with the home missionary.

≈≠ ≠≈

It was late, well on to midnight, and all her friends were sleeping, but Mrs. Roberts still sat in her little private parlor bending over some thin, foreign sheets, giving some of them a third reading. She was planning just how to carry out her husband's suggestions.

The letter was long and full, giving a graphic account of a wonderful evangelistic campaign which was then in progress in London, especially in the interests of young men. After giving in detail the story of a very remarkable conversion, the letter ran thus:

> "And now, dear, I am getting to the special theme of this letter. I am glad that there is no doubt in my mind as to how my suggestion will be received. What sort of a life must it be for husband and wife not to be in accord on such themes as these? Flossy, dear, I cannot get away from the impression that the time has come for us to cry mightily to God in an unusual way, perhaps, for the salvation of our son. Two nights ago I added his name to the public prayer list here: 'Pray for a young man in America who has resisted all appeals, thus far; whose father is in this meeting praying for him.' Since then, I think almost every thought has been a prayer for his conversion. I have made bold to ask that the time might be *now*. I am impressed with the belief that this summer is the crucial one. I

thought of cabling him to join me here with the feeling that the atmosphere of these meetings might reach him; then I remembered that it was not atmosphere he needed, but God; and God did not have to wait for one to cross the Atlantic. Still, we know he does work through means. What I want to propose is that we consecrate the boy's birthday anniversary as a day of special and specific prayer for him; hold that one thought before the Lord *all day*. It happens that on that same date there is to be an all-day meeting here for young men; I need not tell you for what young man I shall especially pray, and I have asked a chosen few to bring him *by name* before the Lord at that time especially. Flossy, dear, I know you will join me; and get the girls to do, if you think it well; also some of their children, Erskine Burnham and his wife especially, and any others with whom you feel that peculiar bond of sympathy. Would that we could ask Eureka, poor girl! I know nothing about the Chautauqua program for that day, and I remember that Chautauqua has the name, of late years, of being intellectual rather than evangelistic in its entire atmosphere; still, the Bishop has not yet gone to heaven; and there are other grand men there this year; beside all else God is there; and however foolish, to human reason, such chains of prayer as we are planning may seem, prayer is one of God's appointed ways for reaching souls; and there is a very special unconditional promise for the 'two or three' who agree. I enclose a letter for Burnham, which please give him on the morning of his birthday."

This was in part the letter over which tears were dropping. Thankful tears, some of them, that "the boy" had such a father to pray for him. Sorrowful tears, some of them, because his mother had not been as constant in prayer for him as she might have been. Not that she had passed a day of her life without praying earnestly for her youngest born, but she knew that she had allowed anxieties as to the outcome of his friendship for Eureka Harrison to hold her thoughts, to the exclusion of more important ones. Especially had this been the case of late, when it began to seem probable that the girl was to be her son's wife. She would never have put the thought into words, but it shocked her to discover that she was almost thinking it useless to pray for a changed life for one who was planning to spend that life with Eureka Harrison!

The foreign mail had been delayed, and there had been but that single afternoon to plan for the concert of prayer. She had found "the girls" in Mrs. Harrison's room and had read to them her husband's letter, omitting only that one sentence about Eureka. They had been sympathetic and responsive to the call—if none of them had expressed strong faith, she could not blame them. One incident had occurred that she regretted.

It seemed that during the reading of the letter Eureka was out on the small porch opening from her mother's room. She had a book in her hand, but she had been dreaming rather than reading, paying no heed to what was going on inside until her ear caught the sound of Burnham's name. Then she had listened, without a thought of impropriety. "Aunt Flossy" was always sharing bits of description or anecdote from her husband's foreign letters, and she was always a welcome listener. So it was that she gave startled heed to the plan as it unfolded in the letter, and sat through part of the talk that followed, before it occurred to her that she was an uninvited participant in a private conference. Then she arose, allowing her chair to make as much noise as it would, and pushing wide the French window, entered and passed through the room, with a scarcely perceptible nod of recognition.

"I had entirely forgotten that Eureka was out there," Mrs. Harrison had said, embarrassed and apologetic, when the door closed after her daughter. "I remember now that she went there to read; I don't suppose she heard what we were saying."

Mrs. Roberts knew that she had tried to say the right words to comfort Eurie, but she also knew that she was sorry that Eureka had heard—if she heard, and was by no means so sure as her mother had been that "of course she would not mention it to a soul."

The name of the missionary from Utah had been added to the prayer chain at Mrs. Harrison's hesitating suggestion, because he was especially interested in young men. Mrs. Roberts had been glad of the suggestion; she liked to hear him pray, she said, because he spoke as one who expected an answer, of course. One or two other special friends who were what Mrs. Burnham called "confident in prayer" were added to the list. They had no fear of inconveniencing anyone, as there was to be no attempt at a formal meeting; each was simply to be asked to give as much time as he could consistently to specific prayer for that one young man.

Mrs. Roberts, after she left the others, had added, on the impulse of the moment, still another name to the list.

24

LINKS IN THE CHAIN

THE impulse came to her that evening as she tiptoed through her daughter's nursery to find two of her grandchildren kneeling with Hazel beside their little beds and paused to listen to their prayer. Here was evidently one who knew how to teach little children to pray in familiar yet reverent language.

Since her coming among them Hazel had made rapid strides into the hearts of these new friends. The children adored her, and their pleased mothers rejoiced together over her discovery. The wish most often on their lips was that they could keep her with them; and they argued as to which of the numerous family groups most needed her; entirely unaware of the fact that the young man, who often listened to them, set his lips in firm lines and told himself that he should like to see any of them keep her! Never were mother and sisters or, for that matter, an entire circle of friends, blinder than these.

Mrs. Roberts called Hazel to her room as soon as the nursery scene was closed and began abruptly.

"Hazel, I know you believe in specific prayer for

others; I want you to join your petitions with ours tomorrow. It will be my son's birthday, and we have set it apart, my special friends here and his father across the sea, as a day of prayer for him. Will you pray for him very often tomorrow, dear child?"

Wide-eyed astonishment was at first Hazel's only answer; then she spoke timidly.

"Are you asking me to pray for your *son,* Mrs. Roberts?"

"Yes, for Burnham; his father and I have prayed for him every day of his life, but the answer has not come yet. His father has been led, through prayer, to believe that this summer will be the one in which he will make unchangeable decisions; and he thinks that this week is a crucial one to him; we are going to call upon God as never before."

"But, Mrs. Roberts, please, I do not understand. Is there a special thing that you want him to do, or not do?"

"My child, we want him to give himself to the Lord."

She remembered always the look of blank dismay that swept over Hazel's face and the faltering voice in which she asked:

"You do not mean that Mr. Roberts is not a Christian?"

"Yes, my dear, I do; he makes no pretense of having the slightest interest in the subject; although when he was a boy of eight I thought him the most sincere little Christian I had ever known. But he went away from home, among companions whose influence was bad; and gradually he gave up all his old beliefs that we had thought were firmly rooted. I know you will remember to pray for him."

Little she knew of the turmoil of soul into which

she had plunged poor Hazel. It was almost as if she had been told that she herself had given up the beliefs in which her childhood had been rooted, so sure had she been that "Mr. Roberts" was a fully developed Christian. All her talk with him had been from that standpoint. In the privacy of her own room that night she went over in detail their conversation but the evening before. Mrs. Roberts had arranged so that she could attend the eventide service, and it had been lovely and helpful beyond what had been described to her. As the crowds were moving away, she had come upon Mr. Roberts waiting for her.

"Wasn't it lovely?" she had said. "I am so glad I heard that man!"

"Why?" he had asked and seemed amused at her eagerness. It had stimulated her to explanation.

"Because he was so helpful and suggestive and original; don't you think so? One often thinks of the power of electricity, but I never heard the thought applied as he used it. But after all, it almost frightens one, doesn't it? To think of the power we might have! 'If a copper wire can carry more than a hundred thousand men, what can a human soul carry when God has hold of him?' Doesn't that make you feel as though we had never let God have real hold of us, after all?"

She remembered now that he had not answered her, but at the time she thought nothing of it and had gone on eagerly, laughing as she spoke.

"Imagine the Doctor of Divinity playing all day with a teddy bear! Wasn't it a capital illustration?" But Mr. Roberts had said that the teddy bear must have come in before he reached there and had insisted on knowing just what was said. She had been very willing to tell it.

"He was speaking of our outgrowing things that we used to fancy we would always want to do; just as soon as we get a real vision of Jesus Christ, we find our tastes changing. 'If they don't,' he said, 'there's something wrong. You watch people and see. If you find me playing all day long with a teddy bear, doing it day after day with relish, you will know at once that there is something abnormal, unhealthy, about me. Apply that to your Christian life.' It was queer, but wasn't it probing?"

She had thought that the reason he made no answer was because others came up just then; the discovery that he had no interest in, no sympathy with, the vital truths that had been thus quaintly pressed home to consciences was so unexpected that it fairly stunned her. She did not wait for "tomorrow" with her prayers. She not only prayed, but wept; and the tears were bitter; they had a personal element; it seemed to her that she had lost a friend.

The garish light of day told all too plainly the story of the night's vigil. Hazel's eyes were red, with dark circles underneath. Her intention had been to avoid the sight of Mr. Roberts, and she had not appeared at the breakfast table. But "Mr. Roberts" had no intention of being avoided. He had delightful plans for the children. It was his birthday, he told them, and he meant to play all day long. He would take them to Celeron on the big boat for a picnic, and a swing, and endless trips in the merry-go-round, and unlimited dishes of ice cream, and a boat row, and—really he did not know what all. Of course Miss Harris was to go with them; did they think he would undertake to keep them from going up in a balloon, or something, without her to help? All in a moment the children were brought from their heaven of delight to the depths of despair. Hazel would hear to none of the plans. In vain Mr. Roberts questioned earnestly; she had no reasons to give, she was simply not going out with the children that day. Norah was to be in charge, and they were not to go away from the children's playground back of the kindergarten. "Oh, very well," he said, the children's frolic could wait for tomorrow. Would she take a long walk with him, away down the shore where it was quiet, to relieve the headache which he saw she had? He had something to read to her that would drive away pain. No, she could not walk that day. She was not going out; would he please let her pass? Mrs. Erskine Burnham wanted her and would be waiting. But he sturdily kept his position and told her rudely to let Mrs. Erskine Burnham wait. "Hazel, I want to understand; something has happened; you have been crying! What is wrong? Have my sisters, have any of those women been nagging you? Then, what is it? My mother cannot—"

She had interrupted him then, speaking with firmness.

"Your mother is the dearest woman in the world, and they are all just as good to me as they can be. I cannot stay here talking another minute."

She had brushed past him and scurried out of sight. Yet she was almost certain that she had done harm. Mr. Roberts would continue to feel that she had been hurt in some way and would not rest until he discovered the cause of her conduct.

Burnham Roberts strode away moodily, paying no attention to the children's calls after him. All his thoughts were occupied with what had happened to Hazel.

When, an hour later he met Eureka, if he had not been too busy with the other problem, he would have noted that she, too, was unlike her usual self. In truth, she was in a mood so strange that she did not herself understand it. Almost it seemed to her that Burnham Roberts was the victim of a conspiracy. What did they mean by singling him out in that way, a dozen of them, making him a special object for consideration all day! It was a scheme about which he knew nothing; she had gathered enough from their talk to be sure of that. Ought not she, his friend, to tell him? Yet—what could she tell?

"You must be on the watch today, for your friends have all combined against you, here and across the ocean; they are going to pray constantly for you all day long." How absurd to go to him with a tale like that! She laughed at her own folly, and then at theirs. What did they imagine would happen to him because they were going to spend one entire day, or one entire week for that matter, praying for him! A company of fanatics carrying things to extremes, as fanatics always did. Why was she so annoyed? She ought to be glad, she supposed; prayer did sometimes help people, her father had been sure of it; and she—yes, she believed in prayer, of course. Burnham at least could not be injured by it; and the boy certainly needed help, often, to keep him from spoiling his life by some folly. Let them pray. Meantime, what attitude should this unknown fellow conspirator take in the matter? She could not pray; her part must be to act. Burnham was mercifully free from the subject of his infatuation today; at least, that was something. She had overheard Hazel explain to Norah that she was to have full charge of the children all day; she herself was not going out; she had sewing and other work to do. What if she, the silent conspirator, should spirit the subject of all this praying away for the day? They might take that long delayed trip to Jamestown, stopping off at Celeron for an ice and any fun they could find. Why not? There would be a sort of poetic justice about it, they two being the left-out ones.

Thoughts like these were in the background of her mind while she exerted herself to charm the moody companion whom she had joined, without waiting for him to ask her.

She waited for him at the bookstand while he went upstairs, ostensibly to hunt a textbook that his sister had left behind, but in reality to read the note from his father which his mother had given him that morning, and which, in his annoyance over Hazel, he had forgotten until now. So, having glanced about the classroom for the missing book, he had dropped into a chair and taken out his letter. It was not lengthy. A piece of paper fell out from it which he crushed in his hand while he read.

"I have but a few minutes to write before the mail closes. I am sending you herewith a birthday remembrance, as I have calculated that the letters by this steamer will reach New York only a few days before that important date. I have spent the time that I would have given to writing on my knees, thanking God for giving my son another year of life and asking him to mark the opening of your new year with so single a gift to you that it shall forever after stand out from all the others—a blessed year.

"Will you think me superstitious, my boy, if I tell you that I am impressed with the belief that you have reached a crisis in your life; a turning point? I believe the Lord has given me this thought. I am asking God if the anniversary of your birth may not be the day in which you will accept his gift, looking up to him for the first time as a son, because you are a 'new creature in Jesus Christ.' Oh, my boy, my boy! Your earthly father's heart is breaking with the longing to have his youngest born a lover and follower of Jesus Christ.

"You know the way, you have known it from your babyhood; I believe you have no foolish modern skepticism to overcome; you have only to *will* to take the Lord Jesus Christ for your personal Savior. A little step, a moment of time would accomplish the transfer. How gladly would I make it for you if I could! I thought as I wrote my name on the bit of paper enclosed, thus making what it stands for forever yours— *provided you choose to accept it*—how gladly your dear mother would write your name with her heart's blood, if by doing so she could secure for you the gift of God that he holds out to you. But it must be your own signature to the paper, *and the call,* that will make the provisions yours. You can turn away from both gifts; burn mine in the fire, if you will, and make no answer whatever to the One who holds out the other, but your father entreats you, dear boy, to accept them *today*.

"I am beginning to feel that it may be at least in a measure my own fault that you have reached the years of manhood without giving your life to God. With such a mother as yours, whose every thought, almost, since she first held you in her arms has been connected with a prayer for you, and who has lived before you the consecrated life she has—it must be your father who has failed. I see some of my mistakes very plainly; often I fear I have been stern and cold, or appeared so, when I ought rather to have shown you God as a patient, forbearing, waiting father. My son, will you forgive me and let me have the joy of knowing that my mistakes have not been fatal, because you have looked past me to your Father in heaven and accepted the provision he has made?"

After reading this letter for the second time, the young man sat motionless, staring at the page like one bewildered, overwhelmed. In truth he was; for years and years, so it seemed to him, there had not come a letter from his father that was not filled with stern, sometimes scathing, rebuke. That his conduct had demanded rebuke and censure he did not deny—although he saw it more plainly at that moment than ever before—yet the fact remained that the tenderness and yearning of a father's heart had been shadowed for him by the critic and judge. Nevertheless he knew, and had known all his life, that, after all, few sons had such a father as his; the thought of his having actually asked to be forgiven gave the young man a strange, choking sensation; and his eyes smarted with unshed tears. But he knew that he must not linger there, he must go back to Eureka who would think his long absence very strange. It was then that he thought of the bit of paper crushed in his hand, his birthday gift; he smiled a little bitterly; he was not having the kind of birthday he had planned. He wished his father had not sent him money—of course it was money—he had been given enough. The idea of accepting not only daily bounty from his father but unasked-for gifts besides, and yet giving no heed to his pleading, was beneath a decent fellow; if he could not do what he asked, he ought not to accept his gifts. He meant to tell his father that his foolish dawdling days were over; he was going back to New York to go to work; at least he could earn his own living at once; and he meant to; but that was not what Father and Mother wanted most. The idea of a day being set apart to pray for him! What did they want? Oh, he knew! Why must it always be something that a fellow couldn't do? If that check proved to be more than a trifle, if it were even fifty dollars, he wouldn't sign it; he would send it back and tell his father he had given him extras enough; hereafter he meant to earn them for himself. He looked at the name; a name so well known and such a power in the business world! Not a bank in New York but would be glad to honor that signature; after all, it was a great thing to have a name of such strength underneath a fellow's life. At last he looked at the face of the draft.

"Pay to the order of Burnham Roberts: twenty-five thousand dollars."

25

A Conflict with "Moral Flabbiness"

BURNHAM Roberts did not know how long he sat staring at the remarkable paper in his hand; nor could he have described the conflicting emotions that it produced. The income from a small property left him by his aunt—while it did not by any means meet his annual expenditures—represented all the money under his direct control. But while most of his wants and very many of his fancies had been supplied, his father had never in his life entrusted him with large sums of money. He had no complaint to make of that; he was fully aware of the fact that his conduct had not been such as to warrant trust. Especially of late years, since he had reached legal manhood, had his checks from his father been drawn cautiously, to be applied to stipulated purposes, and so hedged about that it would not be possible for the monies to be used in other ways. Many of the purposes were such as his father by no means approved, and while he paid the bills, he expressed his disapproval in no uncertain terms. The young man could not recall having received since his nineteenth birthday so much as twenty-five dollars as a gift, pure and simple, unhedged by directions so marked that they almost amounted to commands. Nothing had been plainer or more irritating to him than the fact that his father did not mean to trust him with a dollar if he could help it; yet with glaring inconsistency he had always deep in his heart, below the irritation, exonerated his father and more than once uttered: "He knows I'm not a fellow to be depended upon."

Yet here in his hand was a paper needing only his own signature to make it worth to him twenty-five thousand dollars, a thousand for every year of his life, without a direction or even a hint as to the way it should be treated; trust bestowed on one unworthy!

He went back to Eureka at last, because he must; he was dismayed at the length of time he had kept her waiting, and as he tore down the stairs, imagined her saying that he must have stayed to get the missing book reprinted, or some other sarcasm. But she greeted him sweetly and proposed that they go over to the morning meeting.

"The distinguished Scotsman is to speak, Dr. Johnston Ross. We want to hear him once, don't we?"

Burnham muttered that he did not know whether he did or not and asked what his theme was.

"Oh, never mind his theme; I want to have a glimpse of him because his name is on everybody's tongue. We needn't stay, you know, any longer than we choose."

As they entered the amphitheater the speaker was saying:

> Fatherhood was the earliest conception of God in the world. Divine revelation fulfilled man's conception of it, and the Lord Jesus when he

came infilled it. "Father," "Holy Father," "Righteous Father," he prayed, and these terms give us the true conception of Fatherhood. We who are fathers of children are not *steadily* moral fathers; we make mistakes; we lapse into weakness; our fatherhood needs to be strengthened and stiffened.

Burnham Roberts had gone reluctantly to the lecture because he did not at once see a way to escape; but he meant to escape, both from the service and his companion; he wanted to get away alone. His plan had been to seat Eureka comfortably where she could get a good view of the man whose popularity had made her curious and then to think of some imperative engagement that must take him at once away. Had the theme been other than fatherhood, undoubtedly this program would have been carried out; those opening words held him. If his heart would ever be ready for a message from his Father in heaven, surely it was this morning.

The address was scholarly, theological, abstruse at times, or at least too deeply technical for one who did not understand the ABCs of personal religion—yet it held this young man as no other message concerning eternal verities would have done.

"Remember," said the speaker, "that our Lord has belted human life; he had girded all possible human experiences; and he said of himself: 'He that hath seen me, hath seen the Father.'"

The service over, Burnham got away from his companion, not without difficulty, for although he was manifestly not in a mood to be entertaining, Eureka had a feeling that she ought to try to keep him in sight on this fateful day. She was vaguely troubled about him all day. He did not appear at dinner, and none of the family group seemed to have any idea of his whereabouts.

As a matter of fact, he spent most of the day in the woods; striking off from the beaten paths and plunging into the deepest shade and the most tangled underbrush he could find. He walked fast and far, fighting fiercely the obstructing tangles and over-hanging boughs. Never did the enemy of souls make a harder fight for one than went on that morning. Burnham Roberts's whole being was stirred as never before.

He threw himself down at last on a moss-carpeted hillside, physically tired but in a mental turmoil. He tried to think clearly what it was all about. Why had he broken away from everybody and torn out here alone? Why had his father's letter produced such a strange effect? Certainly its theme was not new; both Father and Mother had harped upon this matter of personal decision until he was tired of the words. Herein lay the puzzle; that heretofore he had simply been good-naturedly bored, able to put it all away and give his mind to other things, while today it would not be shaken off. Well, let him think. Why should he try to shake it off? Why was he fighting it? Why not yield and make his mother and father happy?

"Because," he said aloud, "whatever else I have been, I am not a hypocrite; I cannot pretend what I do not feel." He hunted for his handkerchief to wipe the beads of perspiration from his face, while his invisible companion questioned.

"Who wants you to be a hypocrite?"

"Well, I can't pretend to feel any different about such matters from what I always have."

"Who asks you to? Who has said a word about your feelings?"

"But one can't act except in line with one's feelings without being a hypocrite."

"Oh, what nonsense! Didn't you go exactly contrary to your feelings when you sprang up this morning and hurried with all your might because it was late? Your feelings wanted to lie in bed; did you feel like a hypocrite because you refused to let them keep your mother waiting? In other words, for once in your life you did what you ought."

"Well, what ought I to do?"

"Oh, that's begging the question, shilly-shallying, putting off, just as you have always been doing. You've known since your babyhood just what you ought to do. Why don't you act up to your own beliefs?"

"What do I believe, anyhow?"

"A host of things; among them that there is a moral law that you have broken, and that there is such a being as God who has said that there was only one way for a transgressor of the law to escape, by accepting the substitution offered."

It was a fact that Burnham Roberts believed all those statements; knew he believed them; knew the day and hour away back in his early boyhood when he had felt himself personally convicted of such knowledge; and having been rooted and grounded in Bible theology, not one of the "advanced thoughts" or "destructive criticisms" or any of the "isms" that had fluttered wildly about him through the years had been able to find lodgment in his brain. Moreover, he had had later and clearer proof of the solid rock underneath his early teaching. He had not chosen to tell Eureka that that was not his first introduction to the speaker of the morning; but a single flash of memory at this moment sent him back to the great church into which he had wandered aimlessly to pass away an hour between trains, and to the ringing voice that was saying:

"The doctrine of the forgiveness of sin is not even distantly imitated by any other religion."

It had sounded like a challenge to the idle young man, who had traveled in many lands and amused himself over the peculiarities of many religions, and he waited for the speaker to prove his point. He did it, and did yet more. As distinctly as though the words were being spoken now, came back their echo in the silence of the woods.

"Can a man really forgive himself? Oh, if we are morally flabby, we can forgive ourselves and continue to sin again, and yet again."

Once more Burnham sought his handkerchief to wipe the perspiration; he felt his face burn with shame. He had not thought of that sentence before, since he heard it spoken; he had not thought of it for two seconds at the time—yet here it was convicting him! He had been sinning against his father and mother and regretting it, and forgetting it, and repeating it, all his life. He was "morally flabby."

Other questions asked and answered by those eloquent lips came trooping up to add their testimony.

"Can an honorable God forgive sin?" The answer led by logical sequence to the one way, the expiation, the atonement. "The moral man," said the speaker, "will have nothing to do with *cheap* absolution." And "God could not be a father if he shrank from the consequences of sin."

Fatherhood was facing this young man whichever way he turned. Two fathers had removed all obstacles and were pointing out the path. Would the poor soul step into it?

But the archenemy of souls drew near to thrust his petty obstacles in the way. "However you may decide this thing eventually, you couldn't take any step just now. Think how it would look in two directions! If you take your father's birthday gift, he cannot help thinking, forever afterwards, that your religious professions were made because you could not, in decency, do otherwise. Then there is Hazel; it will look to her, and to your mother, who of course understands her views, that you are just taking a stand because you think she will like it; while, as a matter of fact, she is truth itself and will shrink from anything that she believes is merely put on."

Petty stumbling blocks being placed before the feet of the sinner—they must of necessity be petty, because there were no great ones. This well-taught young man knew intellectually that the *great* gulf between God and the human soul had been bridged. The question was would he stumble, nevertheless, and drop again into "moral flabbiness."

"Is not the bleeding heart of God the greatest thought in the universe?" It was another of those incisive questions that memory photographed and flashed out for him.

Suddenly he sprang up and made a dash through the pathless woods as though an enemy were following from whom he had resolved to escape.

It was late in the afternoon when he reentered the Chautauqua grounds and passed around behind the amphitheater in order to escape the eyes of the large audience gathered there. He had no desire to meet anyone whom he had ever seen before. He felt exhausted in mind and body, yet the fight was still on. He had fallen now into the slough of inability.

"I *can't* do it!" he had said over and over again. "I *can't,* and I know that I can't. Father thinks I am indifferent, unconcerned; that I never had a wish to be a different man from the one I am; God knows better; he knows I have tried again and again, and I can't keep my resolutions for a week; it isn't in me to be any other than the failure I am. It is just as that human dissector of thoughts said: I am 'morally flabby.' I have never before owned this, even to myself, but I have known it all the while." It was in this mood that he was getting in roundabout ways to the privacy of his room. Behold, it was that same "dissecting" voice that was ringing through the amphitheater. Instinctively Burnham halted; he could hear every word.

> The Christian life is not a single act, it is an attitude. The kernel of it is just this: 'I am Christ's. I tie myself up to Christ by every string that I know; and if there is any other string, I want to find it.' That is the continuous attitude of one who has looked Jesus in the face and said: "Thou art Christ, and I am Christ's."

Burnham Roberts did not appear at dinner; nor had any of his friends, so far as could be quietly ascertained, had speech with him since morning. The last one known to have been in his company was Eureka, but what passed between them could only be a matter of conjecture. She was silent—and miserable.

The members of that prayer circle said very little; and that little seemed to be an effort to hearten one another.

"The day isn't done yet," Mrs. Harrison said, speaking softly.

"No," from Mrs. Burnham in the same low tone. "And 'a thousand years in his sight are as one day.'"

Mrs. Roberts said not a word concerning her son to any human soul, but the calm of heaven was on her face.

"Flossy has had her answer," Mrs. Dennis told her missionary brother. "I don't know what it is, except that it satisfies her."

Yet it was not until the great clock on the tower was tolling out twelve solemn strokes that a young man, alone in his room, kneeling, hands clasped in the attitude of prayer said aloud, gravely, deliberately, with all the solemnity of a covenant in his manner: "Thou art Christ, and *I am Christ's.*"

It was the evening of another day before Eureka, not being in the "inner circle," had definite knowledge of the great transaction that had taken place the day before, or speech with the subject of it. She knew that Burnham had taken a late breakfast with his mother and been closeted with her throughout the morning. She also overheard talk that made her sure that he had cabled a message of some sort to his father. As for "Aunt Flossy," the joy in her face made even strangers turn and look again, wistfully. But the one who called herself "left out" was told nothing.

"I am a Samaritan, I suppose, or a leper," she told herself half angrily, half whimsically. "I've a mind to remind them that 'even the dogs eat of the crumbs.'"

Hazel had departed for Jamestown by the early boat with Mrs. Neal Harrison and three of the older children on a shopping excursion. Eureka had been invited to accompany them, but not being at any time fond of her sister-in-law's company, and at all times detesting shopping, had promptly declined. She knew that Burnham went to Jamestown in the two o'clock boat and returned in company with the shoppers soon after five. She sat on an upper veranda and watched their ascent up the hill; the children marching ahead, laden with packages of every conceivable shape and size; Mrs. Neal languidly following them having as much as she could do to carry herself; but the two bringing up the rear were also heavily laden, yet not too much so for earnest talk. At least Burnham seemed to be talking eagerly, and Hazel's cheeks were the color of the carnations in her belt. They had been Burnham's carnations at noon; Eureka had noted their peculiar hue and was sure of it. Her lip curled a little as she watched. Whatever wondrous results that day of prayer might have accomplished for others, it had evidently not made a "new creature" of Burnham Roberts. She was half ashamed and half frightened that this conviction brought a sense of relief. She had not been quite sure how to deal with a "new creature."

It was just after dinner that Burnham, carefully dressed and looking his best in every respect, came in search of her and spoke in his usual airy fashion.

"One good turn deserved another"; she had taken him to the meeting yesterday, and he wished the pleasure of her company this evening at the lakeside service. She went with alacrity; albeit, on the way to the arcade she asked why he wanted to waste an hour of such a lovely evening at a prayer meeting. Hadn't he told her some time ago that he had had meetings enough to last for a lifetime?

He smiled cordially and reminded her that people sometimes changed their minds; that he had special reasons for wanting to hear the speaker and special reasons for wanting a visit with her. He had designs on her for the hour following the lakeside service, if she would grant him an interview. His manner told her plainly that the interview was to be special, and she felt that it would be memorable.

26

"I HAVE SOMETHING TO TELL YOU"

Day is dying in the west,
Heaven is touching earth with rest;
Wait, and worship, while the night
Sets her evening lamps alight
Through all the sky.

THIS was the exquisite song that greeted their ears as
they threaded their way among the throng of wor-
shipers at that lakeside service where earth and air and
tender song of mother birds joined with human
voices in calling to worship.

Yet Eureka, sitting quietly as one of them, apparently listening to the voice of the minister of God—
whose message was for her, if ever a message was—yet
let her thoughts wander from it all and busy themselves with that coming interview. She knew it was to
be eventful. Burnham meant to ask her, at last, in
words, to be his wife; and to that question she had long
ago promised herself solemnly that she would say yes.

She shivered a little at the thought of it. Could she?
Stop! She was not to go over that ground; the decision

was final. There were other things for her to arrange; matters about which she must stand firm. If Burnham had indeed become that "new creature" of which certain dear fanatics were always talking, she would not have to mention the subject; but as it was—doubtless he had made some wonderful resolutions yesterday which he believed, poor soul, that he would keep. But one new departure, whether he had included it or not, must be made and lived up to. All that delightful little flirting with pretty-faced, innocent girls must be given up, at once and forever. She would tell him frankly that he had never done anything in his life of which she was so much ashamed as his continued attentions to that poor little Hazel, and she was firmly resolved to have no more of them. At that moment she was startled into giving heed to what was going on about her by an outburst of laughter from the audience. The speaker was telling a story; and of all stories in this world for a preacher to tell at a religious meeting, it was about a little trained dog in a circus! Eureka felt scandalized. She made no pretensions; she was counted always outside the circle of good Christian people, but she knew nevertheless what was fitting at a religious meeting! Yet she could not help listening. The little dog, the speaker said, had not done his tricks and had been unmercifully whipped by his master. In his agony and terror, looking about for a way of escape, he rushed to the cage of the great Numidian lion and squeezed his little body through the bars. A moment of awful suspense; surely the dog had gone to his doom! Straight up to the monarch of the forest he ran, and that king of his tribe put out his great paw and gathered him gently inside the circle of his protection, uttering as he did so a low, ominous growl to the people outside. The owner of the dog, who had feared for a terrible second that he had lost a treasure, now recovered himself and said gruffly to the lion's keeper: "I want my dog." The keeper looked at him for one disgusted moment, then he said in significant tones: "Oh, all right; I'll open the cage door, and you can go in and get him if you want to."

"I tell you, brother, you who have fled for protection from the blows of Satan to the offered Refuge, remember that the 'Lion of the tribe of Judah' is your protection; and those looking on, if they but understood it, could afford to say to the evil one: 'Get him if you can!'"

No one in that great company laughed more heartily or seemed to more thoroughly enjoy the story than did Burnham; to his dignified companion this was an added proof that he was the same Burnham Roberts she had always known.

The close of the service was reverent enough to please even the fastidious Eureka. The speaker possessed that rare power over an audience which enabled him to turn their thoughts quickly from the story that had amused them to the tremendous truth which it illustrated. But as they made their way out from the crowd, Burnham referred again to the story. "'I want my dog,'" he said and laughed joyously. "Wasn't that the greatest illustration! I think he is about the only man who could do that sort of thing and make the point with it that he did."

"And he very greatly marred his point by using it," Eureka said coldly.

"Oh, I don't think so; not for me; not by a great deal! I tell you, Eureka, I don't suppose you know very much about that enemy of souls, what a beating he can give you even when you are down-and-out. I'm going to be thankful all my life for that story and the inimitable way in which the application was pressed home. 'Get him if you can!' Eureka, that *if* is as big as the world!'" He made only a second's pause then continued eagerly:

"All this puts me into the very middle of a story that I meant should begin at the beginning, and that I thought would be a long one. It isn't, it's very short. I'm the little dog; I fled to him, and he opened his arms and enfolded me. 'He is Christ, and I am Christ's.'"

What was a woman like Eureka to say to this! She tried to make the kind of reply that ought to be made. She said that she was glad, but the words had a strange sound even to her ears. Of course she was glad, she assured herself. And yet—his story had put a sort of barrier between them; she was a woman who had learned many Bible verses in her childhood; the words that memory flashed at her just then were: "Between us and you there is a great gulf fixed."

Suddenly Burnham interrupted what must have sounded to him like platitudes. "I've something else to tell you; shall we sit here, or would you rather walk?" They had been walking rapidly and were near a rustic seat by the shore. For answer, Eureka sat down; she felt that she had no strength to spare for walking; it was coming: what she had been for so long expecting.

"It is something about which I have been for some time intending to talk with you," he said, taking a seat beside her. "In fact I have been rather expecting to have you talk to me."

He laughed as he spoke, but Eureka felt a wave of indignation. Had he expected her to propose to him outright! He was evidently waiting for her to speak, but she let him wait. Then he burst forth impetuously.

"Eureka, I need your help; I feel sure you can help me as no one else can." That surprised and touched her. Despite the marvelous change that he thought had come to him, he did not count her out; he even believed that she could be of service.

"I will help you all I can," she said—and her voice rang true. "But you must show me how."

"I knew you would!" he said gratefully. "I knew you would understand as none of the others can, except of course my mother; she has been more than I could have hoped, but—these things must be very hard on mothers, just at first." What was he talking about?

"She is such a lonely little girl," he began again. "She really has nobody in all the world but me; and I want you to be to her—well, everything that a woman, especially a young woman, can, you know." Assuredly she did not know! She forced herself to question.

"You are speaking of—?" She said inquiringly and stopped.

"Why of Hazel, of course; it could be no one else. I am sure I have shown you all plainly enough what I meant."

Then she found her voice. "Just what do you mean, Burnham? I confess that I do not understand."

He looked at her as one bewildered. "You, too!" he said. "Do you mean it, Eureka? What could I mean but that I am going to make Hazel Harris my wife just as soon as I can?"

She could not help her lip curling a little as she spoke with spirit. "You might have meant much less than that, for all that any of us could know. Remember that you have been on terms of intimacy with 'lonely little girls' before."

"Never," he said positively. "Not in this way. Oh, I have been a fool, if that is what you mean. I have raved over girls to you and Mother and ran after them; I don't excuse myself; I have been an unmitigated fool! But I never for five seconds thought of marrying one of them, and they knew it. I never spoke a word of love to any other girl in my life or tried to make her think by my actions that I loved her. Why, Eureka, I was with them just as I have been with you—only you and I are closer friends than any of them ever were— and imagine people misunderstanding our friend-ship!"

Uppermost in Eureka's heart at that moment was the hope that he would never by any chance discover how utterly she had misunderstood. He went on eagerly.

"Those friendships were long ago, anyhow; they seem ages ago to me; since you and I have been close friends, chums, you know, I haven't cared for any other friendships; and I never loved any woman in my life except Mother, until I met Hazel."

They talked long, sitting there until darkness gath-ered, and after that walking slowly down the nearly deserted avenue toward the hotel. He told her of his hopes and plans, not fully matured but glowing before him in the hazy distance. Of what he wanted her to say to people who needed to know things and to decline to say to those who had no right to ask; and above all to be to Hazel just the shield and escape and help that a young girl needed. "As if you were her sister, you know; the child never had a sister."

Eureka listened and questioned and promised, en-tering into the spirit of his mood as best she could, and apparently to his entire satisfaction. Arriving at the hotel, she went straight to Mrs. Roberts, who was standing in the doorway of her own room and bending, kissed her lovingly as she whispered:

"Aunt Flossy, I want to be the first to congratulate you."

Mrs. Roberts reached up to return the kiss, speaking quickly. "Oh, has he told you? You kept his secret well, dear, I did not know—I did not dream of any such thing."

And Eureka, who knew what this mother had feared, felt the joy of discovering her fear to be mistaken swallowed up some of the motherache over the certainty that she was never again to be first in her son's life.

There was still Hazel to be met, and the girl dreaded it; what was the first thing to be said to her? It arranged itself. She was flying along the hall, getting to the privacy of her own room, for her mother was still lingering belowstairs with a group of friends when she came face-to-face with the girl and her lover.

"Eureka," he called as she was passing them. "Wait! Come back; I am just telling Hazel that you are the first, the very first, one to be told our secret, and the only one to whom I shall volunteer confidences."

Something must be said, and Eureka had no words. She bent and kissed the girl on both glowing cheeks, then put both arms about her lovingly and kissed her again.

"There," she said. "Tomorrow I'll say *words,*" and fled.

She heard Burnham's joyous laugh; he was satisfied.

At last, in her room alone with the door locked, she tossed off her wrap, pushed the window higher, and said aloud deliberately, "'Hazel Harris Roberts'; it sounds better than the other." And the uppermost feeling in the heart of this young woman was relief. She had escaped the consequences of her own decisions. Blessed are those who, having made solemn decisions without other guidance than their own, escape from their consequences in time.

The next few days proved to be some of the strangest, the busiest, and, in certain respects, the most eventful of Eureka Harrison's checkered life. Among other things, she found herself the very center of the not small circle of friends that had been shaken to its center by the announcement of Burnham Roberts's engagement. Those who had looked upon it as a settled matter that he was to marry Eureka Harrison were amazed at discovering her to be the closest confidential friend not only of himself but the lady of his choice. From being looked upon by certain ones with disfavor, as a girl who was carrying a very doubtful friendship to an extreme that she must know would make unpleasant gossip and cause discomfort to her friends, and by others as a foolish young woman who refused to be counseled and was heaping to herself unhappiness that they were free to declare she would richly deserve, she became the hopeful subject of all sorts of information that they were eager to secure and was expected to join in the outburst of laughter at their own expense. Notably did her brother Neal indulge in merriment and congratulation. "If you aren't the slyest puss! I thought I knew you, but I give it up. We never dreamed of such a thing! Why couldn't you have given a fellow a hint when I was lecturing you that day for all I was worth?"

Eureka, as she listened and smiled and made what replies she could, rejoiced that neither Neal nor his wife would ever have to know why she had given him no hint.

One of her unique experiences grew out of what she called a "family tryout." The scheme was Burnham's own.

"Don't you think I am right, Eureka?" he had called as she was passing the corner where he and Hazel stood talking.

"I'm insisting that this child should explain matters to her aunt before I call upon her formally. It isn't the thing to spring a fellow upon her without any warning, now is it? She may not even know of my existence."

"But I don't know how to do it," was Hazel's shamefaced response. "There is no chance in that cottage to see Aunt Sarah alone for a moment. If I could get her away somewhere."

Burnham caught at the words.

"All right, let's get her away; we'll go out for a drive. Let's go this afternoon; there's a splendid new turnout at the stables that I'd like an excuse for trying. We'll bring up at the Thompson House in Mayville in time for dinner; I'll phone them right away to give us a separate table. It's a capital place to dine; Stebbins and I have tried it several times; never found better service anywhere. Let's see, there'll be five of us: Mother, Eureka, and your aunt, besides you and me."

Eureka's protest that she was not needed and would be one too many was promptly overruled. Hazel was already learning to depend on her in emergencies, and Burnham explained that the livery man would be deeply grieved; part of the charm of the new outfit lay in the fact that the seats had been planned for three occupants. In undertone he added: "I want you along to sustain my mother."

It is doubtful if even Hazel appreciated the flutter of satisfaction in which her aunt made ready for that eventful drive. She did not fail to make careful explanations to her neighbor, Mrs. Adams, as they lunched together at the Arlington.

"I can't be at the five o'clock lecture; I'm going to drive with Mrs. Evan Roberts.

"Oh, yes, my niece is still with her; they think the world of her. I told her last week that the next thing I knew she would be deserting us altogether and going to live with them!" Little did Mrs. Bradford imagine how true were the words spoken in sarcasm!

The stream of information flowed on. "My daughters will have to eat their dinner in solitude tonight; we are to dine at the Thompson House in Mayville. Have you heard what a very fine house that is? Really exceptional, I am told; but I suppose dining there is just a little device for giving dear Mrs. Roberts and myself a quiet hour together; we live in such a whirl here that there is really no time for social functions."

Apparently, however, Burnham Roberts was not planning for that "quiet hour." He seated Hazel in the backseat beside his mother and placed Mrs. Bradford in front with Eureka and himself; and those two, both of them adept at entertaining others when they chose, exerted themselves to the utmost to give the good lady a happy afternoon. When, after a delightful drive along the lakefront, they finally drew up before the Thompson House, Mrs. Bradford's eyes were bright, and there was a color on her somewhat jaded face. She had never in her life before ridden in so fine a turnout nor been so charmingly deferred to and entertained.

It was after the excellent dinner was concluded and they had gone to the veranda to view the sunset that Hazel called her aunt to the farther end of it to look at an ambitious vine which was climbing to the second story and forgetting it entirely when they reached it, began breathlessly:

"Aunt Sarah, I have something to tell you that I think will surprise you very much. I have promised— that is I—Aunt Sarah, I am engaged to be married."

"The idea!" said Mrs. Bradford, startled out of her eagerness to make quick work with the vine and get back to Mrs. Roberts.

"What do you mean? Whom have you found so soon that you think wants to marry you? Child, you are too young to talk about such things! What do you suppose your uncle would say to such nonsense? Do *they* know—I mean the Robertses—what you are up to?"

"Yes," said Hazel with a nervous little laugh, "oh, yes, they know."

"And what do they say? Do they know him—the fellow—and is he—decent?"

"Aunt Sarah!"

"Well, such questions have to be asked, I can tell you, if there's anything to it. Your uncle will never in the world consent to your marrying some worthless fool of a boy who can't support a wife. What's his name? Where does he live?"

"Aunt Sarah, it is Mr. Roberts."

"What! *Who* is? You don't say he's got the same name as the family! Is he their hired man? What are you talking about, anyway? Why can't you tell a straight story?"

"It is Mr. Roberts himself, Aunt Sarah; Mr. Burnham Roberts, the one who brought us out here today."

But at this point the look on her aunt's face was too much for Hazel; she broke into hysterical laughter that was very near to tears and summoned Eureka with a beseeching gesture to her side.

27

◄━━✦━━►

MEMORIALS

WHILE Eureka explained and explained again and listened to incoherent exclamations and answered what questions she could and exerted her skill to the utmost to get the good lady calmed down into ordinary speech and manner, Hazel slipped away and joined Mrs. Roberts at the other end of the long veranda.

For the homeward drive, Burnham, without asking any questions, placed his mother and "Aunt Sarah" on the backseat, leaving them to get on together as best they could, while he devoted himself exclusively to the ladies in front. But he put the aunt into another nervous flutter by saying to her, when he handed her from the carriage as if she had been a princess, "May I call upon you tomorrow at about ten o'clock, Mrs. Bradford?"

Busy as she was during that strange week, Eureka nevertheless found a little time for her own interests and was amazed when she thought it over afterwards, to realize how absorbed she had been in the numerous missionary conferences and missionary "talks" and even missionary prayer meetings held at the various denominational houses. It was not until she had been to several of these meetings that she awoke to the consciousness that always her escort seemed to be Mr. Dennis, the missionary from Utah, and that they went and came without other company; also that both of them were in the habit of lingering on the veranda or in one of the small parlors for an hour at a time, asking and answering questions, and apparently enjoying each other's society to the utmost. What aroused her to this state of things was the discovery that she was the subject of remark and of curious surmisings. Some of the bolder lookers-on began to rally her, after the fashion of their kind. Mrs. Neal Harrison, for instance, more bold perhaps than others by reason of being her sister-in-law, asked her outright when she expected to go to Utah, and if she felt very sure that even a missionary could always withstand the temptations peculiar to that state. The coarseness of the insinuation made Eureka indignant, yet it was not those words that sent the blood racing through her veins with such force that she turned suddenly giddy; it was the scarlet line on the face of her mother and the very peculiar look that passed between her and Mr. Dennis, who at that instant entered the reception room.

Lying outwardly quiet beside her mother that night, Eureka was in inward turmoil. She was translating that exchange of glances between the missionary from Utah and her mother and deciding that she understood. Her translation fitted in with a remark made to her by Mrs. Dennis but a few hours before.

"Do you think," she had asked, "that your mother would like to live in the West?" The tone was peculiar, and she knew now that it was significant; but she had been stupid.

"In the West?" she had repeated. "I am sure I don't know; she has never had any reason to consider such a question. Why do you ask, Aunt Marion?"

But "Aunt Marion" hadn't chosen to answer and had immediately changed the subject. Now it was all very plain. They wanted her to marry the missionary from Utah! Her mother wanted it and had been allowing herself to talk over the possibilities with the man himself! What else could that exchange of glances have meant? Mother was so anxious to have her married and settled in life that she would be willing to have her go to Utah, or to China, so that she need be worried over her no more. Perhaps Mother was disappointed that her daughter was not to be Mrs. Burnham Roberts; it is true she had always heartily opposed their friendship, but that might have been because she feared that Burnham was simply flirting. Poor Mother! She was very much alone in this big, hard world and had very little of this world's goods. Perhaps she worried over the future; in truth, Eureka knew that she did; she had nothing to lean upon; the others were—well, they were married and settled, and of small account so far as her mother's comfort was concerned. Did she believe that a home missionary would be able to support a mother-in-law? Was it possible that Mr. Dennis was really thinking of such things? He must be; he must have talked with her mother! She went hurriedly over the days since she had known him intimately. Certainly he had sought her out, taken trouble to secure a walk or a talk with her; now that she forced herself to go over the days in detail, his attentions had been really marked. It must be that he wanted to marry her! And—poor Eureka—it was plain that her mother wanted her to marry him. No wonder that speech failed her that night; and, after lying perfectly still as long as her nerves would bear the strain, she arose, slipped into a wrapper, and, going softly to the little porch, bared her burning face to the dews of night. Another terrible problem was before her, and her common sense told her that a decision of some sort would soon have to be made. What should she do?

There was no question of her liking the missionary, she liked him very much in every way; and she was more deeply interested in the work about which he had told her than in anything that she had ever heard of before. She was sure that she could help in it, even as she was. "And I am not—" she began in her thought and stopped with a strange feeling at her heart. Without herself realizing what had been taking place in her mind during those few strange days, she knew that the evident and very strongly marked change in Burnham Roberts had moved her powerfully. Deep in her inner consciousness, this carefully taught child of believing parents hid a firm belief in the fact of regeneration. She knew that there was such a thing as becoming a "new creature." She had looked on at transformations and had learned to scoff and sneer because there were apparently so few of them; so few Christians who lived up to her ideals. These days since Burnham had begun to pray, and to live, had left her feeling alone and lonely. The hidden thought of her heart had been: "If I had anybody to pray for me as they prayed for Burnham, I might—" then her well-trained intellect had reminded her that she was the child of many prayers, and that Jesus Christ himself was her Advocate at this moment. "He ever liveth to make intercession." Hadn't her own father explained the meaning of those words to her long ago when she had learned the verse as a "golden text"?

But the immediate problem was whether she could possibly marry Mr. Dennis.

He was a great deal older than herself—she did not care for that. Poor Mother! To be disappointed twice in getting rid of her troublesome daughter would be hard. Would he be willing to marry her if she told him that she respected him very much, believed in him fully, liked him better than any of her friends, but as for loving him, she was different from other girls and had never loved, and assuredly never expected to really love anybody? He must be going to ask her to marry him, for surely Mother would never have been confidential with him unless he had gone to her. Was marriage sometimes just a fine friendship between self-respecting people? Would it be right for her to secure in this way a home for Mother and the protection for her old age that men could give?

These questions did not follow each other consecutively; some of them were not definitely thought at all; they just floated through her consciousness hurriedly, like problems that must be taken up if—. Morning brought no relief to her perturbed soul, but her nervous unrest sent her to the morning conference on missions, to the afternoon question hour on home missions—at both of which gatherings Mr. Dennis was the chief speaker—and finally to the home-mission prayer meeting at one of the denominational houses. Little she heard of the talks or the prayers during that hour. She had met Mr. Dennis at the door, and he had asked if he might take her home after the meeting and would she give him an opportunity to talk with her on a very private and personal matter? He began the talk the moment they were out of hearing of the multitude.

"My dear Miss Harrison, I have really been seeking

this opportunity for the last two days, and I fancy you know fairly well what I want to ask of you."

If she had not felt too much troubled, she could have laughed. Here was another who supposed her to know people's thoughts before they were spoken! He waited for no response but went on hurriedly.

"I have noticed with the greatest joy your deepening interest in the general subject of home missions, and I cannot help feeling that there has been a special interest in my own field. I have sometimes hoped that you would like to live in the region where my work lies; and I am sure that you would take the greatest possible interest in the young women we are trying to reach."

There was a pause as if for reply, but Eureka felt that she could not have spoken a word to save her life. He cleared his voice ever so gently and went on.

"In short, my dear Eureka—I may call you 'Eureka,' may I not? I have dared to hope that you would help me to reestablish my broken home and be to us all—to my children especially, perhaps—the friend we all need."

Still was Eureka tongue-tied; this was so utterly unlike the way she had imagined he might speak, that there seemed no place for her words. But he did not wait, this time, for response.

"I think I can realize to some extent how your mother feels about this; knowing, as she does, that you gave up your dearest hopes for her, and feeling sure, as she does, that whatever arrangements in life you might make she would be always your first thought— of course she thinks first of you—but I have ventured the hope that, so far from my putting an obstacle in the way of your care for her, you would be willing to trust me to do everything for her comfort and happiness that a man could do. Not only that, but I—we have both hoped that you would be willing to come and help us make a united home and work with us for other homes that Satan has despoiled. Have I presumed upon my knowledge of your real character, my—*may* I say daughter?"

Once more in the solitude of her room, her mother having been left with Mr. Dennis on the porch below, Eureka locked her door, drew down her shades, and dropped into the first chair she saw. Then she laughed. Not bitterly, not gloomily, just a free, hearty laugh with a touch of relief in it. The tremendous tension of the day was over at last, and she could afford the reaction.

"To be refused twice in one week is too much!" she said aloud and laughed again. "Eureka Harrison, you would do well to stop planning other people's lives for them and give yourself to being thankful that you are to be allowed to remain Eureka Harrison to the end of the chapter. *'May I say daughter?'* Think of it! Oh, Mother, *Mother!* But I shall go to Utah all the same and help some of those girls; see if I don't."

⇒+ +⇐

Burnham and Hazel were out for the afternoon. The days were very busy ones, for the Chautauqua season was drawing to a close. Only one whole day more and then "home" for all the members of "Aunt Ruth's party"; to several of them the getting ready to begin other homes and utterly changed lives for more than one of them. Hazel had been left to travel in Mrs. Roberts's care; her aunt and cousins having departed two days before, being driven to the railroad station in excellent style and established in the luxurious drawing-room car with all the appliances of modern luxury about them: the latest magazines, the choicest fruits, and every other aid to comfort that Burnham Roberts could secure.

"It is awfully different from the way we came," said Isabel as she leaned back in her luxurious chair and munched chocolates.

"I should think as much!" from Josephine as she turned the pages of the latest *Harper,* "and to think that we owe it all to that little mouse of a Hazel! Doesn't it seem almost like witchcraft, Mother?"

Mrs. Bradford adjusted her head comfortably among the cushions and closed her eyes to enjoy the luxury of rest as she said dreamily:

"Hazel is really an unusual girl; I knew there were possibilities in her; she takes after the Bradford side of the family."

But despite the busy closing days, those two had found time for a special afternoon together. They wandered into the Hall of the Christ to enjoy its solitude.

"It is simply shocking," Burnham said as they mounted the steps, "that you have not been to any of the meetings held here. It is the place of all others where I should have expected you to spend your leisure time, until I stole it all."

"I had no leisure time," said Hazel, laughing. "And if I had, why should I spend it here? What is this place?"

"It is the Bishop's heart, as nearly as I can make out. Here, I can read you what he wants it to be."

He took from his notebook a scrap of paper and read:

> The Hall of the Christ is, first of all, to stand in the center of Chautauqua to represent Christ as the center of all learning and all true living; the Key to the true and eternal wisdom.

"Do you notice that the books in the library here have all of them to do with Jesus Christ? The aim, I am told, is to gather the best writings of all ages—past, present, and, as they come out, future books—that bear upon his life and his work. Pictures, too, you know—copies of the great masters. The Bishop, they say, wants one, very large and the very greatest, to cover that space back of the archway. Somebody will give it someday—I wish it could be us."

"Perhaps a great many 'somebodies' might do it, of which you could be one."

"That's an idea, a class picture, *our* class; we have four years in which to work it up. Let's take hold of it."

She laughed deliciously. She had not yet grown used to the joy of hearing this man say we and us.

"It is a beautiful thought," she said, looking about her. "A hall where Jesus Christ is enthroned, where only his story is allowed; told in print and picture and sculpture and the human voice. Isn't it grand!"

"We will help to tell the story," he said eagerly. "You and I; let us begin now and lay aside a certain sum each year that shall help to make this building vocal with his praise. Wouldn't that be a good way in which to memorialize this special year?"

"A beautiful way!" she said. "Burnham, I do know about this place; isn't it here that the Bishop speaks on Sunday mornings? Well, do you know that Eureka came here last Sunday to the early morning meeting and heard him speak some words that I don't believe she will ever forget? Have you begun to pray very especially for one person yet, above all others, one who doesn't know the Lord? Oh, you will! I think it is one of the very first things he gives us to do. I hope he will want you to take Eureka. We *can't* let her go on alone any longer! Burnham, I want her for Christ, as a souvenir of this year."

28

"HE IS CHRIST, AND WE ARE CHRIST'S"

THEY walked from the Hall of the Christ toward the lakeshore and presently found themselves near the bell tower, in the very spot where Hazel had thrown herself on the grass in all the abandonment of bitter weeping. She was thinking of it when Burnham answered her.

"I am afraid they are not all at work for Christ; but, dearest, let us pledge ourselves that there shall be at least two members of the class of 1916 who will give themselves to the swelling of that company."

"Yes," she said, "oh, *yes!* Isn't it blessed that we have the opportunity? In the first talk that I ever had with your mother, she asked me what I was going to let Chautauqua do for me. The question startled me because I had supposed that I hadn't a thing to do with it; but she asked if I did not know that opportunities did for us what we let them, and that sometimes we just let them slip. That was what I was doing; I told her that I hated Chautauqua! Then she said that part of my inheritance was here; what God meant for me, you know. Burnham, it almost frightens me when I think of all that he has given me here."

"Think of me!" Burnham said, much moved. "I have been letting opportunities slip all my life. Hazel, let us do as the 'Four Mothers' did when they came here years ago as girls; consecrate all that has come to us, all that we have and are and ever shall be to the service of our Lord."

They had turned and were walking toward the sunset. There had been clouds part of the time, but the king of day had broken through them and was flooding the earth with golden glory. They climbed the hill to see it bid their world good-night. They were among the tall old trees, and all about them was the hush of sunset and the gentle twitter of birds giving good-night calls. They stood enthralled by the beauty of earth and sky.

> Sing a song of ages,
> Eternities to come!

softly quoted Hazel.

Burnham answered with an apparently irrelevant quotation, but they two understood each other. "He will convince the world of sin because they believe not on *me*. 'Master, is that the only sin?' No, but it is the crux of all sin. If you can get a man in a right attitude toward Jesus, all other sins will right themselves."

Hazel knew by heart the story of that crucial day; she knew whose human voice had been used of God to turn this man to the "right attitude toward Jesus."

As the sun dropped away and the afterglow spread and deepened, bathing all the hushed and worshiping earth in unearthly glory, the two clasped hands and, moved by the same impulse, repeated the declaration that had been used to anchor one of them to the Rock.

"He is Christ, and we are Christ's."

THE END

Don't miss these Grace Livingston Hill Library romance novels by Isabella Alden